FRANZ ANTON MESMER
Physician *Extraordinaire*

FRANZ ANTON MESMER
Physician *Extraordinaire*

BY ANN JENSEN AND MARY LOU WATKINS

Garrett Publications/HELIX PRESS/New York

Copyright © 1967 by Garrett Publications
Library of Congress Catalog Card No. 66-28499
Manufactured in the United States of America

❖ ACKNOWLEDGMENTS ❖

ALTHOUGH hypnotism has been known and practiced for centuries in one form or another, to Franz Anton Mesmer, M.D., A.A.L.L., Ph.D. (1734-1814), belongs credit for the introduction of hypnotism as a tool of modern medicine.

Like sleep, the trance state of hypnosis has never been fully explained. And as with electricity, an astonishing amount is known of how to use hypnosis in spite of the fact that we do not know what it is.

The authors of this book wish to acknowledge their gratitude to the many highly respected and fully qualified medical persons who have made extensive use of hypnotism and recorded their findings.

In particular, we are indebted to Margaret Watkins, M.D., Cert. Orthopedic Surgeon, '46, who gave so generously of her time and knowledge—to the point of reading grubby first drafts of our manuscript.

To Andrew Jensen, M.D., Cert. O.G., '59; to Herman Kantor, M.D., Cert. O.G., '44; to Dechard Turner, Bridwell Library, Southern Methodist University, who also read and advised with us; to the gracious librarians of Southern Methodist University and Southwestern Medical Foundation—and especially to Dr. Harold Crasilneck, who lectures in both of these schools—our heartfelt thanks.

THE AUTHORS

FRANZ ANTON MESMER
Physician *Extraordinaire*

CHAPTER I

FRANZ MESMER picked up Papa's valise and allowed himself one last look at the tiny cell that had been his home for the past three years. He walked through the door and smiled to himself when he realized that he was reluctant to close it. His eyes misting with tenderness, he took a deep breath as he walked across the campus to Father Emmanuel's study.

"I felt this same excited sadness when I left home three years ago," Franz remembered. Mama was happy when she said good-bye. "My prayers are answered, Franz. You will be a good priest," she had said. And Papa had brought out this old, worn, red valise and helped Franz pack it. He gave the valise a small pat.

"I'm proud to have a son going all the way to the Jesuit College in Bavaria," Papa had said. Franz paused at the Shrine of the Holy Family. He crossed himself, but he could still hear Papa's voice. As old men do, Papa had started to reminisce, "If I hadn't met your Mama, I might have been a priest today instead of a forester."

"Now, Papa," Mama had interrupted. Franz laughed out, recalling. He noticed the fall leaves dancing in the sunlight of the mid-morning breeze, then rapped on Father Emmanuel's door.

"Come in, come in, son," Father Emmanuel's hearty words boomed out from a lusty and wide diaphragm. He embraced Franz. "Not much time to lose, son . . ." Father clapped Franz on the shoulder. "Let's be off, we're to meet the Baron at the village inn."

"The Baron? I thought I was taking the stagecoach."

"My lad, did I fail to tell you I arranged a ride with one of our patrons?"

"A Baron?" Franz repeated.

"Yes, an art collector, as well, and a man of considerable influence in Munich."

"You are kind—that stagecoach . . ."

"Yes, I know, my son, it's always late, and sometimes it never comes." Father laughed. "The Baron will take you straight to Munich and from there you will take the stage to Ingelstadt."

"I've never met a Baron. He is a Baron?"

"Yes, indeed, yes."

Franz opened the monastery gate and stood aside for Father Emmanuel to walk through. Once on the village road, Father slowed his pace.

Fumbling in the folds of his voluminous robe, he brought forth a book, handing it to Franz. "Here's a parting gift, great words of fire."

Franz took the book and read the title page: *Sensible Thoughts on the Effect of Nature*, by Christian Wolff. He looked up. "Christian Wolff, I never heard of him."

"Naturally, naturally, that's why I'm slipping him to you. The Church will have no part of him." Father had dropped his voice to a stage whisper. The sly grin on Father's face amused Franz, and he wondered just how Father had managed to smuggle in all his contraband literature. It was through Father's good graces that he had been permitted to devour Descartes and many others forbidden by the Church.

"What's wrong with Wolff, Father?"

"A thinker on a new path, son . . . that's all . . . the Church frowns on new thought."

Franz nodded as he recalled how Descartes had caused the stars to shine with new meaning for him. He remembered the hours he had spent on such questions as "What do these stars do in their remoteness, or can it be they are not remote . . . but near . . . near enough to quicken my pulse, or to start a new thought forming in my brain. . . ." Franz turned the book in his hand, "Ah, Father Emmanuel, thank you for this parting gift. You have given me many books that have made me question deeply."

"I hope they fill your soul with an exquisite longing . . . but to Wolff, as the time permits—"

"Yes, Father, I want to know about him."

"He is one of our greatest philosophers. In this modern age we need more thinkers."

"Yes, Father?"

"As a man grows, his faith must grow; his faith will grow as his mind becomes free to seek. This, lad, is what Wolff is saying in this book." Father Emmanuel tapped the book under Franz's arm.

"Is Wolff a teacher?" Franz asked.

"Was—a professor of mathematics at Halle—gave a lecture to the students on the philosophy of Confucius." Father hurried his words and slowed his steps. Time was running out; they were almost at the inn. "Being a mathematician, Wolff found reality in precise patterns, rules and principles. He saw these same symbols in the ethics of Confucius."

"Did he say this in his lecture?" Franz asked incredulously.

"Yes, and added the fact that both systems were the product of the mind of man." Father caught Franz's arm emphatically. "He gave evidence of the power of human reason to attain moral truth by its own efforts and thus fulfill the will of God—sans priest, Catholic devotion, and Divine intercession."

"Whew!" Franz whistled softly. "That must have caused a furor."

"A furor!" Father snorted. "Some of the professors nearly died of religious indignation. Those old goats were so steeped in dogmatic pietism that they screamed for Wolff's dismissal."

"I can almost hear them."

"Yes, they claimed he had desecrated their sacred portals with his tribute to a pagan religion."

"Has he been dismissed?"

"Yes, but the truth he spoke cannot be dismissed. Always listen to the voice of truth wherever it's spoken; honor it; and Franz, above all, never fear it, for Truth is the Voice of God!"

Father Emmanuel's own voice stopped as an elaborate coach drew up. Franz had no chance to reply, for an elegantly dressed man of middle years greeted Father Emmanuel.

The next few minutes were devoted to introductions. The Baron was cordial but formal. The red valise was stored, and Father Emmanuel gave Franz a bear hug of farewell.

"Education, nothing like it. Nothing like it except experience, young man."

Franz listened to the Baron rumble in schoolboy French as

they rolled away from the gate. Franz had learned his French from a master, and his excellent accent gave him a feeling of comfort in the luxurious interior of the coach, so obviously and expensively French.

"This is a beautiful carriage, sir," Franz touched the tufted upholstery and delighted in the silky feel of it.

The Baron nodded happily, "Yes, it's nice. The ladies love it—God bless them. By the way, you are such a handsome lad; how do you get on with the ladies?"

Franz stammered out what he intended as a denial, but the Baron apparently misunderstood his French. He pointed to Franz's hand at the carriage window and said, "You have the kind of hands women love. Ever notice how you can drive them mad for you just by using your hands?"

They were jogging along at a rapid pace. Franz was relieved that the Baron was looking away, for he felt his face turning red.

"See, I have nice hands, too. Madame Roussault says the lines of power in my palms are unusually strong. You've been to Madame Roussault's house?"

Franz felt safe with this prosaic question and assured the Baron that he had never been in Munich.

"Ah, what a pity. Madame's house, with German cooking and your choice of French girls. What more could mortal man ask? I'll take you there! By all the holy angels, we'll change horses and drive straight through to Munich." The Baron lifted the tube and gave orders to the coachman in German.

Franz didn't protest—he couldn't—he was caught in a delirium that robbed him of reason.

The Baron continued, "Madame Roussault is a gifted astrologer and uses this gift in a unique way—what's your birthday, lad?"

"May the twenty-third, sir. 1734—I'm eighteen."

"Gemini, by all that's holy—the same as mine. Madame will know exactly how to mate you, with the blessings of the stars."

"The stars, sir?"

"Oh, yes, I know that as good churchmen we are not supposed to be interested in their influence—but I had a chart made and it's astonishingly accurate in its predictions. You are a scholar. At the university you might pursue some astrology along with your philosophical study."

"Theology, sir." Franz felt a reluctance to correct him, and a sense of shame for being reluctant.

"Theology? The priesthood?" The Baron seemed amazed as Franz nodded; then he protested: "But you don't look the part. You are a man for women, for amour, for a home and children, perhaps—*ach!*—the priesthood!" He shook his head.

In a moment he brightened. "Oh, well, you can come in and meet Madame Roussault, even if you do not wish to avail yourself of her services."

Franz swallowed hard but found no words. "You will find her a charming woman," he heard the Baron continue in a confidential tone as he laid a fatherly hand on Franz's knee. "Don't forget, lad, you have not yet taken the vows of celibacy."

The Baron turned his unending flow of talk to other matters—the fall crops now being harvested, the price of malt, the theatre and music. Franz was only half listening. Something in his nature cried out for a new experience. He often had vague half-dreams with which he dealt harshly and with shame. Now, out of the misty vapors of his imagination, every stillborn dream came flooding back. He closed his eyes.

The Baron must have thought him tired. "That's right, lad, sleep a bit," he said.

Franz appreciated being released to his thoughts. He would have to get command of himself; he must regain control of his emotions.

Later on he dozed as they drove along, for the next thing he became conscious of was the crunch of gravel as the coach turned into a driveway. He opened his eyes as they pulled up in front of the most magnificent establishment he had ever seen.

"Is this a palace?" Franz asked the Baron, as a footman opened the carriage door.

"This is Madame Roussalt's," the Baron laughed. "Let's go in."

The interior was sensual beyond anything Franz could

have dreamed. The great hall was filled with roses, and the soft music of a harp drifted in from the closed doors on the right. This must be a salon—Franz presumed—something he had read about but never hoped to see. The servant recognized the Baron and was effusive in his greeting.

"Madame will receive you immediately. Will you follow me to her sitting room?"

The Baron motioned Franz to accompany him. They climbed a short flight of stairs and stopped behind the servant at a gilded door. The man knocked, pushed open the door, and stood aside.

"My dear friend," Franz heard a voice, warm and gay, call out to the Baron. The Baron moved quickly to the lady with the lovely voice as she held out her hand, saying, "I have been expecting you."

Franz watched the Baron click his heels together and bend to kiss her hand. Then he turned to present Franz. Franz hesitated only a moment before clicking his heels and bending over the white, jeweled hand of Madame Roussault. Her room, too, was filled with the odor of roses, but Madame's hand had a delicious smell of blended perfumes. Franz wondered at this. He had never smelled ladies' perfumes before; it moved him strangely.

Madame's voice came like music to Franz's ears. "You are tall and handsome, young man. Those eyes of yours impel me to foolish thoughts. I must not delay in selecting a young lady of suitable age for you. When is your birthday?"

She turned to her ornate desk, but not before she had smiled deeply into the eyes of the adoring Baron and motioned him to a comfortable chair. He settled down with a pleased sigh.

"Sit here by me." She smiled at Franz and pointed to a small chair beside the desk. "Your birthday?"

"May the twenty-third."

"Oh, the cusp." Franz saw her twinkling eyes seek the Baron's. "Two of you—the vigor of the Bull—the poetry of the Twins." She turned back to Franz. "You love music, is that not so, my dear?"

"Yes." Franz wondered how he should address her.

"You are deeply religious, too, but neither music nor religion will be your life's work." Franz felt his face redden under her searching eyes.

She continued, "You are handsome beyond dreams. Women will swoon for you always. Count yourself fortunate in this, for you have within you a lust for the flesh which you will not be able to deny."

She laughed her musical laugh. Franz wanted to cry out a protest, but it stuck in his throat as she pointed to an impressive chart of the stars.

"I think I have just the girl for you—delicate, lovely, full bosoms, rounded hips." Franz coughed. "She sings like a nightingale. Shall I send for her?" As Franz hesitated, she urged, "The stars know this will be a night you can never forget. Trust my knowledge of their influence. Lisa is your astral mate and she is well trained in amour."

The Baron had made no comment to all of this; yet Franz, while feeling his presence, was unwilling to look at him. He murmured, "Send for her." Now his ears seemed to fail him. He could hardly breathe. He felt his heart beating against his ribs. Madame Roussault and the Baron were making small talk that he didn't even try to follow. His eyes were on the door, waiting—waiting—and finally it opened. He felt his feet on the floor and knew that he was standing—and he saw that she was lovely.

Franz never remembered how he took leave of Madame Roussault and the Baron, or how he arrived at Lisa's own little sitting room. He only remembered that her voice was light, her French perfect, and that her hand on his arm burned into his flesh. She closed the door and bade him sit. As one moving in a dream, he found the sofa she indicated. The dream continued as she poured wine into a glass and pressed it into his hand. She sat beside him and gently ran her hand down his arm. Then she leaned forward to place her hand on his thigh.

"Are you worn from your long drive?" Her voice caressed him. Franz couldn't answer. His eyes were on the low-cut gown that revealed most of her bosom. He swallowed the glass of wine, feeling the warm glow that it brought to his body. He realized that this was the first time he had drunk wine not cut with water.

Lisa took the empty glass and placed it on the floor beside her. She took his hands in hers and spread them open, caressing each finger.

"How beautiful," she murmured.

Franz remembered what the Baron had said about his hands. This and the wine gave him courage—and perhaps some undue finesse. Gently he touched her left breast and whispered, "How beautiful."

◆ CHAPTER II ◆

FRANZ BOARDED the stagecoach with remorse the next morning. He found his place and closed his eyes against a world that had changed overnight. He rode along, heartsick and full of bitterness, with sudden little shafts of remembered passion piercing his reverie like thin slivers of ice flying from a tall tree. He prayed fervently, but there was no peace. He entreated, he pleaded, even while remembering with nauseating delight the feel of Lisa in his arms.

Franz tried to remember yesterday. What had he thought about before the ride in the Baron's coach? How had his days been filled? There must be a panacea for this agony. Father Emmanuel could help him. What was it he used to say?—God is the Father of the sinner as well as the saint. And then, as though Father were speaking beside him, Franz heard him say, "The confession, my son."

With this, Franz felt the first pang of hope of cleansing, but then his wayward mind recalled the smooth delight of Lisa's limbs. "Oh, merciful heaven, come to my aid."

Franz was actually ill when he arrived at Ingelstadt, but before going to the infirmary he requested the rite of confession. He poured out all the details of the outrageous night. Even as he confessed, the events seemed to burn more and more brightly in the fires of his memory.

Then came the penance—"A year, my son, of sleeping on the bare floor with only one blanket. Every hour free from study must be spent on your knees in the chapel—and may God have mercy on your soul."

Gratefully Franz received this sentence. And released from an agonized sense of sin, he was in no way surprised to realize that his fever had left and that the pains which had plagued his body were gone. Franz reported to the headmaster instead of the infirmary.

The year in Ingelstadt taught Franz much. He found no Father Emmanuel here to emulate, but he did try to discover a release from self that Father Emmanuel had said would come with diligent study and mental dicipline. He steeped himself in religion and spent hours in prayer. On some days he was centered in Being. He knew the Presence of God. On other days he fought fiercely to keep Lisa's body from intruding between a "Hail Mary" and a "Holy Mother." The cold nights on the floor did not serve their purpose. The priest must have thought that passion was no problem to a cold body. How wrong he was! The cold floor kept Franz from sleeping well and, when he did sleep, his dreams were often of Lisa—though sometimes they went back to earlier days when Mama would pull him from his warm bed to assist in a bleeding.

Time slipped by. At first Franz was too rushed to make close friends among his classmates. They were kept busy with routine, and on holy days they were dedicated to silence. A Father John had taken over where Father Emmanuel had left off. But whereas Father Emmanuel had given companionship and devotion, Father John gave sarcasm and demerits.

Father John was tiny, French, and high-tempered. He was forever doing penance in prolonged fasts and mortifications.

Franz had observed that Father John was a dedicated servant of the Lord—and he tried to win his favor. "He must know how sinful I am, and this is his way of showing his disapproval," Franz reasoned with himself. "He's different from Father Emmanuel, but if I keep trying. . . . Anyway, he is an excellent teacher, and as he continually points out to me, he is only critical for my own good."

Father John had a peculiar lilt to his voice that disturbed Franz. He felt that he had heard the voice before, and under unpleasant circumstances, but he couldn't remember where or when.

"Why do you insist on reciting the *Pax Domini* as though you were mouthing a childish jingle?" Father John demanded of him, once. Another day he raged at Franz, "This paper you turned in reads like a businessman's report—where is your religion?—Remember, I speak for your good," he chided.

Franz tried to find the right words. He looked out the window and Father John's voice came across the classroom, "You are intellectually cold" . . . the word "cold" rang with a teasing half-memory of his first day at Ingelstadt—the confession and the penance. Could it have been—oh, no, no!

For the next few days Franz pondered whether he should take steps to avoid Father John as an instructor, but he decided against it. "I know a priest will not judge—I know he acts as an intercessory—he is an agent of God—but why does Father John go out of his way to humiliate me?" Franz considered writing to Father Emmanuel for advice but decided against that, too. He smiled to himself as he acknowledged, "I can't explain that confession yet."

Franz longed for the strength of Father Emmanuel. He could remember Father striding into a classroom, his face lit with enthusiasm—the way he gathered the entire class into the joy of his nature—while homesickness fled, doubts disappeared. Poor papers were examined in the light of the students' aims, and help was given . . . and Franz was his confident, his favorite. Why was he displeasing Father John? Did Father John know Franz's carnal thoughts . . . that lustful night . . . his remembering?

Franz, in mental torment, walked alone under the chestnut trees . . . "Does Father John, in his purity, see my evil nature?"

Father John continued his harassing. Franz met each crisis with what he hoped was Christian fortitude, and each crisis became more difficult.

"You will proceed from your class to the chapel. You will stay there on your knees until the last bell; perhaps foregoing your evening meal will improve your Latin translations."

Franz noticed the brotherly understanding of each classmate as he walked from the room. Haribert, a young, blond German giant, had the temerity to grin at him. Franz responded with a sudden lift of his spirits.

The chapel was small and dark; incense hung like a rich drapery in the warm air. Franz sat in contented silence, his rosary in his hand. His wayward thoughts drifted as effortlessly as clouds on the wind, straight into the salon of Madame Roussault. He caught himself up with a start and fell to his knees, while the beads on his rosary started a frantic rotation. Then, as suddenly as he had gone to his knees, he settled back in his pew. . . . "Truth . . . listen to it, Franz . . . it is the Voice of God." Father Emmanuel's voice spoke to him across the distance of miles and days.

The truth? Long he thought and questioned. . . . "The truth is," he whispered at last with amazement, "I'm not repentant . . . I remember with delight. . . ."

The realization of his unrepentant state plunged Franz into a black despair. For days he prostrated himself before the altar, and with his entire being he cried out the Prayer of Contrition.

"My Lord Jesus Christ—Thou hast made this journey to die for me with love unutterable. . . ." Franz felt his tears on his face. "So many times . . . abandoned Thee . . . love Thee with my whole heart . . . I do, oh, I do . . . I know . . . Oh, my God . . . I do know you. . . ."

In his distress Franz sought the morning and mid-day mass, the evening prayers. He fasted and prayed. He turned to his music with renewed vigor and wrote a number of compositions with a religious theme. He walked alone and watched the sun go down. He listened in the stillness of the night. He asked for enlightenment with the first dawning of a new day. At times his heart would be heavy, but sometimes it seemed that he was lifted completely above all heartache and separateness and placed firmly in the presence of the Most Holy.

Father John's lilting voice interrupted even the most sacred communion, and Franz came to know what a thorn in the flesh could be. . . . "That's it . . . that's all he is . . . a thorn, easily removed—but passion of the flesh is. . . ." He sought for a fitting word, and was brought back to the classroom with a sharp reminder from Father John.

As he left the classroom, he was stopped by Haribert. "Walk across the campus with me," he invited.

Franz fell into step, "Speak a few kind words to this unworthy creature," he begged, mimicking Father John's high, lilting voice.

Haribert laughed, "You sound just like him . . . I'm going into town tonight. If you're free, why don't you come?"

Franz hesitated briefly. Tonight he had liberty; it would be a change.

Haribert continued, "I know a girl, Ingebord . . . she has a friend, Greta. We will go to their home . . . you need. . . ."

Franz felt a familiar tightening of the throat. It was like that night at Madame Roussault's—the same closing in his ears. "I'll go," he found himself answering.

On the way back to the seminary, at midnight, Haribert walked jauntily ahead, singing a popular song. Franz felt no remorse, no sense of sin. He felt a mild astonishment at his attitude. "Have I become calloused so easily? Why can't I berate myself? Can it be that I have relived the sin with Lisa so many times that I have become blasé? It is true, I have relieved this sin with Lisa almost daily for a year," he told himself.

Haribert called over his shoulder, "Was Greta satisfactory?"

"Yes," Franz answered, almost indifferently. Then he probed, "You are studying for the priesthood, too?"

"Certainly." Haribert slowed his prancing and questioned Franz. "Why do you ask?"

"But—tonight—the girls?"

"Oh, that! Well, I just think I haven't taken any vows yet, so I'm not breaking any . . . and I'll go to confession . . . pray like crazy, and be ready for my next liberty . . . as simple as that. What's troubling you?"

"Do you want to be a priest?" Franz asked.

"Yes, more than anything."

"Why?"

"Because I love the life. I love the sacraments, the masses, the obligations. I love people . . . I want to serve—"

"But, tonight?"

"Tonight . . . was grand. Ingebord is a delight. Be happy, Franz."

"When you take your vows, what then?"

"I don't know, Franz . . . but God will take care of me . . . I just trust."

Franz slept soundly all night and awoke feeling happier than he had since leaving Father Emmanuel. "This isn't right . . . I think—" He shook his head. His eyes fell on the title of Wolff's book, *Sensible Thoughts on the Effects of Nature*. He read it over again, aloud this time . . . then he laughed.

Father John assigned his class a paper on the meaning of the Crucifixion. He gave them until the beginning of the Lenten season to finish it. Franz set to his task with a devotion he had never felt before. He spent hours making the stations of the Cross; he read and reread the scriptures. He stayed for long periods on his knees. When he wrote, it seemed to him that a master hand held his, and that the words were words of fire burning his heart. "Words of fire" reminded him of Father Emmanuel. They were words Father used to describe any writing he considered exceptional.

Franz sat looking into space, seeing the years he had spent learning from Father Emmanuel—the walking and talking method of instruction. How he longed to find this companionship with Father John. He lifted his essay again and read the words over softly to himself . . . "Father John will know now . . . the Blessed Savior Himself has given me these words . . . Father John will. . . ."

Before Franz turned in his paper to Father John, he made a copy of it and sent it to Father Emmanuel. For the next few days he felt jumpy and irritable. He wasn't sleeping well . . . and when he did sleep, Greta wore Lisa's face in his dreams.

Then Franz and Haribert went into town again and were met by their cheerful, laughing friends. After a few dances, Franz and Greta wandered off. "I know a place," Greta whispered eagerly. "The family is away. . . ." They hastened to the home.

"She is like I am," Franz consoled himself, as he removed his tight student's jacket.

On the way back to the campus, it was Haribert who asked, "You are going to be a priest?"

"I'm asking myself that question now. I'm torn—completely torn—between piety and passion," Franz answered.

They walked in silence; then Franz continued, "I can't obey two masters. It's the world or the priesthood. . . ."

"For some it's like that, Franz; I'll pray for you. . . ." Haribert's voice was full of sympathetic concern.

Father Emmanuel's letter came.

My Beloved Pupil:

Your paper on the meaning of the Cross fills me with great pride. I find myself at a loss to say more than this, for I am so deeply touched by your vision and comprehension of the "love expressed and released to all life everywhere" that words cannot contain all I hold in my heart.

May this Lenten Season bring you into full communion with our Blessed Savior. This is the prayer of your old teacher.

Father Emmanuel.

Franz read and reread the letter, then gently folded it and whispered, "Bless you." Confident and expectant, he hastened to Father John's class. He had never felt happier. Father John held the stack of essays in his hands. He handed back several, with nods or brief words of approval. Then he held up Franz's. "Here is one that deserves no mark; but because of the Holy Season, I'm passing it. Franz Mesmer, think well before you take your vows. This shows no gift for priesthood . . . trash—just trash. . . ."

Franz felt the world whirl around him. He thought for a moment that he was nauseated, and with a blinding flash of insight he knew . . . Father John hated him. His next thought was, "I must see Mama and Papa."

He asked for and received, as a special dispensation, a two-week Lenten holiday to visit his parents in Switzerland.

On the stagecoach he read his prayer book, said his beads, studied a musical score, prepared the next month's work in astronomy, and then settled back to flood his being with all the unanswered questions that plagued his soul.

Father John is not a happy man, he thought; not even a successful one. He has the beloved habit of our Order—the seclusion from the world, with the beauty and sanctity of constant communion available to him—but he is harassed and bitter. Why?

The Baron is a worldly man who follows his desires. He is jovial and warm-hearted. He supports the Church, but he is not a captive of it. Why?

Why did I grovel in shame after having Lisa and feel nothing but relief after Greta? Was it the luxurious setting which made the affair with Lisa sinful and the careless, happy interlude with Greta seem more like playtime? Can it be that a visit to a house set apart for lust is more evil than a coming together in shared joy?

What will I say to Mama and Papa? They've been happy,

believing me to be preparing for the priesthood . . . how can I speak of my doubts?

Then, too, there was Father Emmanuel. Franz covered his face in his hands, "How can I tell?" he kept asking, but no answers came.

Then he was home. The cottage seemed a little smaller at first, the mountains and trees larger, but Mama and Papa were the same.

"My son, my son, how big you are!" Mama wiped her eyes.

"Mama thinks of you as an infant. 'My Baby,' she says. . . ." Papa laughed noisily, then blew his nose.

For the next few days Franz gave himself to his parents. He listened to Mama's village gossip and attended Papa on his daily chores. There was an outward pleasure in being home, but underneath the sense of joy was the dull hammering of his unanswered problems.

It was Papa who spoke of it. "My lad, you are not at peace." They were alone, high in the forest.

Franz stopped the denial that sprang to his lips: "No, Papa . . . I am unsettled . . . worried," he admitted.

"Your work—it is——"

"No, Papa. There are just many unanswered questions . . . I seek answers."

"A wise man asks the most important question first." Papa stood by a seedling; he carefully studied the bark, then moved on.

"And then?"

"Then he awaits his answer. Foolish men keep asking questions, never listening for the answer." Papa caressed another seedling.

"See these young trees—they don't question, they just know . . . nature . . . son. . . ."

The next day Franz slipped off alone. He walked through the garden and climbed over the wall and started up the gentle incline toward the mountain.

Up the slope, he recalled, fifty paces from the garden wall, a gentle ravine parted the face of mother earth. Between the lip-like banks of this furrow bubbled a spring which ran off in two directions as a brooklet, only to disappear into the earth again a few feet on each side of its source.

As a small child, Franz had found this spot and had named it the Holy Place. He remembered how he had prostrated his body in thanks to all Being. He had lain flat on the cold earth, his mouth against the silken grass that felt somewhat like Mama's hair. The odor of life had filled his nostrils, and song was everywhere. Strength had flowed through his bones as water flows in a river bed. He was part of the flow. The flow was part of him. Strength had been in his being—and a knowledge without words.

Franz remembered telling Mama and Papa about it that night at supper. He had finished his last bite of cheese when he had heard himself blurt out, "I found God today."

"You found whom?" the parents gasped together.

"God, you know, our Father. I found him." Franz had carefully removed the largest grape from the bunch and crushed it between his teeth.

"Today—alone up there," Franz nodded to the slope outside the window, "I found Him. I was lying on the ground watching the clouds—trying to see God or hear Him, like Moses did." Franz remembered how he had paused and sought out the next largest grape. His parents waited.

"Suddenly I heard the music of the brook, and I knew it was the voice of God. It said, 'Franz, I am life. I am rushing forward to meet the world. Soon I'll be the great Rhine River, and then I'll be Lake Constance; and then again, I'll be the Rhine. I shall see all of life; I'll be all of life; and yet I shall always be here, too.' Papa, I felt this song a long time today. I know it is true."

Franz tried to find the exact spot he had lain on as a child . . . he stretched out. The sun seemed very near and intense. He lifted his thin, white hands to its rays . . . the fohn, that alpine wind so welcome in spring, seemed to sway his arms. Franz felt comforted.

"I hate to bring out my questions now," Franz confessed to himself, "Papa said a wise man asks only one question at a time. What is my first question; it must be why does Father John find me unworthy . . . yes, that's my question—now I've asked it; let me listen for the answer."

Franz turned on the damp ground. He sniffed in delight

the perfume of the earth's spring. He listened for the message. His thoughts went back to the classroom . . . *Father John's irritability . . . irritated me except when I'd been with Greta . . . sex . . . relieved . . . irritated? . . . me . . . Father John irritable . . almost as though he were jealous . . . irritable . . . sex . . . the confession* . . . Franz felt a chill pass through his body and then a flush spread over him . . . he felt his face grow red, then pale with emotion. At last he knew . . . it was Father John who had heard his confession. No, no . . . I have no right to question . . . a holy man of God . . . Listen to the voice of truth . . . it's the voice of God. . . .

Franz lay still, his arms stretched out, palms down. His face pressed against the earth. He knew his first question was answered; he knew he didn't like it.

His second question must follow. . . . Did he want to be a priest. . . . Does Father John want to be a priest . . . or is he forcing himself to be one . . . does he long for the world . . . his disciplines and mortifications . . . what do they mean? Father Emmanuel wanted to be a priest. Haribert wants to be a priest . . . Franz would not be a Father Emmanuel . . . the truth of the matter is . . . Franz turned over to face the warmth of the Switzerland sun. *He would be a Father John!* A man trying to be a priest . . . I can't . . . Merciful Jesus . . . I can't. . . .

It was at the supper table he told them—just after grace.

"Mama, Papa . . . *I can't be a priest."*

Mama caught her lower lip between her teeth and stared at her plate. Papa looked out the window into the forest, black with the evening shadows.

Franz felt the silence grow big. He wished to break into it, to shatter it into bits of rainbow lights and make the world happy again, but he could not unsay his words. He couldn't change his mind. He watched the silent steam rise from the fondue dish. Mama had made it with pride for the son who made her proud. Her son, Franz, a priest. Papa's large hand was flat on the table; against the white of the cloth, it looked very brown. His nails were strong and pink—they were healthy hands that knew how to work. Franz remembered Father John's hands

—impatient hands—small, white, and clasped tightly in a prayer.

"What is prayer, Papa?" Franz's voice cut through the silence. It rippled the dying steam from the cooling fondue; it loosened the grip on Mama's lips, and Papa moved his hand. Franz didn't wait for a reply. He answered, "Can't prayer be service, labor, love, laughter?"

Mama crossed herself and looked at Papa. Papa looked at Franz, as Franz continued, "All things beautiful can be prayer—music, nightfall, Mama's fondue. . . ."

Franz knew his parents were listening. "Mama, I want love, like you have loved. I want children, a home. I want God within my own walls, belonging to my loved ones."

Franz's eyes turned from Mama. "Papa," he implored, "I want to stride up and down the land as you do—meeting my friends and my troubles as you do. Papa, I want to be like you. . . ." His voice broke. Franz angrily shook his head, embarrassed at the weakness he was displaying. He gave up, pushed his plate back, put his face on the table, and struggled to keep from sobbing like a child.

Mama's arms enfolded him. Papa's big hands comforted him.

"There, there, Mama understands," and Papa was not to be outdone. "Just what I've been wanting . . . my son in the world—living a good life . . . grandchildren." They laughed together.

Before he went to bed, Franz composed a note to Father Emmanuel.

Beloved Teacher:

I bring you disappointing news. After your careful tutelage and hours of instructions, I have decided against the priesthood.

Mama and Papa have asked me to return to Ingelstadt to complete my education in philosophy, music and law.

Can you forgive your suppliant?

Franz.

CHAPTER III

RENEWED IN spirit, Franz returned to Ingelstadt for four more years. He studied philosophy and received a doctoral degree. Then he turned to music and received his master's certificate. Not content, he read law and eventually took a degree in it.

Then Franz went home to Papa and Mama. He felt empty. He couldn't explain, but Mama and Papa urged him to rest.

"I can teach in any university, I can play in any symphony, or I can practice law in any court," he told them, "but I don't want to."

Day after day he sought the mountains, trying to find his answer. "What meaning is there for me? What am I to do?" Again he wouldn't allow himself the comfort of conferring with Father Emmanuel.

Franz remembered his childhood. Papa was a forester for the Archibishop of Constance. Papa knew the secrets of the wild creatures in the forests, the life habits of the trees, and the treacherous beauty of the storm-swept mountains. He had taught Franz. For miles and miles, Franz had tramped behind his sturdy figure as he talked of things at hand.

Yes, Papa knew the earth; but sometimes at dusk when they turned homeward, his thoughts as well as his eyes strained upward to the sky.

"Paracelsus," Papa would say, "Paracelsus knew about that."

"Did you know him, Papa?" So many times Franz had asked this question, always hoping Papa would answer yes. But always his father had answered, "No, no, my son. Paracelsus died two hundred years ago. I'm not quite that old."

"Tell me about him, Papa. Tell me like your grandfather used to tell you."

"As I know the paths of this forest, Paracelsus knew the paths of the stars. In some strange way he drew upon the heavenly bodies for strength—or wisdom, for the two are one. 'Man is like a magnet. He can draw from the astral flow either good or evil.' Paracelsus said this, for he was a philosopher as well as a doctor. In his practice of medicine, Paracelsus used magnets to draw disease from men's vitals. Some people laughed at him. You see, he wasn't trained in a school of medicine."

"Did he mind being laughed at, Papa?"

"Ah, son, even a strong man needs approval. But Paracelsus fought for his beliefs like a true son of Switzerland."

Paracelsus and the sky. Papa and the earth. Franz remembered that, as a child, he had sometimes felt caught between them—tiny and breathless and insignificant.

Franz remembered the village doctor—a fascinating man, Franz thought. He must have been a very kind one, too, the way he let me follow him from patient to patient. I even carried his little black bag; and then there were the days he let me help him roll pills and put them in bottles. He was a patient man. I was happy then . . . happier than I have ever been. Mama, Papa . . . Herr Doctor and the patients he shared with me . . . Franz smiled to himself.

Franz remembered, too, how he had often assisted in bloodletting. The doctor as well as the neighbors had felt that he had some power over the flow of blood. He remembered one cold night in particular.

"Franz, Franz." Mama was shaking him.

"Yes, Mama," he had answered her as he burrowed into the warm covers.

"We must go. Herr Doctor has decided to bleed little Gretchen again, and he wants you to come."

"But, Mama, it's cold. Let's wait until the sun is here."

"Child, the angel of death waits not upon the sun." Mama had pulled the covers back.

Franz remembered how Gretchen's weeping mother had hurried them down the village street. She led them into the bed chamber where her fat, pimple-faced child of fourteen was threshing about on the high-canopied bed. The old doctor was laying out his bleeding instruments on a table beside the bed. He nodded to them and turned toward the patient. From his pocket he pulled a large handkerchief. He folded it carefully and tied it around the girl's feverish upper arm. The vein stood out against the puffy flesh. Quickly he slashed. The blood spurted. The doctor untied the handkerchief and placed a receptacle under the arm.

"The blood is sluggish," the doctor said, as he motioned Franz nearer to the bed. "Come, Franz."

Franz could still feel himself walking toward the bed and then placing his hands on the girl's head. She grew suddenly quiet and blood gushed from the wound. The doctor nodded his satisfaction.

"Enough!"

Franz moved his hand from her head. The blood stopped. The wound closed. It appeared as a small scratch. Gretchen smiled drowsily.

"A miracle, a miracle," the mother whispered over and over as she clutched her beads.

"Can't we go home now, Mama?" Franz had asked.

"What had happened?" Franz questioned himself now. He stretched out his well-shaped white hands and studied them. "Did I have a power here, or was it superstition?"

As time went by, Franz slowly groped his way—unsettled intellectually, disturbed physically by the never-ending lust of his body, yet yearning spiritually and reaching out always for God's wisdom. Again and again he sought the quiet haunts of his childhood. He was lying by the familiar little brooklet when the answer to his own problem came to him.

"I'm going to be a doctor!" he cried aloud, exultation filling him.

In 1759 Franz entered the University of Vienna. His new masters were physicians of renown in the Vienna School of Medicine. Maria Theresa, Empress of Germany and Archduchess of Austria, had brought these famous men to Vienna. Doctor Girard van Swieten had organized the clinic, and Doctor Anton de Haen had followed him from Holland. It was Doctor de Haen who first advocated the consistent use of the clinical thermometer with every patient. These men were especially generous of their time with Franz. In a letter to Mama and Papa he wrote:

"It seems as if I had spent all my previous years preparing for this experience. My academic accomplishments give me a certain standing with the professors, yet I often feel that they expect more of me than of the other students. For this reason, and because of my own desire to learn, I work hard."

Franz completed his medical examinations when he was thirty-two.

"What are you using for your graduating motto?" one of his colleagues asked one day as they left the clinic together.

"*Multa renascentur quae, quae jam cecidere cadentque, quad nunc sunt in honore,*" Franz quoted.

The student whistled, then translated perfectly, "Many expressions which have now fallen into disuse will rise again, just as those which are in honor will fall. Isn't that Horace? You surely are not applying it to medicine. How does it fit in with your thesis?"

"My thesis is entitled, *De Planetarium Influxu*. I'm writing it in Latin."

"But what's it all about? What are you trying to say?"

"I'm trying to show that the planets have an effect on our lives. I'm wondering if some of the old sages could have been right when they said that the sun, the moon, and the planets have a great deal of influence upon us, our thoughts, our ways of living, even the formation of our bodies. Not wishing to improve upon Paracelsus, I wonder if these heavenly bodies do not give off some sort of emanations—*I call it fluidum, which flows into all life or through life.* If this is true, then is it not possible that the human body carries this same fluidum? If the ebb and flow of the tides and the flow of a woman's menstrual cycle are determined by the moon, why is it that. . . ."

The student was staring at Franz as though he were deranged.

"And what is your thesis about?" Franz asked abruptly.

The student explained that his thesis had to do with the use of hemlock and other poisons and the possibility of their use in small quantity for curative purposes.

Franz couldn't help smiling as he recognized the pharmacological approach of their teacher, Doctor Anton von Stoerk, but he listened carefully. One of his Jesuit disciplines had been to learn to listen carefully, to refrain from argument, to control anger, and to suffer silently.

Franz's dramatic thesis created a stir among the faculty. It stimulated talk and speculation. Dr. van Swieten was obviously referring to this when he embraced Franz in farewell and advised him.

"Settle down to good medicine as it has been taught to you, Doctor Mesmer. Leave your visions for entertainment. Don't try to establish new schools. We need good, solid physicians with such training and background as yours."

Franz decided to establish his practice in Vienna. Mama and Papa helped him to select an acceptable office. Mama was busy and felt important supervising the establishment of "the Doctor's" office; Mama always referred to Franz now as "the Doctor." Papa wandered about, getting in the way and complaining of the city life.

"Too much noise—not enough good clean air."

"But the music, Papa," Mama protested.

"Ach, yes, the music," and Papa smiled. "I think that's why Franz chose to practice here."

"You're right, Papa," Franz conceded. "I've never been happier," he declared over and over.

After Papa and Mama went back home, Franz decided it was the right and proper time to contact Father Emmanuel. He wrote:

September 19, 1766.

BELOVED FRIEND AND COUNSELOR:

Although I have not heard from you for a long time, you have been with me in my daily work and nightly prayers. I wrote you of my decision to leave the priesthood. I have longed to tell you the reason for this decision and ask—no, pray—that you will be magnanimous in your forgiveness.

I wonder if dedicated men of God, such as yourself, can know the torment some men suffer in the battle of the flesh? This has plagued me for years now. Right from the first, at Ingelstadt, I was torn between heaven and earth. I would come from the highest and holiest communion, dazed with spiritual insight and filled with divine exultation, only to be betrayed by the devil into an animal desire for a woman's body. Even the severest rigors of penance could not assuage this desire entirely—for you see, Father, I had sinned and knew the carnal delights. Confession and penance and self-imposed tortures availed me little when the madness was upon me. I recalled in joyful sequence each step in her love play and my response. At times I would call out to Almighty God to show me a more soul-stirring experience than the naked body of a beautiful woman in close embrace. God has been patient with me, Father. Can you be less?

My medical training is now complete and I am establishing in Vienna. I have rooms in which I feel much pride and I would love to show them to you. Also I would find peace in knowing that you wished absolution for me. Can you soon visit your humble and affectionate

Franz Mesmer.

Father Emmanuel sent a reply by return post.

MY ESTEEMED PUPIL AND BELOVED FRIEND:
Your letter gives me new evidence of God's Eternal Wisdom. All men could not be celibate priests, or the world as such would soon cease. You have fought a good fight or you would not have won your present position. I not only forgive you and pray for your absolution, I shall even refrain from saying 'go and sin no more.'

Thank you for your kind invitation. I shall avail myself of it and join you for a fortnight after Easter—six months hence.

God be with you.

Father Emmanuel.

Many of Franz's patients were poverty-stricken, but even at the beginning of his practice he had invitations from the wealthy. Such calls increased, now that he had time free from study and was able to accept some of the dinner invitations received by any educated, unmarried man in social Vienna.

But his social life expanded more rapidly than did his medical practice. After the first few months, Franz sometimes felt as if he were treating patients by rote—as if medicine had become the means by which he earned his daily bread while he looked for the wine of life elsewhere.

Franz took up his music again. He learned the conventional steps of the decorous dances used at court balls, and he accepted every invitation extended to him by wealthy or distinguished personages.

Some of these invitations Franz was able to return in a small way with musical evenings in his rooms. He grew proficient in the use of the glass harmonica—a new instrument invented by an American, Benjamin Franklin. This music machine consisted of a set of graduated glass spheres which revolved in a water container. One played them by running a moistened finger around the rims of glass. The instrument was a fine one, and Franz used it to draw visiting musicians to his parties. It was in this way that he met Christoph Gluck and Joseph Haydn.

Franz became quite proficient, too, in all the little social graces which bridge the gap between the cottage and the court. He clicked his heels and kissed jeweled hands, among which was the hand of Frau Marie Anna von Bosch, one of Vienna's wealthiest and handsomest widows.

A few days after Franz met Frau von Bosch, there was a rap on his door and a man announced himself as Karl Weber, the manservant of Frau Marie Anna von Bosch.

"I've come to fetch you, sir." The man had a dignified bearing and spoke in such cultured tones that Franz bade him sit while he got his medical bag.

"Is Madame very ill?"

"Not Madame—her son, whom we call Junge. . . ."

To make conversation, Franz asked, "A little boy?"

"No, sir. Junge is nearing manhood. Nineteen, sir. . . ."

Franz liked the man, Karl Weber. "There is something about him," he thought, as he pulled on his coat and gloves to go to the von Bosch residence. "He has strength . . . I like him."

Before Junge had recovered, Franz was hopelessly in love with his mother. She honored him by attending his next musical evening. Franz had given in to an extravagant impulse and bought another new instrument, an offspring of the harpsichord. This amazing instrument was called a piano-e-forte, because one could produce soft or loud tones at will by simply striking the keys gently or firmly.

Franz spent hours practicing. One day he was interrupted by a loud bang on his door. He waited for the servant to answer, but the banging came again with even more insistence. Franz left the piano-e-forte and opened the door to a man with gloved fist raised to continue his pounding.

"Here, here, my good man," Franz said, and grabbed his hand.

"It's time you 'here, here' me, I'm dying . . . yes, I'm dying. . . ."

"Come in." Franz smiled at the man, who resembled a well-wrapped package.

"Won't you remove your wraps . . . it's quite comfortable in here."

"Cold as purgatory—that's what it is . . . I can't get warm—chilled all night . . . can't breathe . . . nose stopped. Look —can't breathe at all."

Franz had piloted the man into his office. He pushed him into his examining chair near the window.

"Now open your mouth . . . say Ah-h-h . . . Uh huh"— Franz put his ear on the man's chest and said, "Now cough."

"Did I come here to play games?"

"Cough!"

The man coughed.

"Your lungs are clear. The congestion is here in your throat and nose. Nothing serious. Do you know how to prepare a mustard bath, Mr. . . . Mr.?"

"My name is Leopold Mozart. I am a choirmaster from Salzburg."

Franz smiled, "Ah, my friend, being a musician, you will recover in a hurry when you see what I have in my music room. Come . . . see my piano-e-forte." Before Mozart left the music room, they were dedicated friends.

Franz asked Leopold Mozart to play that first evening Marie Anna von Bosch came. She was enchanted. She promptly asked Mozart to come for a musical evening in her home, and he asked permission to bring his eleven-year-old son Wolfgang.

"Could this possibly be the child who toured the capital cities of Europe five years ago?" inquired Marie Anna.

"The same, Madame."

"But he is famous!"

"Was famous, Madame. The public forgets easily. We have not been able to afford another concert tour."

"But he has continued in his study and practice?"

"And in his composing. You may have heard that he wrote a minuet when he was five years old. This is true. I set the notes down for him as he played them."

"And a genius such as this lacks patronage?"

"Professional musicians doubt him, Madame."

Franz was delighted that Marie Anna did not doubt. She and Franz were drawn together by their interest in this talented man and his gifted child. They were together as much as her social life and his profession would allow.

Franz's admiration for Marie Anna grew. He saw in her the beauty, fire, and grace of Lisa, plus the tenderness and spirituality of Mama. "With this woman I can become whole," he persuaded himself. "Gone will be the torment. Earth and heaven will come together in her arms."

One night after the opera they were driving home in her carriage. Franz looked at his hands, remembered Madame Roussault, and his passion could no longer be denied. Tentatively he stroked the rich embroidery of her cloak. Emboldened by the fact that she did not chide him or draw away, he touched the warm curve of her throat and gently turned her face to his. The moonlight gave her flawless skin an unearthly glow.

"You are too perfect to be human," and his lips were against her cheek. He sought her mouth. It was soft and full—but closed. In an instant she withdrew her lips and in a cool, restrained voice said—

"You forget yourself, Doctor."

But as if to soften the blow, she laughed lightly and tapped Franz's arm gently with her gloved hand. He caught it and cradled it in both of his. Then he slipped off her glove and kissed each delicate finger.

Franz spent his days seeking ways to please Marie Anna. He bought small gifts to make her smile; he composed a love song and inscribed it to her; he catered to her slightest whim and was extravagant in his open adoration.

True to his promise, Father Emmanuel came for a visit.

"Franz, what an abode you have here. I'm proud of you. My, there must be many wealthy sick."

"True, there are many sick, Father, and I manage to see that the wealthy ones pay for the care of the poor. I do my best for all."

Father admired in turn Franz's library, his expensive laboratory, his set of musical glasses; then he walked to the piano-e-forte. He touched the keys, ran his fingers over the inlaid case, and then picked up some sheet music from the rack.

"Wolfgang Mozart—hmm—who is he?"

"Listen, and then you tell me."

Franz sat down at the piano and opened the manuscript. He played it through. Then he lifted his hands from the piano and sat quietly. Father did not speak. Finally Franz turned to him.

"You find it moving?"

"The man is a genius. I am transported." Father Emmanuel wiped his eyes unashamed. "Mozart . . . he is a great talent."

"Yes, I believe so, too. I have known him only a short time, but he has endeared himself to me not only by his genius but by his gentility and his unassuming nature. Would you like to speak with him?"

"It would be a privilege—a very great honor. He is one of the immortals; this I know. Where shall I meet him?"

Franz smiled and thought, "Now is the time to tell Father about Marie Anna." How should he start? Franz moved from the piano over to his musical glasses. Absent-mindedly he rubbed a finger over one of the rims. It sang out in the silence and Father started.

"Always reminds me of lost souls. Excuse me, son, perhaps that was an ill-timed remark. What do you want to tell me?"

Franz took a deep breath. "Father, I'm in love. You shall meet Mozart this evening in the home of my beloved."

"Excellent! Excellent! Tell me about this beautiful young lady."

"Beautiful, yes. . . . Young, no. Father, I must talk with

you." Franz poured two glasses of wine and they pulled their chairs close.

"The lady is Frau Marie Anna von Bosch. She was married to a Privy Councillor who died and left her wealthy. I was called in to see her son—a youth of nineteen—but I continued calling long after he was well. For months I have known she was meant for me."

"Meant for you?"

"I have never been so attracted to a woman."

Father turned his wineglass in his hand. He made no comment, and Franz blurted out, "and she has done me many favors."

At this Father raised his eyebrows and pursed his lips.

"Oh, not that, Father. I mean she has introduced me to well-born friends and urged them to call me in as physician. She has done much for my practice."

Father's face did not change.

"And she is beautiful, she is elegant in her dress, she is gentle and kind. . . ."

Father smiled again at last.

"How much older than you, my son?"

"Ten years—but this makes no difference."

"Not to you, I'm sure."

"Nor should it to her. I'm not a child, Father, and age really knows only three stages—infancy, maturity, senility."

"True, son, true. I congratulate you and wish you all the happiness you are capable of enjoying, and I look forward to this evening when I shall meet both your paragon and your genius."

"As to the genius, Mozart—he is barely eleven years old."

A look of utter amazement came over Father's face; then he threw back his head and laughed so heartily that the sensitive strings of Franz's new piano resounded with his merriment.

Marie Anna outdid herself. The dinner was excellent, the wine superb, the guests scintillating. Franz kept watching Father Emmanuel's face, hoping to see a reaction to his beloved; but

Father's face was bland, his voice friendly, and he appeared in no way swept off his feet by Marie Anna's beauty.

A young servant passed the liqueur. As he served Marie Anna, his pocket caught on the back of her chair. Franz saw a glass tip; he sprang to catch it, but the contents spattered Marie Anna's white gown.

"You pig, why don't you watch what you're doing," Marie Anna hissed; then her voice turned saccharin. "Don't worry; no harm done," she laughed, "I was only startled. If you will pardon me, I'll go change."

She left the room. Franz glanced at Father, expecting to see his admiration; to his astonishment, Father looked exactly as he used to when he caught a boy cheating.

The days of Father Emmanuel's visit were at an end. Franz hated to see him leave.

"There've been so many affairs for you. I'll miss you, Father, and long for another visit. All my friends love you."

"You are well situated, Franz, and very popular."

"You sound like a warning."

"Do I?" Father smoothed the sleeve of his robe.

"I've felt you had something on your mind," Franz said.

"You have?"

"Yes."

"Sometimes it's better not to speak."

"But if I've been amiss—"

"Not you, my lad, not you."

"But who. . . . ?" Franz heard Father take a deep breath.

"Franz, are you certain of Madame von Bosch?"

"Certain?"

Father Emmanuel stood up. Franz arose, too. Father touched Franz's arm.

"My son, she is beautiful and clever; but I sense a coldness; there's a certain quality—perhaps spiritual deformity . . . I hate to speak. . . ."

Franz felt no anger—only an amazement that Father Emmanuel, who had so much perception, should be completely myopic now.

"Perhaps I'm wrong, Franz. I'm sure I shouldn't have spoken—"

"Please, Father. Never, never say that. Always speak . . . even if I don't agree with you."

Father's face relaxed; he laughed—but he also muttered something that Franz thought he understood as "Maybe she won't say yes."

CHAPTER IV

FRANZ BEGAN to believe that Marie Anna loved him as he did her, for otherwise why did she always accept his invitations? She listened to his conversation with avid interest, and even more convincing of her love were her attempts to please him. He was thinking about the attractive little theater she was building in her garden.

"You can help unknowns or honor the great by your patronage." He had been merely dreaming out loud, but Marie Anna must have given orders that the theater be built at once.

"My dearest dear," Franz smiled at her when he saw the first scaffolding of the building, "if you were not so beautiful I'd think you a witch, the way you get things done"; and he kissed her hand, letting his love shine in his eyes.

It was Leopold Mozart's distress that had caused the comment. He'd been at Franz's earlier that afternoon, raging in his disappointment.

"Travel—concerts—travel—drafty halls—meager pay—and still more travel. We are wearing ourselves to the bone and no one takes us seriously. Wolfgang is no dancing bear that I should lead him about the country from now on. My son is a genius. I tell you this from my heart, Franz, he is a genius. He must have commissions to compose operas. He must have peace and quiet, and time to develop his rare talent." Leopold paced the floor.

"You are right. Many of us recognize his gift and see his need."

"Not many—no, not many—only a few have eyes to see and ears to hear. The rest just sit quietly while he plays—a cat would do as much—and when he has finished they pat him on the head and make silly noises." Leopold's voice grew harsh with anger. " 'So sweet,' the ladies say. Bah!"

Franz knew Leopold had never pressed for recognition of his own talent, but now he was ready to fight for that of his son. Leopold's fury boiled over; he kicked a foot stool. It flew across the room and landed in the midst of a table holding Franz's medical instruments. The sudden clatter of falling instruments was followed by a moment of dead stillness; a servant rushed in, but Franz waved her away. Leopold's anger was gone. He stood pale and contrite, staring at the wreckage; then he sighed and began to pick up the pieces.

"I'm sorry, Franz. You see, I'm just a country bumpkin; no place for me in polite society." Leopold held a broken box and tried to fit the pieces together. Franz walked over to him, took the box out of his hand, and tossed it into the fireplace.

"Forget it, Leopold . . . no harm done," Franz smiled.

"Franz, you are not displeased with me? Ach . . . this peasant side of me. It and my temper will be my undoing."

"Leopold, do you think I could know you so long and not check you against the stars?" Franz asked.

"Astrology! Are you interested?" Leopold was diverted.

"Yes—yes I am. Paracelsus believed in the stars. I've been studying."

"Do you use it in your practice of medicine?"

"Only to check my records and research."

"What do they tell you about me?" Leopold demanded.

"You are Scorpio. The stars gave you that temper." Franz laughed.

"And Wolfgang?"

"Is Aquarius. He'll do his best to cover up his extreme sensitivity to public opinion."

In an instant Leopold returned to his distress about Wolfgang. "Franz, a musician must not cover up; he must express, express." And Leopold banged his fist on Franz's desk for emphasis.

"Then we must try one more concert. Wolfgang shall play only his own music."

"Only his own . . . dare we?"

"We dare, my friend, because we must."

Franz sought Marie Anna's help. He told her of his talk with Leopold.

"Will the little theater be finished in time for the concert?"

"I'll see that it is." Marie Anna's voice was imperious, but Franz knew that it was her enthusiasm for Wolfgang.

"My beloved, I knew I could depend on you." Franz's arms reached toward her but clasped the air, for Marie Anna had moved to a mirror to inspect her coiffure.

"We'll start our guest list with the Emperor himself," she smiled from the mirror to Franz.

The concert was a glowing success. Poor Leopold wept with pride when Emperor Joseph embraced Wolfgang and announced to the assembled guests, "I am publicly asking, nay entreating, this golden genius to compose an opera for us."

Leopold and Wolfgang set to work at once. Occasionally Franz dropped in on them to see how the opera was progressing, and once he took Christoph Gluck with him. Success sat well on Gluck's fashionably-tailored shoulders, Franz thought, and Gluck was able to impart his own sense of self-assurance and well-being to others. Only six short years before, he had become famous for his *Orfeo and Euridice*, the first opera to blend arias into a story or play. He had followed this production with several more successful reform operas, and his encouragement meant a great deal to both Mozarts, as Franz had hoped it would.

"See," Leopold pointed out to Franz and Gluck, "I only help my son put the music down. He does all the composing. I explain this to you, my friends, for many donkeys accuse us of fraud. Even our own Archbishop doubted until the time he had Wolfgang locked alone with paper and clavier."

It was Gluck who suggested to Franz that Wolfgang's completed opera be informally reviewed by a few of their musical friends. Franz never knew whether Marie Anna had invited Afligio, Director of the Imperial Opera, or whether he had simply come with one of their close friends. At any rate, he was there when all gathered about the little stage in the garden.

Franz was glad that Nannerl, Wolfgang's sister, was in Vienna at the time. She was four years older than her brother and sufficiently mature to take a part in this informal production.

Wolfgang played, explaining parts of his opera as he went along and introducing the arias sung by Nannerl and Leopold. *La Finta Semplice* could not have been produced more simply, but it was charming. Leopold had a great natural voice, and what Nannerl lacked in volume she made up for in purity of tone.

Franz was delighted to see that Gluck was as enthusiastic as he was. Most of the guests were generous in their praise . . . not so, Afligio. He did not even approach the stage when the performance was over. Finally, Leopold sought him out. Afligio's curt reply carried to the ears of Gluck and Franz.

"The opera has very little substance. A boy of twelve is too young. . . ."

Franz motioned Gluck to come with him to Leopold's rescue, but they turned toward the two men just in time to catch the full fury of Leopold's answer. He referred to the Director as an unspeakable part of a donkey's anatomy, as a mere chicken's droppings when it came to musical appreciation, and as a pig—a castrated pig.

Franz was pleased that Marie Anna rushed her guests into the house as he and Gluck sought to calm the two men.

After the concert Franz did not hear from Leopold; he assumed, therefore, that he had made his peace with Afligio through the Emperor. Franz knew that Emperor Joseph II was an easy man to see. Not only did he move about freely in Viennese society; he made himself available to his people at regular office hours—as a professional man would do.

It must have been three weeks before Leopold called upon Franz at his office and said, "The Director of the Imperial Opera has refused to produce *La Finta Semplice*."

"Refused?" Franz couldn't believe Afligio would carry his hurt pride this far.

"Yes, in his own way. He delays, he criticizes, he suggests changes, and all the while he is spreading gossip about me in court circles. Oh, my friend, it's no use—no use."

"Let me see what I can do, Leopold. Don't worry, and don't blame yourself." Yet, even as he reassured Leopold, Franz was disturbed.

"Ours is a highly moral court. Could word of Leopold's outbursts have offended the aging Empress Maria Theresa?" Franz asked himself and prepared to call upon Emperor Joseph—for he shared the throne with his mother, the Empress.

The situation was not as bad as Franz had feared, but

Emperor Joseph did explain to him that he limited his patronage to those artists who were recommended by his advisors.

"My beloved mother introduced me to each of the Muses, Doctor Mesmer," he said, "but none of the introductions ripened into a love affair. I must depend upon Afligio's judgment. Now, if it were a matter of land reform. . . ." and he smiled. His enthusiasm for land and social reform was well known.

Within a few days the Emperor sent Leopold a small sum of money, one hundred ducats, for Wolfgang's work on the opera. Franz knew then that they must abandon hope of seeing *La Finta Semplice* produced at the Royal Opera House during Afligio's directorship.

Franz saw that the Mozarts were heartsick, each too weary and broken in spirit to console the other. Wolfgang took refuge in playing dreamy little pieces, to which he added nonsensical chants of rhyming words. Leopold came down with digestive attacks. Nannerl stayed in Vienna, fluttering over them both. Franz found himself deeply concerned for the whole family.

He had just left Leopold's bedside one evening when he came upon Wolfgang, huddled in a tight little ball on the outside stairs; the boy's knees were drawn up under his chin and his thin arms were folded about his legs to press them close to his body. He was rocking back and forth, humming a doleful tune.

Quietly Franz closed the door behind him. In the darkness he moved over to the boy and sat down beside him. They sat thus, neither of them speaking. Finally, Franz broke the silence.

"Tell me, Wolfgang."

"I have failed . . . I have failed! It is over . . . I have failed!"

Franz was startled; he recognized in this child's voice the music of his little brooklet streaming across the years from the haunts of his childhood: "I am Life—I am Life." It stirred him with holy awe.

Reason left Franz—for suddenly he was Life. All the power and surge and rhythm of Being swept over him in that moment. He grasped Wolfgang by the shoulders and pulled him upright. He stared into the boy's eyes and spoke in tones as measured as the beat of his pulse.

"You are a genius. You are great. You are loved. In your

music, you are immortal. Tomorrow you begin again. You will write another opera. You will write and write—and this opera we will produce, together."

As suddenly as the spell had come it was gone. The boy burst into tears, grabbed Franz's hand and kissed it, and rushed into the house. In a daze, Franz walked to his waiting carriage.

"How could I have given Wolfgang this assurance when I no longer have it in my own life," he asked himself, amazed, for Franz was tired and filled with a nostalgia for the dreams he used to have . . . for his faith . . . for his prayers . . . maybe for youth, too.

"I don't know. . . ." In great weariness he leaned back against the carriage seat. If he could find the courage to ask Marie Anna . . . with her as his wife. . . .

The boy must have set to work right away, for when Franz next saw the Mozarts they were full of talk about the new opera *Bastien and Bastienne.*

"You heard part of the music for it that night," Wolfgang told Franz shyly.

Franz did produce *Bastien and Bastienne in* Marie Anna's garden theater. He wrote Father Emmanuel about it, "This little opera has considerable charm. To my mind it does not show the full development of the boy's genius, but I do not doubt that it will take its place among the great dramatic works that are products of our generation." Franz sealed the note to Father. He felt restless. He sat at his desk and made a few jottings. He picked up a book to read but felt relieved when he heard a knock at the door. He was delighted to find Karl Weber, Marie Anna's driver, on his step.

"Madame von Bosch is in the carriage. She would be happy if you would join her for a drive," Karl said as Franz reached for his hat and ran to the carriage.

"How kind of you . . . how thoughtful, my dear." Franz kissed Marie Anna's hand, then held it in his own. Karl was driving through the Vienna woods and life became a miraculous thing. Franz smiled at Marie Anna. She smiled faintly, then dropped her eyelashes and turned her head away from him.

"Oh, no, my dearest. . . ." he let himself breathe the words.

He turned her face back to his, "Never turn your beautiful face from me . . . why, if I live to be a hundred, I can never look at you long enough . . . close enough. . . ." There, he'd almost said it.

For a moment she seemed to melt against him. He wanted to cry aloud with the upsurge of joy at this response—to sing praises, even to tell Karl Weber, the good man who was driving them, that the most beautiful woman in the world loved him . . . him!

His lips brushed her hair and he followed her gaze out the window—"See, the forest; there we should be wedded. The trees would be our guests, the birds our music, and love our sacrament." He allowed himself to finger the smooth curve of her throat. He kissed her lips, her hands, her closed eyes. He felt her tremble.

"Franz?"

"Yes, my sweet." He was surprised that her voice was composed; he thought she had been as shaken as he. She pointed lightly. "There is St. Stephen's Cathedral."

"Yes, precious. It is imposing—a magnificent spire—can be seen for miles. . . ." He kissed her hand.

"It is in the precise center of Vienna, and all street numbers radiate from it."

He frowned. What was she driving at?

"Franz, we shall be married at St. Stephen's on January 10, 1768." Marie Anna announced her decision with authority and finality.

Too enraptured with her consent to care, he kissed her hand and sought her lips.

She permitted him a brief kiss on her cheek.

It would be different later, he promised himself; he was just impatient.

Marie Anna's gown subtly revealed the dimensions of a body which delighted even his professional eyes. He permitted himself the luxury of swiftly appraising her trim feet and slim ankles as she alighted from her carriage. But she was so demure, so spiritual, that he felt he must plan each step in the gentle wooing which would bring her to the full release of her passions.

The weeks passed slowly, but at last the wedding parties, the pomp, and the ceremony were over. Franz was alone with his bride. The cruel nights of waiting were at an end, but Franz restrained his eager impulses and poured his wife a glass of wine. He remembered Lisa. After pouring a glass of wine for himself, Franz knelt at Maria Anna's feet and looked up in worshipful adoration. He caressed her hands, and shyly he touched the bosom concealed by her wedding gown.

"My dear, shall we retire?"

"Yes, Franz, it has been a wearing day."

She moved into her dressing room. Franz changed into night attire and awaited her. As she came back into the room, Franz's senses reeled as he whispered in wonder, "My wife, my beautiful wife."

Marie Anna slipped off her satin robe and daintily slipped between the bed covers. Franz extinguished the lights and moved in beside her. The bouquet of her body came to greet him as he reached out arms to enfold her . . . but her voice stopped him. Cold and impersonal, it came.

"Not tonight, Franz. I'm tired. Another night, perhaps?"

Franz did not speak. She went quietly to sleep while he lay motionless beside her, bathed in a cold sweat of pain that turned to bitterness.

"Why didn't I see? . . . I should have known. Father Emmanuel saw . . . he warned me. Of course, she's cold . . . never has she returned a kiss . . . even a pressure of the hand . . . never even once . . . what a fool I've been . . . I wanted love . . . warmth . . . she's incapable. . . ." Before daylight he moved into the rooms she had had furnished for him in another wing of the house

The stately mansion, No. 261 Landstrasse, had been a wedding gift to Franz and Marie Anna from her father. They moved politely through the following days—receiving friends, accepting congratulations, dining with guests, and retiring separately to their own rooms.

Finally there came an evening when Franz had had too much wine. As Karl closed the door on the last guest, Franz whirled and caught Marie Anna up in his arms.

"Franz, put me down, Franz!" But he held her tightly,

stalked up the stairs, and bore her down upon her bed. She fought and bit and scratched; but he prevailed. Finally she whimpered and lay passive. Slowly Franz was filled with self-disgust. He left her rooms and never returned.

Two months later he wrote Father Emmanuel—

March 10, 1768

BELOVED FRIEND AND COUNSELOR:

Were you to visit me now you would rejoice in the material changes in my life. Our house is a well-ordered castle in which I have my own apartment, a magnificent laboratory for experimental work, and my medical rooms.

My wife excels in the social graces. She takes hours to plan a menu, days to arrange a musical, weeks for her gowns. Her servants are well trained and well paid. They slave to keep a gracious background for their lovely lady. Even our gardener chooses flowers to complement Madame.

I, too, am part of the setting. My knowledge of mathematics, astronomy, philosophy, and music is cleverly exploited by Madame to make our parties the most stimulating in Vienna. How perfectly mated we must seem—yet our marriage is a failure. How right you were . . . had I but listened.

Marie Anna is stupid, too—stupid beyond endurance. There, I've said it at last, and I want to go on saying it again and again—pyramiding the words until they crash the very gates of heaven. Stupid . . . stupid . . . stupid!

Can it be that all women are like this? Do they not know that a man's soul cries out to his beloved through his body? How can anyone deny this reaching out of one human being toward another for completion?

I look at our friends and wonder. I think back to the quiet kindliness my parents showed one another, and I question. Was Papa hungry at times for a fulfillment he never knew? And did Mama know this yearning, too? Mama was a haven for me. Was she less for Papa?

Oh, my oldest and my best friend, Mesmer's heart is empty. His vision of rapture was only a mirage. Pray for him.

Franz.

CHAPTER V

SOCIAL VIENNA began to absorb more of Franz's life. Night after night Marie Anna had plans for them. There would be a small dinner, or an important banquet, a grand ball, the opera, the symphony, or the theater.

"Sometimes I feel like a child's ball—bouncing, bouncing all the time," Franz complained.

"But you do enjoy it, Franz," Marie Anna laughed at him.

"Yes," he admitted reluctantly, "but I'm behind in my work," he protested.

Many evenings, after all the festivities were over and Marie Anna had climbed the graceful staircase to her suite, Franz walked to his laboratory. Here, with his medicines and notes he sought peace. Sometimes he wrote up the records of his patients of that day. At other times he just sat and let his liberated mind go off in any direction it chose. . . . "I do not have to be social in any sense here, saying 'Madame, you dance divinely,' or 'Ah, sir, what a wit!'" At times he recalled his childhood activities. Most often he would recall the days when Mama would hustle him off to the bedside of sick friends to assist in the bleeding.

"What resource did I tap in my childish ignorance?" There was nothing special in these experiences; yet, something happened to the patients. What? Over and over he relived these instances, hoping to catch an insight into some manifested power.

The very first time he had helped with a bleeding, he must have been about ten. One of his friends had had to be bled. Franz stayed in the room because he was curious, and because, too, the adults thought he might be a comfort to his friend, who was frightened. Franz recalled taking the boy's free hand in his. He felt the beat of his pulse through his thumb, "or was it the beat of my own heart that I felt?" Franz asked himself, then continued his remembrance.

"At any rate, I winked one eye, the eye away from the doctor, at my friend in time to the rhythm of this beat. At first he grinned in response; but as the doctor proceeded, my friend's face lost all expression. I looked over and saw the blood flowing."

Franz remembered feeling suddenly sick. He dropped his friend's hand and moved to the window. Then he heard the excited, whispered conversation behind him.

"Hot packs, quickly, the flow has stopped."

"Is he dying? Oh, doctor, is he dying?"

"My friend dying!" Franz recalled how he had rushed back to the bedside and had laid his hand on the boy's forehead. "Beat, beat, beat," Franz had whispered to his friend's heart, and the doctor had looked up in startled disbelief.

Such a childish act—commanding that which is beyond man's ability to influence, much less control. Yet the doctor had looked up in startled disbelief, for once more the blood was flowing.

Franz loved this genial old doctor who had brought him into the world. He remembered how he had followed the doctor's footsteps from the first day he had been allowed to play with the doctor's medical case. The bottles and boxes fascinated him. He smiled, remembering that he hadn't even protested too much when the doctor painted his sore throat and prescribed a mustard plaster for his chest.

"He must have been a great doctor, with only a minimum of training," Franz thought. "Anyway, he did possess considerable professional curiosity, for I remember he commanded, 'Franz, move over to the window again.'" Franz had done as he was told.

"Now come back here and put your hand on this boy's head." He returned.

They had repeated the performance several times, and each time the flow of blood had come and gone with the pressure of Franz's hand.

There were several witnesses to this episode. Franz never recalled being questioned about it, but the story must have been widely told. After that, mothers of sick children often sent for him when their children were to be bled; and soon even the old doctor began requesting his presence.

These and other scenes from Franz's childhood filled his mind when he was alone in his laboratory. As he meditated, his soul was filled with longing; yet he knew not for what. He did want to practice better medicine. He had respect and admiration for the Vienna school, but he felt that they were not exploring to the fullest all the sources of information available to them. The current theories of science and medicine seemed too mechanical and drab to Franz. They were explanations of patterns on the surface of life, mere cover-ups for the ignorance of the Life Force itself, which ran deep, powerful, and mysterious within. It was this Force that Franz longed to identify with. He knew that there was a God—but he felt he had lost personal contact. He also missed the time he used to spend in prayer. The God of his childhood had disappeared. No longer did he look up at the sky, hoping to see God's face—as Moses had. Now, in maturity, it was not the face of God for which he searched, but for His eternal Presence.

"Can it be that I question too much, that I don't live as naturally as I should; like Papa says of his trees, 'nature takes care of her own'? But my life here with Marie Anna—this is not natural . . . it is against my nature, but what can I do?"

Father Emmanuel's reply came:

MY SON, MY SON:

"For the Lord disciplines him whom He loves, and chastises every son whom He receives." Hold fast to these words of scripture while I pray that they will come to have reality for you.

Such Force as is given into our mortal bodies comes not from our own efforts, but from God Himself. To you, much of this Life Force has been given. In this you are blessed. Give thanks and pray that you will soon find release in your work. Work, my son, work—pour out your seed upon the world of medicine and music.

I pray for you.

Father Emmanuel.

In his heart Franz knew that Father Emmanuel's advice was sound. He determined to discipline his own thoughts and energies as they had been disciplined for him by his schoolmasters in former years. He set up a rigid schedule. In addition to regular office hours and clinic visits, he offered his services as physician to the cathedral orphanage. He allowed time for laboratory work which he had been neglecting, plus one hour a day for study.

He got out his old thesis, *De Planetarium Influxu*. Just the sight of it reawakened his interest in the scientists and physicians of ancient times: Hippocrates, Galen, Paracelsus, and even Newton.

"These are the men whose writings I must study," he told himself. "This is more important than being a background for Marie Anna. She can indulge her passion for social affairs as she did before I came along. I must work . . . work . . . Marie Anna . . . How can I avoid? . . . But I will."

A letter from Mama provided a temporary answer, for Mama wrote, "Papa isn't at all well; can you come?"

Franz's days of introspection and work were overshadowed by his deep concern for his beloved parent. He was grateful to Marie Anna for sharing his concern, and for her help in arranging his journey. Franz asked another doctor to see his patients while he was away. Marie Anna insisted he take the large carriage and Karl to drive.

"You must hurry, Franz," she told him. Karl made the trip in record time.

Franz found Papa quite ill with pneumonia, but he responded in a miraculous manner to Franz's treatment.

Franz brought Papa a new book on astronomy and a map of the skies. They spent hours poring over them. In a few days Papa was up and about the house.

Franz felt refreshed and stimulated. Mama cooked his favorite dishes and told him all the village gossip. He would draw her out. "Has the widow Schmitt convinced Herr David that he has mourned long enough?"

"Would you believe it, my son, since Frau Becker died last winter the widow Schmitt has eyes only for Herr Becker; and, this I know you will not believe: after she has run after Herr David for fifteen years to no avail—why, he wasn't even polite at times—now, when Herr Becker is returning her long looks, Herr David is as moony as a sixteen-year-old, but the widow Schmitt spurns him." Mama hadn't even paused for breath during her recital.

Franz laughed with delight. "Mama, you should write stories."

Franz stayed until Papa was ready to work again; then he

told them good-bye. He embraced Mama. "I feel rested and very much alive—this has done me more good than I have done for Papa." Then Franz turned to Papa. "You are a better conversationalist, Papa, than any of the Emperor's men."

As Karl drove off, Franz directed him to the road to Dillingen.

Franz found that the old monastery at Dillingen had changed very little—draftier, perhaps, after the luxury of Vienna, but the mouldy smell of the place was so comforting to him that he did not mind at all the coldness of his feet.

Father Emmanuel assigned Franz a cell near his own where he could rap on Franz's door each morning as he went by at five. Franz rose in the icy darkness and plunged into his clothes in time for the mass. He breakfasted in silence with the priests, who one by one left the table as they finished. Franz, too, had outside chores to perform before he was free to go into Father Emmanuel's rooms to read. Soon Father would join Franz in the little library and then they would talk.

"Healing is the subject closest to the hearts of both of us, Franz. You work with the body and I with the soul, and the mind is the vast unknown between the two."

"Father, it's this vast unknown between the two that I'm concerned about."

"Concerned? I find it exciting." Father rubbed his hands together with eagerness.

"You remember my childhood ability to influence the flow of blood?"

Father nodded.

"What is this ability?" Franz asked abruptly. "You see, Father, I'm disturbed because I think—that is, I know—I still have it."

Franz rapidly recounted his experience with Wolfgang. Father kept nodding until Franz had finished; then Father cleared his throat. "Franz, how is your religious life?" he asked.

"I go to mass, Father, and. . . ." Franz stopped.

"And?"

"That's it, Father, that's what I miss most, my prayer life. The time spent apart. I need it. My soul cries out in longing, and yet there are the sick waiting, the poor to be cared for, a social life to be maintained, and my family to think of."

" 'In as much as ye do it unto the least of these,' " Father quoted.

"I know, but in giving I am depleted—something flows from the inward me. I have no time to regain this supply before there is another need. If I only knew the source . . . if I could but understand. . . ."

"Franz, do you see the connection between medicine and religion?"

"Yes, Father, I do. A physician is a better doctor if he enjoys the grace of God. Then there's the patient with a troubled soul." Franz shook his head. "Of course, we have many physical explanations for disease and we shall discover more of them." Franz paused as though looking for words. "Paracelsus just might have been close to such discoveries when he suggested that the stars and the planets give off forces which affect man's body." His voice was slow and deep as he explored his own thoughts.

"Remember, too, Franz, that Paracelsus also said, 'You must know that will is a powerful adjuvant in medicine.' "

"Yes, he did. I've wondered if he was referring to the doctor's will, or the patient's will? Or perhaps the Divine will?"

"The three can become one, Franz. Such was the case in the person of Jesus."

Father Emmanuel moved a book on his desk and restacked a few papers. Then he gave Franz a sharp look.

"Your married life, Franz?"

"It's as I wrote you, Father. I presume that even the servants of the household have no idea. Certainly society accepts our marriage as above reproach." Franz smiled wryly, then added, "Marie Anna is charming, and remote as a maiden aunt to me."

"Well, that is some consolation. From the gossip that drifts into these walls, I judge some women make their homes so torrid that hell would seem a mountain resort to their families." Father laughed at his joke.

Father walked over to his little Chinese cabinet and drew out a bottle of wine and two glasses. When he had filled the glasses he offered one to Franz, who lifted it to his lips. It was at this moment that Father Emmanuel asked, "And, of course, you are living the life of a celibate?"

Franz swallowed hastily and choked. "This man knows everything," he thought to himself. He had a fit of coughing, then regained his composure.

"This is excellent wine, Father. It must be of reputable vintage," he remarked politely.

Father's eyes twinkled, but he only said, "Thank you."

"Now, Franz, let us return to your depletion. You feel you give something of this flow to each patient?"

"Yes." Franz hesitated. "I really hadn't thought about it before, but I do . . . not as dramatically as with Wolfgang . . . but . . . even with Papa . . . he recovered almost immediately."

Father Emmanuel was silent for a few minutes.

"My son, the only comforting words that come to my mind are those of our Saviour—'Knock and it shall be opened to you.' Keep on seeking, Franz. God has given you a talent. Remember the parable of the talents? You can't bury your talent, but God will attend you, replenish you. . . ."

The men sat in contented silence; then Father asked, "Franz, would you be willing to travel a bit out of your way to visit with a priest healer in Klosters?"

"A friend of yours?"

"No, we have not met, but I am much interested in his work and have kept up with it rather closely. I would like to know what you think of his methods."

"Tell me about him."

"His name is Gassner, but I'd prefer not to say any more, Franz. Go see with your own eyes, and evaluate for yourself."

"Father, why don't you come, too? The carriage is large and comfortable. Karl is a good driver . . . it will be a holiday."

Father frowned in deep thought. "That it would, lad, I would like to go. . . ."

"And so it's settled!" Franz moved fast so that Father would have no time to change his mind or his mood.

When they arrived, mass was over at the cathedral in Klosters, but still the people waited on their knees. Suddenly Franz heard a scuffling noise in the back of the chapel. As he turned to look, a peasant woman jerked from the hands of two men who appeared to be holding her—half running, half dragging herself down the aisle toward the altar. The woman's left arm hung lifeless at her side, and her ungainly pace seemed to be caused by a partial paralysis of her left limb or foot. On her face was a look of utter terror.

This amazing spectacle so absorbed Franz that he did not see the priest return to the chapel by a side door. Franz had risen to go to the assistance of the peasant woman when the command, "*Cessett!*" rang through the cathedral.

Franz settled back by the side of Father Emmanuel.

The woman dropped to her knees, and then Franz's startled eyes beheld the priest. He was robed all in black. Before him, and slightly aloft, he held a crucifix—his eyes fixed on the face of the peasant woman—and slowly, slowly, he moved toward her as he began a chant.

It couldn't be! . . . it was . . . the rite of exorcism. The priest was commanding the devils to leave this child of God. Now he stood in front of the woman, lowering the crucifix as he finished the chant. As the last words fell from his lips, he touched her on the forehead with the crucifix. She fell on the floor in a swoon.

"Move your left arm," he instructed her in Latin. She moved the arm freely. Franz noted that it was the same arm that had hung useless at her side only a few moments ago.

"Move your left foot in a circling motion." Still he spoke in Latin. The woman raised her foot slightly from the floor and described a circle with her toes.

"Your devil has left you, and you are cured of your afflictions," announced the priest at the end of this amazing ceremony. "Arise." And he blessed them, one and all.

Franz watched the woman walk from the chapel. Her face was composed, she did not limp, and she carried her shawl over her bent left arm.

Franz never knew why he and Father did not go immediately and talk with the priest—for this was Father Gassner, whom they had come to Klosters to see—but they did not. Instead, they sought out their carriage and started the trip back to Dillingen. Franz was troubled.

"I think I'm repelled by this theatrical use of one of the church's rites," Franz complained.

"But, Franz, my lad, do you realize that peasant woman obeyed his commands spoken in Latin?" Father's voice showed his respect. "Surely you were impressed."

"I can't believe she was possessed *by a devil*," Franz protested.

"You can't? Why?" Father's voice was cold.

"Maybe he's a fraud . . . maybe it was all staged."

"Franz! Shame. This priest is famous everywhere; country people flock to him for healings."

"How does he do it?" Stubbornness clung to him.

"They say he just drives out the demons, always addressing them in Latin; I suppose the demons can't speak German." Father laughed, and Franz joined him half-heartedly. Then Father continued, "The patients always swoon; sometimes they even have convulsions . . . bad convulsions." Father jerked his rotund body, demonstrating the convulsions.

"Are they always healed?" Franz asked.

"No, Franz, not always; but all of them say they feel better. Oh, yes, you will also be interested to know that a physician came here from Switzerland to investigate. Father Gassner showed that doctor!"

"How?" Franz asked, hoping he didn't sound too skeptical.

"He ordered a possessed woman to slow her pulse, while the doctor counted; and then to increase it to 120 beats a minute!" Father sat back, looking pleased with everything.

"It's hard for me to accept, Father. Demonic possession, indeed!" Franz shook his head.

"Our Lord drove out devils." Father's voice was soft.

"But he was using the terminology the common people understood," Franz protested.

"Can it be that Father Gassner is doing the same thing?" Father demanded.

"Father, I give up the argument." Franz shook his head. "I am at a loss to explain anything right now," Franz acknowledged. "I remember years ago reading a statement made by a Bavarian doctor, George Ernst Stahl. He wrote '*disease is a disturbance of vital functions caused by misdirected activities of the soul.*'"

"Now, my lad, that could be called demonic possession." Father slapped Franz on the knee. "Why don't we stop at the next inn and drink to it?"

"I'll buy you a drink, Father; but remember, I have to accept as truth these words of Hippocrates: *'Disease comes from natural causes and not from demons or angry Gods.'* And I shall continue my search for these natural causes.

CHAPTER VI

Franz returned to Vienna filled with enthusiasm and vitality. "I feel like a whole new world is opening for me," he thought.

He was at his office early the next morning and found it crowded.

"Everyone, except the emergencies, waited for you, sir," explained Karl.

Franz felt a warm glow of appreciation for these loyal patients.

The first one he saw was his friend Joseph Haydn. "Don't tell me your good music hands are wearing out on you?" Franz joked to hide his concern.

"No, Dr. Mesmer, it seems to be my heart that's wearing out . . . it jumps and stops . . . I have trouble breathing."

"Remove your jacket and shirt, and I'll listen," Franz ordered; then to put Haydn at ease, he said, "Madame Mesmer and I were speaking of you last evening. We want you for dinner Thursday. Madame has sent you a note."

"Ah, doctor, you should send me a board bill, too. I've eaten so many delicious meals with you." Haydn was fumbling with his buttons.

Franz studied the man's face. Lines of heartsickness and despair cut through the healthy-looking skin. "What ails this man is not organic—that I know—the texture of his skin, his pink fingernails—no. All that drawing room gossip can't be false; from all reports, his wife is a hellion—" He sighed. "Marie Anna is never a hellion; sometimes I wish she were—a little excitement—" He caught himself up from such things and, frowning slightly, he applied his stethoscope to Haydn's broad, bare chest. He listened for a few moments to Haydn's great heart beating in strong rhythm. Then he tested his reflexes; he peered into the famous throat; he asked Haydn to lie down; then he punched him all over the abdomen and bowel regions. All was in perfect order.

"You may replace your clothing." Franz sat at his desk until Haydn had dressed and tied his cravat.

"Sit down, my friend." Haydn sat down. "How shall I begin?" Franz asked himself. He used the physician's method of gaining time by scribbling a few lines on a convenient pad. Then he leaned back in his chair and said, "Haydn, an unhappy man is never a well man. Unhappiness chokes," Franz lifted his hand and made it into a tight fist—"like this. See?"

Haydn eyed the fist and nodded his head.

Franz felt a rush of pity fill his heart. How he longed to help his friend. "Unhappiness constricts, and this slows the ebb and flow of the life force. Your heart, dear friend, is a good one; it will last for many a year."

"But this irregularity—I can't be mistaken—it does go too fast."

Franz was touched by the distress in Haydn's voice, but how can you tell a man that he is letting his wife kill him?

"How came you to marry?" Franz asked abruptly and was pleased to see that Haydn looked surprised.

He hesitated a moment. then answered Franz's question as though he were glad to speak. "Perhaps I should tell you, doctor, that once I was completely devoted to my wife's younger sister. Although I idolized her, she could not respond to me or understand my physical love, looking only to God as she did for her passion. She went into a convent."

"You were miserable?"

"Oh, Franz. . . ." Haydn threw out his hand in an act of utter desolation.

"But, why the marriage to her sister?"

"I don't know. Perhaps in blind pain I stumbled into her available arms."

"Is it true that she is unsympathetic to your work?" Franz probed. "It is necessary for a doctor to see the wound."

"Well, all of Vienna is laughing about her cutting up my last completed music score to make curl papers for her hair." Haydn smiled wryly, "A servant told that story, Franz, with very little exaggeration. Yes, she hates my music."

"Then she was not distressed by the fire at Esterhazy?" Franz recalled the recent fire at Prince Nikolaus' (Haydn's patron) in which much of Haydn's work had been lost.

"On the contrary, she reveled in my loss and taunted me with ugly talk about God's wrath being turned upon me."

"But God has permitted you to recover a large portion of this work?" Franz asked gently. He not only admired this great musician; he loved him.

"It's hard, Franz, picking up again when so much has been destroyed."

"Has anything really been destroyed? The music lives in your heart. Write it down again, dear Joseph, and as a coda enter your personal triumph over despair. This can be your resurrection, your Easter."

"My Easter." Haydn seemed to taste the words. Franz saw his face brighten.

Franz handed Haydn a small vial and instructed him take nine drops in a glass of water thirty minutes before dining. A patient feels better if the doctor gives him some ritual to perform.

Franz began to feel as if he were performing some type of ritual when he went to medical meetings. The papers presented always had to do with the most recent developments in science, but seldom was any attempt made to bring these developments into direct bearing on the problems of healing.

For instance, there was the Leyden jar; it had been a central theme of discussion at the meetings. The jar had been developed in 1746 through the experiments of Pieter von Musschenroeck at Leyden University. More recently, however, Benjamin Franklin had declared that the electricity it demonstrated was a single fluid and that it was one and the same thing as lightning. Previously, science had referred to vitreous electricity and resinous electricity, but Franklin declared these to be aspects of the same force—positive and negative, or plus and minus. Franklin expected to harness this force.

"Nonsense," declared one of Franz's colleagues.

"Ridiculous," snorted another. "Why, my wife would hide under her feather bed if I brought this jar into the house. Can you imagine my suggesting that she cook with bottled lightning?"

"Perhaps Franklin has given up this notion. I hear that he is in England now, and that he and Dashwood are planning to revise the Prayerbook," offered a third doctor.

Franz joined in the general laughter, and the talk drifted off into idle gossip. Franz had given up trying to arouse any interest in his notion that this electrical force might be one with the fluidum of which he had written in his thesis some years ago. His speculations had been ignored. He knew the stars were too far away to interest his colleagues.

He began to spend more and more time in his laboratory at night, poring over his patients' charts and checking them with the signs of the zodiac. The case of Frau Ost was especially intriguing to him.

Franz noted that her birthday was July 15—the sign of the Crab, Cancer. She was a lovely, feminine creature with just a touch of autumn about her body. An unfortunate marriage had been terminated by the death of her husband and the full force of her possessive love had been turned upon her son. Now the son wanted to leave her and marry. She could not bear what she termed "losing him." Franz knew these things because she had told him.

Franz examined Frau Ost's delicate hands and smiled when he realized that he was visualizing them as crab claws. A crab attaches himself to something and hangs on until he conquers it or loses a claw.

"Can I deflect this woman's possessive love? Can I find her a new interest and loosen her grip on her son?" Franz asked himself.

Frau Ost was troubled with insomnia, upset stomach, gas, indigestion, and leg cramps. These were not her only physical problems. In addition, her eyes troubled her at times, there was a vague uneasiness in her breathing; she feared that her teeth were bad, and didn't the doctor think her hair dull?

Could these be the signs of the Crab losing a claw? Franz almost prayed as he asked her—

"Frau Ost, is it not right that you are agile with your hands? The harpsichord? Or perhaps the pen?" I've got to release that son, he told himself.

"Oh, no, Herr Doctor, not the harpsichord nor the pen." She was responsive. Franz smiled, because his books taught that all Cancers are responsive. "But my friends do think me clever with brush and oils."

"I wonder if you could do me the honor of illuminating a manuscript?" Franz handed her a volume of poetry. "I wish it as a gift for Frau Mesmer."

He gave her, too, the little vial with instructions to take nine drops in a glass of water thirty minutes before dining.

In a very few weeks Frau Ost returned the manuscript. Her illuminations were exquisite beyond anything Franz had visualized. He was also pleased that Marie Anna was delighted and displayed the volume proudly.

It was not long before Frau Ost was busily decorating things for several ladies in Vienna. Franz heard that she did greeting cards, sheets of music, and finally some dressing rooms. She also made friends with other artists and ultimately took up with a fellow artist—a middle-aged man in need of mothering. Her claws were intact, but the son was now free. He married with a minimum of distress on his mother's part. Franz recorded the Ost case with much satisfaction.

Fredrick Hauffer came to Franz complaining of chest pains which had moved about and finally settled in his left shoulder. His birthday was December 26, and he was a true son of the great Capricorn. He was a sturdy, handsome man who had made a late and unsatisfactory marriage; and since by nature he was secretive, Franz did not easily gain this information about his personal life.

Franz prescribed the nine drops—but having in mind the mystical inclinations of Hauffer's being, Franz headed him straight to the cathedral by asking if he would assist in the orphanage by teaching wood carving to a small group of the boys.

Only a week later Franz saw him there, surrounded by an adoring group of youngsters. His pain was gone.

Franz did not persuade himself that all physical ills might be so easily resolved. All of this was purely speculative—a research—nothing conclusive—but interesting, definitely interesting. He saw a good many organic disturbances which he could not ascribe to the influence of the stars on man's nature. Too, he was finding no distinguishing features in the physical make-up of babies born under the same sign. He observed and charted children from several age groups and found nothing in bodily structure, skin color, height, or girth to distinguish Pisces people from Virgo people.

It seemed to Franz that only after maturity was the seal of life set upon man's physical features. True, one person might be blond and the other dark, one tall and the other short, but in the features and the set of the body there were distinguishing characteristics. Rarely did Franz miss when he mentally classified the person according to his or her sign of the zodiac, and always he checked by asking. Naturally he did not confront his patients with his findings in their horoscopes, nor did he tell them why he recorded their birth dates with such care.

Only Franz knew how he longed to find answers to the questions his observations aroused. *What strength had the fluidum that it could put its mark upon the living flesh?*

Christoph Gluck was the one person who listened long and patiently to Franz's theorizing. Inevitably he ended his monologues by grumbling because none of the doctors of Vienna would hear him out on his theories. "Just you, Christoph—only you will listen."

"In an audience, quality is worth more than quantity," Gluck would remind Franz, and they would laugh.

This was not their private joke. All of Vienna had laughed at the story of Prince Kaunitz, advisor to Maria Theresa, commanding Gluck to perform a whole opera which only the Prince would hear.

"But, sir," Gluck had protested, "performers need an audience."

"Herr Gluck, I alone constitute an audience," the Prince informed him haughtily. "Quality is worth more than quantity."

Franz, forgetting his own frustrations, inquired about the Prince.

"You know how handsome the scoundrel is, Franz," Gluck said. "He has a naturally regal appearance, which he enhances by lavishing every imaginable attention on his toilet. He guards his complexion as zealously as if he were a belle. And that enormous wig, have you seen it lately?"

"No, not in months."

"Then he has added something new. Each morning, after he has completed his dress, he dons the wig and a long satin powder-coat to protect his clothing. Slowly he walks down a double line of servants, each of whom is armed with a vase of wig powder. The powders are of various colors, and as the Prince moves along each servant adds another color to the already well-powdered wig."

"It must look like a rainbow!" Franz said.

"That it does. It is nothing less than astounding, but perhaps what is even more astonishing—the man's bearing is so dignified that one feels inclined to admire rather than laugh."

"Undoubtedly he has a way. He excels as a diplomat and as Chancellor. The Empress and Joseph both judge him indispensable in spite of his eccentricities and vanity."

"Good theatre, Franz. The man knows the value of dramatic staging and how to use it to further his own ends. Perhaps you should make a study of his methods."

"My good friend Gluck—always he has just the story to shake me out of the doldrums," Franz said, still chuckling when he and Gluck parted.

CHAPTER VII

Franz discussed his concern with Gluck. "The stars—I need to know more."

"You need to study astronomy like I need to study the scales," Gluck joked. "You know more about Paracelsus than anyone."

"But I must know more of the later theories. I must keep abreast."

"If you insist, I'll take you by to meet my good friend, Father Hell. He is Professor of Astronomy at the University of Vienna. It's not far to his place . . . shall we walk by?"

"University? He should be well informed. . . . Yes, let's do visit him."

"He's well informed on a variety of subjects. By the way, he is also Court Astronomer to Maria Theresa."

Franz liked Father Hell from the first. This big, clumsy, happy priest bargained with Franz. "I'll take you as a private pupil in advanced astronomy, if you'll translate these into good German." Franz took the papers and glanced through them. It was a manuscript, written in French, on the art of French cooking.

"I'll do it," he agreed. "You enjoy cooking?" he asked.

"More than anything except stargazing." Father Hell looked thoughtful. "We need a new telescope . . . I've been looking at one . . . it's just what you need. Ach, my friend, if you knew what a good telescope can mean. . . ."

Before Franz fully realized what he was doing, the beguiling Father Hell had him promising to visit Herr Riemann's emporium to inspect the very best telescope in all of Vienna. Franz saw that Gluck only listened and smiled.

"I can see that Father Hell's need for excitement makes him an interesting companion," Franz said after they had left Father Hell.

"Let me warn you, Franz, he is unorthodox and frequently in trouble with the hierarchy."

"That, dear Gluck, is recommendation enough for me," Franz laughed.

Franz bought the very expensive telescope at Herr Riemann's and he and Gluck mounted it on Father's small balcony. As they took turns peering through the instrument into the moonless, star-studded sky, Father Hell ("loquacious as ever," Franz thought, "not even the stars stop him") talked of Paracelsus.

"Paracelsus theorized that the stars had a connection with magnets."

"I recall." Franz knew that Father Hell was aware of his interest in Paracelsus, but Franz had been careful not to reveal his interest in the astrology which Paracelsus mixed with his astronomy.

"Paracelsus thought that magnets had a sidereal power, an astral nature."

"That is right." Too late Franz realized he had fallen into Father Hell's trap. "Paracelsus used magnets for healing."

"Yah, yah," Father Hell said in his exclamation-point voice, "and he did heal, too—sinus troubles, dropsy, jaundice—even cancer, remember? Yah, he said that magnets had a hidden power, that a magnet possessed a belly and a back."

"Today we speak of this as a positive side and a negative side."

"There is a difference! No! Properly applied, magnets can yet give energy to the human body."

"Careful, Father Hell, remember the trouble Paracelsus got into with this belief. The doctors of his time—"

Father Hell snorted and leaned over Franz to make an adjustment of the lens. Franz stepped aside, but Father Hell motioned him back to the telescope as soon as he had fixed it on a new point of interest. Franz returned to his stargazing as Father Hell resumed his talk, but now Father's voice dropped to confidential tones.

"The Earl of Grosvenor sought me out at the University today." Father Hell paused; then his voice dropped even lower, "He and his lady are visiting here in Vienna. The Duchess suffers from a chronic kidney ailment. Usually she handles it with very little difficulty, but since arriving here the humor has spread to her ankles. They are badly swollen, making the pursuit of her social activities an impossibility. She is confined to her bed."

"Has van Swieten seen her?" Franz gazed steadily through the telescope. The Cassini division seemed actually to be frolicking around Saturn. "This is a fine instrument, don't you think so?"

But Father Hell answered Franz's first question, "No, they have called in no one. The Earl came to me to ask if I would procure some magnets for the Duchess."

This so astonished Franz that he deserted Saturn in orbit.

"Magnets?" Franz knew his voice was incredulous.

"Yes, magnets. You know we have just been talking about magnets and Paracelsus," Father Hell reminded Franz testily.

"But whatever would the Earl want with magnets?"

"To heal with, doctor, to heal with. The Duchess needs them."

"Can you get them?"

"Indeed I can. I put Ganser on the project and the magnets will be ready tomorrow. I plan to deliver them myself."

Franz's curiosity was aroused. "Can there be some new discovery in England?" Franz questioned himself. "Will you be able to observe the use of these magnets?" he asked Father Hell.

"Indeed, yes!"

"Will you keep me informed?"

Three days later Father Hell called for Franz in the Earl's carriage.

"Come and examine the Duchess if you wish. She is cured."

Father Hell's excited account of the healing was substantially the same as that given Franz by the Duchess and corroborated by the Earl.

"But how was it that you knew enough about this illness to ask for the magnets?" Franz inquired.

The Duchess smiled. "Once when I was a small child I fell and suffered a sprained ankle. My Nana applied two magnets to the ankle and assured me that within a short time the pain and swelling would leave."

"And it did?"

"Oh, yes. That is why I knew that if we could find the

magnets I would be well again. See—" She stood on her small feet and twirled in a childish little half-step.

Franz and Father Hell were on the street again before Franz questioned him further. "Why did you have Ganser make two of the magnets in the shape of kidneys and the other two in ankle shapes? Do you feel that these shapes have anything to do with the cure?"

"Who knows? They have to be in some form—so why not let them represent the ailment they are to heal?"

"The Earl requested this?"

"Oh, no. I just felt it wise." Franz watched in amusement as Father Hell puffed out his cheeks a bit and stood a little straighter as he continued, "I plan to use some magnets on Grandmother Mehrtens. You know she is badly bent and suffers considerably with her back. You may go with me to call on her if you wish."

"Thank you." Franz hoped he didn't appear too curious.

A servant admitted them, and the gentle little old lady arose with great difficulty to greet them as they entered her private rooms. She was about to order tea when Father Hell stopped her by saying:

"Absolutely no tea today, Grandmother. Ours is not a social call. I have found a new miracle treatment, and I have come to straighten your back."

Father Hell excitedly undid the package he had been carrying. Franz felt as amazed as Grandmother Mehrtens looked, for there before them lay a long iron magnet shaped exactly like a backbone.

In his gusty manner Father Hell commanded, "Grandmother Mehrtens, undo your bodice and flip off that bustle."

"Father!" she gasped.

But Father Hell was a forceful talker and a persuasive one. In no time at all he had Grandmother Mehrtens lying on the couch with her backbone revealed. He knelt beside her, talking in his most winning voice.

"Now, this may be somewhat painful, my dear. As I apply the magnet to your back you may feel a great deal of pain. However, the pain will come and then go as you find yourself bathed in a cold sweat of healing. At that point I shall wrap you in blankets. When the crisis passes, you will feel alive, alert, and free from pain. You will feel the blood coursing through your body and you will feel younger than you have felt in years."

Father Hell applied the magnet and sat back on his heels to watch Grandmother Mehrtens' face. Within a matter of minutes it was contorted with pain. She bit her lips and made little moaning sounds deep in her throat. Franz was alarmed—and then he saw the moisture forming in beads on her upper lip. He reached for the blankets.

Grandmother Mehrtens' tiny body was still limp when Father Hell removed the magnet, swathed her in the blankets, and carried her over to a big lounge chair. He and Franz stepped outside when the maid came at Father Hell's call. "Dress her," Father Hell said to the maid, "and then see that she has her tea."

Franz half expected the maidservant to refuse them admittance when they called again the next day. On the contrary, she greeted them cordially, "Madame was hoping you would return today."

Grandmother Mehrtens rose to greet them. To Franz's medically-trained eyes, her movements appeared as stiff as before. There was, however, a new lilt in her voice and enthusiasm in her facial expression as she welcomed them.

"My very good friends, be seated. I must tell you immediately about the miracle you have wrought with your wonderful treatment."

"Your back is free of pain," Father Hell anticipated.

"No, Father Hell, no. Something even more wonderful has happened. For the first time in years—in years, mind you—my bowels emptied this morning without flushing. If you could know the joy, the pleasure . . . oh, my friends, I am so grateful to you."

Franz dared not look at Father Hell. The dear little lady was so seriously and happily describing her physical relief—she might have been confiding the intimate details of a satisfactory love affair. Franz knew he would burst into laughter if he looked at Father Hell; and, of course, neither a doctor nor a priest may laugh, no matter how ludicrous the situation a confessor recounts.

Franz had again overestimated both Father Hell's sense of humor and his interest in science. For Father Hell was not amused, nor was he concerned that he had obtained unexpected results. Primarily he wanted action; and, of course, he had gotten action.

"Excellent." Franz listened to him enthuse. "Excellent, Grandmother. After tea I shall give you another treatment."

It was more than a week before Franz called again on Grandmother Mehrtens with Father Hell. By this time she had received a total of ten treatments. She rose easily to greet them; she walked erect; and she declared her back to be completely free of pain. Furthermore, each and every morning she was experiencing a "delightfully normal" bowel movement.

"From here I go to Baron von Stahlman," announced Father Hell as they left Grandmother Mehrtens.

"But I am treating the Baron myself," Franz protested, "he has asthma."

"No matter." Father Hell waved his hand in lofty dismissal of asthma. "The Baron has called for me. Don't be jealous, Herr Doctor. Soon all of Vienna will be calling for me. Of course, you must feel free to use my magnetic treatment on the sick who have not heard of me yet. Ah, yes, we must cure the sick."

Father Hell's self-importance was showing, as was his lack of medical training. Franz knew Father Hell wouldn't understand this, but there is nothing of which a medical man is more suspicious than a universal panacea. Even before Harvey detailed the circulation of blood in 1628, doctors knew that certain specific ailments occur which respond only to certain specific treatments. Preceding Harvey by almost a hundred years, Vesalius had accurately described the human anatomy and some of the malfunctions to which certain organs fall heir. "But there's no need to tell Father Hell this," Franz murmured, surprised at his own reluctance. "Father Hell expects to cure *all* the sick with magnets—nonsense." Franz went along to see the wheezy old Baron, whose main trouble, in Franz's opinion, was the dissolute living by which he was gradually destroying his whole body.

There was an earthy quality about Father Hell to which the

Baron responded. Franz felt this at once; moreover, he knew that certain lusty people speak readily of body functions, but the opening conversation between the Baron and Father Hell exceeded the limits of professional good taste. Franz tried to bring some measure of dignity to this meeting by interrupting the Baron's lewd recital of his woes.

"I left you a nose and throat spray for your asthma, Baron. Was it not effective?"

The Baron snorted, "About as effective as an old woman's efforts to piss against the wind."

Franz kept his professional questions and opinions to himself after that. Later he was thankful that he had done so, for to his amazement both the Baron's asthma and his prostate pains were relieved by the magnet treatment. This was exactly what Father Hell had expected, but Franz was astounded, and his astonishment grew as cure followed cure!

Some of Franz's colleagues heard of Father Hell's cures and were surprised that Franz had accompanied him on calls. They came to Franz with questions.

"Something happens," Franz assured them, "but I have only the beginning of a theory of what this something is."

The doctors pressed Franz for answers. He sought for an explanation. "Paracelsus used magnets to cure. He used them because he knew that magnetic iron came to the earth from meteors. Paracelsus believed that the stars had an influence on man, and he felt that these bits of magnetic meteors partook, somehow, of the stars' astral nature. In applying the magnets to the human body, Paracelsus believed that he was combining this astral nature with man's terrestial nature to achieve a condition of harmony." He pointed to his texts.

"Paracelsus spoke of a fluidum, an invisible fluid in which everything exists. Perhaps magnets exert a force on this fluidum and cause it to ebb and flow in the body. This force is almost certainly something like electricity, with which we are all so familiar."

None of his colleagues agreed with his reasoning, Franz saw quickly; however, he was thankful that they did not make a point of disagreeing. They accepted his statement that something was happening to Father Hell's patients, but they needed an explanation in terms of a something they could see or taste or smell or measure.

Nor were they as familiar with Franklin's electricity as Franz had assumed. He discovered this fact one day when Doctor van Swieten stopped him in the hall of the clinic and questioned him about his theorizing, which his colleagues had repeated. Somehow they had given the doctor the impression that Franz was experimenting with electrical black magic. Although he tried to reassure Doctor van Swieten, Franz was pondering another possibility. He wondered if the magnets were acting so as to bring on a crisis. Several diseases demanded that a crisis be reached before any healing could be expected to begin. Could it be that this was true of more types of body ailments than medicine realized? And if such were the case, could the magnets effect an artificial crisis after which healing would immediately begin?

These and many other questions were pounding in Franz's brain the day old Herr Mueller came to his office with a toothache. Herr Mueller was a quarrelsome fellow under the best of circumstances, but today he was intractable. Three times Franz readied himself to pull the offending tooth, only to have Mueller spring suddenly from the chair.

"A sound beating if you increase the pain in the pulling." He waved his finger threateningly. In vain Franz argued and reassured. At last, in desperation and anticipation, Franz sent Karl to fetch Father Hell and his magnets.

As he met Father Hell in the hallway, Franz shrugged with dismay.

"Just leave the good man to me, doctor," Father Hell replied as he unwrapped two magnets, took one in each hand, and stalked through the door to confront the unruly patient.

"Sit down in that chair, Herr Mueller." Father Hell's voice had the ring of authority. The patient obeyed. "Now look at me. Observe closely. I have here in my hands two magnets. I shall apply one to your left jaw, thus—the other to your right, thus. You will feel a magnetic pull, first from right to left, then from left to right. Back and forth . . . back and forth. . . ." At this point Herr Mueller's head was wagging slightly—right to left—left to right.

Father Hell continued talking, his voice authoritative but smooth as silk. "Slowly, very slowly, I shall now remove the magnets. Now you are magnetized to the point of no pain. You will feel no pain as you open your mouth and permit the doctor to remove your offending tooth."

To Franz's astonishment, Herr Mueller opened his mouth. Quickly Franz stepped up and pulled the tooth. Still Herr Mueller sat with his mouth open. Working rapidly, lest the patient's mood change, Franz staunched the blood flow and packed the gum with a clove oil pad.

Not until Father Hell clapped him on the shoulder with a "Not bad, old fellow, not bad" did Herr Mueller close his mouth. For a few moments he sat quietly gazing at the decayed stump of a tooth, with its long bloody root, which Franz had placed in his hand.

"No, not bad, not bad at all," he said, "but if I had been God I sure would have done things differently."

"How is that?" Father Hell raised his eyebrows.

"I would sure have fixed it so a man shed his pecker instead of his teeth in his old age. An old man ought to at least have left to him the pleasure of chewing."

In spite of Father Hell's aid, this was the only time Franz called him in, for Father Hell and magnets had attracted so much attention that Vienna doctors complained to his superiors in the Society of Jesus. Father Hell was admonished by the church for working outside his own science of astronomy. Franz was told that Father Hell had protested that he had only been assisting Dr. Mesmer and that it was really Mesmer who had directed the magnet treatments. Understanding Father Hell as he did, Franz could not be angry with him for this attempt to clear himself. "My robust, tempestuous friend—he has such need to be in the good graces of others," Franz explained to Gluck, and added, "Who knows, perhaps this very quality endears him to God. Certainly it could make him an excellent servant of God."

"At any rate, Father Hell did have Ganser make me some very fine magnets, which I plan to use experimentally."

CHAPTER VIII

THE FIRST person on whom Franz used the magnets was Franzl Oesterlin. Franzl was twenty-eight years old and unmarried. Her big violet eyes peered timidly out at the world through a curtain of heavy black lashes. These unusual eyes were Franzl's only distinctive feature. Her personality was so retiring as to be almost drab, and her pale, bony hands seemed to set the pattern for the balance of her bodily structure.

"No two women were ever more unlike than Franzl and Marie Anna," Franz thought; yet they had been close friends for several years. He couldn't understand it.

Marie Anna fretted over Franzl's poor health, and finally she brought the girl to live in the Mesmer home.

"Fine food and a full social life—these are Marie Anna's prescriptions for any and all ailments," Franz teased Franzl, as he coaxed her to eat.

Franzl's health did not improve. "She suffers from a variety of symptoms which stem undoubtedly from hysteria. She has occasional fever with which come convulsions, attacks of vomiting, and abdominal cramping, bloating and inability to pass urine, violent toothaches and earaches, and sometimes paralysis which lasts for several days," Franz thought to himself. He had learned to foresee her attacks, but he was powerless to forestall them.

"I know that they have some connection with her female cycle, but none of my pharmacopoeia compounds are in the least effective," he told Marie Anna.

"If you tried, Franz, really tried, you could find some way to help her," complained Marie Anna. "I seldom ask a favor of you. Surely you can do this for me. Must I call in another physician?"

"As a matter of fact, I have discussed Franzl's case with two of my colleagues," Franz admitted as kindly as he could, "but they can suggest nothing which I have not already tried. There is one thing. . . ." and Franz told Marie Anna of the magnet treatment.

"Then you must use the magnets," Marie Anna decided emphatically. "I insist."

Late that same night Franzl went into one of her spells. She was in acute pain when Marie Anna called Franz. Together they described the new treatment to Franzl, and Marie Anna persuaded the girl to let Franz try it.

Franz tied two magnets to Franzl's feet and then hung another one, a heart-shaped magnet, around her neck. Marie Anna unfastened Franzl's nightdress and Franz settled this heart-shaped magnet directly between her breasts, pressing it firmly against the flesh. As he worked, he talked to Franzl quietly—explaining the crisis which they might expect, for he feared her fright when the crisis should come.

"You must expect pains—hot, blistering pains which will shoot up your limbs from your feet to the upper rim of the iliac bones." Franz placed his free hand on her body and touched the spots. Immediately the crisis began. She writhed in agony.

"Next the pain will come up to here." Franz touched her breastbone.

"Pain will come from either side to join the pain which radiates from the legs. And finally the pain will come up to here." Franz touched the part in her hair. As he did so, she groaned and cried aloud; but Franz continued to talk. "The pain is as coals of fire burning throughout your body, burning out all illness. But soon will come the sweat. Soon your body will be bathed in perspiration which will cool the burning." Franz could see that Marie Anna was alarmed, but in his heart he felt strangely confident. Franzl was responding properly to the magnets!

"Soon, now," Franz consoled his patient and was gratified, for he saw the moisture beginning to form on her brow. Within moments her hair and nightdress were drenched.

"Change her clothing, quickly," Franz directed Marie Anna, as he withdrew to wait in the adjoining room.

Franz waited for Marie Anna to tap on the door; then he returned. Franzl lay as one in a stupor. He addressed her. "Now you are going to sleep. I have removed the magnets that drew the sickness from your body. You are well and you will sleep soundly. You will awaken with tomorrow's sun, happy and free from pain."

Franzl smiled drowsily and closed her eyes in sleep.

Marie Anna went to her rooms, but Franz sat at Franzl's bedside all that night—watching, wondering, thinking. His mind went all the way back to a book which Father Emmanuel had given him at school, *Sensible Thoughts on the Effects of Nature*. The magnetic force was certain to be a function of nature. There had to be a natural explanation of the cure he had just witnessed. Left alone, he felt quite sure Franzl's attack would have endured for at least three days. That the attack had terminated in a matter of minutes was no supernatural mystery. Somewhere, somehow, magnetic force was certain to fit into the great natural laws of cause and effect.

"Am I a praying man?" Franz thought to himself there in the night. "I do not speak of prayer often, perhaps because prayer is difficult to talk about after one has passed the childish stage of visualizing a God in man's image." Yet he still returned in memory to the voice of the brooklet which he had first heard in his childhood days. Franz touched Franzl's relaxed hand and noted it was cool and moist.

Yes, he returned to the voice of the brooklet when he needed help. Sometimes it spoke to him through the formal prayers in the cathedral. At other times it seemed to echo faintly through his body and he would feel a sudden need to reach out and touch his rosary.

Then there were days when he slipped off to drive through the Vienna woods. He would leave his carriage and walk alone in the expectant quietness of the forest. Here his mind would have to be stilled before he could hear the music of the spheres. He would walk and walk, becoming more and more a part of the Everlasting Song. Time had no face—for all was of now.

Sometimes it seemed that he had joined the Blessed Lord. The noblest physician ever to walk this earth knew both suffering and triumph. In the soul of Franz, he could hear:

"For if ye love them which love you, what thanks have ye?

For sinners also do even the same—
But love your enemies and do good and lend, hoping
for nothing . . ."

Hoping for nothing? Franz's eyes sought the relaxed face of the sleeping Franzl. "Blessed Jesus—You, too, were a physician. You used the healing force. Pray with me, Saviour. Have I a healing force? Is this of You? Help me to use it if it is . . . help me to understand it . . . help me to describe it to the world."

Franz realized that he had tears on his face.

The next evening was a gala one. Franz never felt more joyful. Franzl was glowing with health, and the Vienna Symphony was presenting Haydn's new work *The Farewell* for the first time. Haydn's conducting was superb. Franz felt his throat tighten with pride. Even Marie Anna was caught up in the rollicking gaiety of the music, and he saw her lean forward in her seat expectantly when one of the performers in the brass section blew out the candle on his music stand. Haydn appeared not to notice as the musician walked from the stage.

Next a man in the strings laid down his violin with much show. He, too, leaned over to blow out the candle on his music stand. This time the "puff" sounded clearly over a *pianissimo* passage. Haydn appeared startled. His head turned as he watched the violinist stalk from the stage.

Franz knew that Haydn's inborn humor was bubbling forth in this delightful work, but those in the audience who were not familiar with *The Farewell* watched with some consternation as two more musicians blew out their candles and left the platform.

Haydn did not miss a beat, but his head turned from side to side as he watched his musicians blow out their candles and desert him. By ones and by twos they left him, until only two violins remained to carry the melody of the music.

"What now?" Franz wondered. "Would all the men return in a body for the ending?" It was a dramatic moment. Then, with one accord, the violinists lifted their bows from their instruments in the middle of a passage. They blew out their candles simultaneously and disappeared from the darkened stage. Haydn stood alone. His shoulders drooped—and then suddenly they straightened. He flung his baton on the floor. It clattered across the boards as he blew out his one remaining candle and stomped from the podium.

There was a moment of silence—and then the audience went wild. Never had Franz heard such laughter and applause. All the men bravoed themselves hoarse, while the ladies squealed their delight.

"No doubt about it, this orchestra will get the vacation for which it is asking," a man near Franz remarked, "and during the period of rest its musicians will be the darlings of the Vienna drawing rooms."

But there was no vacation for Franz. His gala evenings were becoming more and more widely spaced by the pressure of his practice. He had his old patients, plus those who had turned to him from Father Hell, plus some "incurable" cases he had sought among the poor.

It was autumn of 1775 and the City of Dreams was swaddled in gloom. Leaves drifted down from the trees to their death and decay in the gutters. "Fall depresses me," Franz admitted to himself as he picked his way through the filth strewn alleys of the slums.

"Late fall," Franz continued his brooding, "is the same as old age—as compared to the springtime of youth. And why should it be depressing? Why should not the finishing of the race be more exciting than the start of it? When one looks upon the whole picture, does one regret that it was painted? Or having heard the entire symphony, can one mourn?"

Franz tapped on the door of a hut. Hinges creaking, the door slowly opened to dirt and disease. Two wispy children stared big-eyed from the floor. The woman smiled a mirthless greeting and motioned Franz toward the bed. He crossed to it, dragging a stool with him.

"You are better today, Johann," Franz told the man. The man turned his head slowly in Franz's direction, but there was no recognition in his face. His empty eyes moved to the ceiling and then drifted back to Franz.

"Will you give him another treatment today, doctor?"

"Yes. Please fetch me the tub of water." Franz opened his bag and lifted the three large magnets to put in the tub. "Help me turn him to the side of the bed as we did the other day."

The children stopped their play and edged up against the wall near the bed to watch. Franz and the wife placed Johann's feet in the tub. Together they stripped off his night dress. From its case Franz took a new magnetized wand—a slim, highly-polished steel rod tipped with copper—and began to move it slowly over the man's body, watching him with grave concern all the time.

"My good friend, soon you will be well and strong again. This is but a bad time that shall pass away. You will soon be well to do your work, and you will be happy. Soon your small ones will have food and clothing again. Soon, Johann, soon—" Franz continued soothing words as he slowly passed the wand over the man's body.

"Notice, doctor." The wife pointed to a quivering bit of flesh on Johann's shoulder.

Franz noted, too, that Johann's lips were trembling. Then his eyes began to roll about and moisture gathered in large drops on his forehead. Within moments he was in a violent spasm.

"Good," Franz reassured the wife as the violence of the spasm increased. Suddenly Johann moaned and fell back upon the bed. Swiftly Franz dried his feet and bundled him into a blanket.

"Suzanne, what is wrong?" asked Johann as he opened his eyes. He pushed back the covers and reached for his trousers hanging on the wall peg. A smile came to his face as he noticed the children. "Why, you little mice. Come over here to your papa and help his lazy bones out of this bed. I'm well and strong again, and now I must go to work."

The giggles of the children mingled with the happy laughter of their mother. She wiped tears from her eyes with the ragged edge of her apron and asked, "How long, doctor, will he know us?"

"Last week it lasted three days, no?"

"Yes, doctor, and then his mind was gone again."

"I expect it to be six days this time, but before long we shall have him cured."

"God bless you." She grabbed Franz's hand and kissed it. He patted her shoulder.

Outside again Franz drank deeply of the night and found it sweeter than before. He lifted his eyes to the stars. "You and I have a secret that must be shared with the world. We must work slowly—cure upon cure until the evidence is proof—and then we'll give them our secret."

Franz reached for his beads as he thought: "Death is as natural as birth and in no way more painful. But disease and insanity are not natural things. They are interruptions in the smooth ebb and flow of the life force. They are blocks in the fluidum." Franz's feet seemed to rise and fall in the measured cadence: ebb—flow—ebb—flow.

Stories of the magnetic cures spread, and Franz was unable to work as slowly as he liked. He was not even able to record proper case histories of the people he treated, much less spend time in his laboratory meditating on the theory of magnetic cure. Daily the street in front of No. 261 Landstrasse was jammed with coaches, carriages, and carts. A few of the poor even brought their sick to him in wheelbarrows. The halls of his rooms were seldom empty, though Franz arranged for medical assistants to aid him in the magnet applications.

Karl still drove Franz, but he had long since given up the care of Franz's rooms and clothing. When they were not in the carriage, Karl was busy with such medical records as he was able to make. Franz was pleased that Karl had developed a system of note-taking which would have been invaluable to Franz if he could have found time to study Karl's records. Franz questioned Karl about this secretarial ability and discovered that he had served Marie Anna's first husband similarly.

In the beginning, Marie Anna was overjoyed with the success of the magnetic treatments. As Franzl blossomed, so did Marie Anna's enthusiasm over Franz's work. She appeared pleased with the thought of having a part in the development of a technique which would revolutionize medicine. Gradually, however, as the weeks passed and Doctor van Swieten gave

Franz no recognition, her interest cooled. She was extremely upset when the Berlin Academy refused Franz's application for a hearing. Finally she began to fret, and then to quarrel about the crowds of people who gathered daily for treatment.

"Today, Franz, they tromped all over the garden, destroying plants, just as the swarms of locusts did in Abraham's time." Marie Anna knows as little about sacred literature as she does about medicine, Franz told himself.

In all fairness, he could hardly blame her for her petulance. Their way of life was changing rapidly. He rarely had time to take Marie Anna to the elaborate balls which she loved so dearly. Seldom did they go to the opera now, or to the receptions at court. The Mozarts were not in town; and since Franz had become too busy, other musical friends no longer dropped in for tea.

Franz's days were filled with a never-ending stream of diseased, pain-wracked bodies. Some of them he turned away or treated without charge because he recognized organic disturbances which were too far advanced to be helped by magnetic treatment. Occasionally, however, he would take even these cases and treat them for relief of pain. Always, of course, he had to see, to feel, and to reassure each patient. Franz thought proper diagnosis an important element in the placement of magnets on the body. A magnet placed exactly on either side of the humor seemed to increase the ebb and flow of the fluidum and bring about a faster crisis—and always this was the thing he worked for.

On the Landstrasse near his home, Franz had bought a plot of land for a hospital. He made some preliminary sketches for the building but could not seem to find time to complete his plans for the structure. At last he turned this project over to Karl. Karl secured the services of an architect, and the two men designed a building most admirably suited to Franz's needs. Franz authorized its construction and put Karl in charge of the project.

About this time, too, Franz hit upon the idea of handing out magnetized articles for the waiting patients to hold in their hands. This seemed to assist in bringing on a faster crisis, once the sufferers had received the regular treatment for which they had waited. Then he added music. He engaged a group of young musicians, who took turns playing. Their melodies drifted out over the garden on warm days, caressing the tortured bodies and easing the pain. To rest himself, Franz sometimes played for his patients on the musical glasses. He had always believed music to be a medium for healing the soul, and he thought it possible that music could help in healing the body as well.

On one of Franz's rare visits to the Vienna clinic, he again met Doctor van Swieten in the hall. "What sort of a carnival are you holding at No. 261 Landstrasse?" he inquired. "From the crowds you draw, I gather it must be more lucrative than medicine."

This time Franz smiled but did not attempt to explain.

As the number of patients increased, Franz tried to think of more and more ways to speed up treatment. Since he believed that magnets had power, he tried to find ways of surrounding himself and his patients with this power.

Instead of using the magnetized wand, he took to wearing a small but powerful lodestone magnet on a chain around his neck. It was encased in a leather pouch.

Soon, too, Franz designed and had made a device which enabled him to treat a number of patients at the same time. He called this device a "baquet." It consisted of a number of jars of water into which he dropped small magnets. The jars sat in a wooden trough which was covered by a top into which holes had been bored. Steel rods ran from the jars of magnetized water up through the holes in the cover of the trough. Loosely joined to these rods were other steel rods which extended out to the patients who sat round the "baquet."

It was well known that both water and steel were conductors of electricity. Franz reasoned that these mediums would also conduct the magnetic flow. Rubbing or friction produces electricity, and so Franz had his patients rub with the steel rods the particular areas of their bodies that were affected by disease or pain. This was most effective.

Franz also magnetized the fountain in the garden. Many of the ill obtained relief by simply bathing their faces, hands, and arms in the fountain.

Franz seldom felt fatigue, so buoyed up was he by the joy

in this miracle of healing. There were nights, however, when he would throw himself across his bed to think—and awaken the next morning fully dressed. Franz realized that he had gone to sleep praying for help. "This thing is too big for me to handle alone. I desperately long for the aid of medical doctors and other men of science who are willing to observe, investigate, and experiment with magnetic healing," Franz told the sympathetic Gluck.

As if in answer to prayer, Doctor Unzer of Altona and Doctor Harser of Geneva came to visit. Gratefully Franz received their questions. Though he could not answer them all, he supplied the doctors with information with which they could return home and test his theories themselves. This they did, with such success in treatment that their letters were warm, humble, and enthusiastic.

Both of these doctors wrote and published erudite papers on the subject of magnetic healing. The papers won for Franz many new converts and investigators.

"What I need is a dramatic case that will startle all of Vienna," Franz declared to himself. "That should convince the doctors."

CHAPTER IX

EARLY ONE morning, lovely young Fraulein Weber came in for treatment. She had a lung congestion, slight fever, and a hoarse nonproductive cough accompanied by a stabbing pain that Franz felt must be pleurisy. He asked her to remove her bodice and undergarments. She made an attempt to do so, but even this slight exertion caused her to cough and gasp with pain. Franz began to assist her, talking as he did so in order to calm her fears.

"I know the pain is bad now, but it will not last long. It will soon be gone and your fever will disappear with it. Try to rest and do not fight the pain. It will soon be gone."

Franz placed his right hand under one breast and his left hand on her back. As he talked, he was testing for signs of pneumonia. He moved his hands over the upper part of her body, pressing here and tapping there—all the while reassuring the sick girl.

He realized that the coughing had stopped for the moment and that her breathing had become as regular as in sleep, but it was not until he put his ear to her back that he noted her skin had grown cool and moist. Franz stepped back and regarded her curiously. She blinked her eyes, shaking her head slightly at the same time.

"Doctor, did you catch me napping? How silly of me, going to sleep sitting upright. I didn't even know when you applied the magnets. Thank you, anyway. I feel fine." Chattering gaily, she donned her clothing and tripped out the door.

Franz was badly shaken, too startled to explain to his patient that he had not yet given her a magnet treatment. She appeared healed! What had happened? Suddenly Franz recalled the lodestone he wore around his neck. "Could it be that this small magnet carried enough force to charge my hands?" He felt for the leather pouch. It was not there!

Franz locked his door and sank into a chair. Step by step he recalled the events of the morning. He had been breakfasting in his room when Karl had called him to attend Fraulein Weber. "'An emergency,' he had said, 'the girl can barely breathe.' I dressed hurriedly—ah, yes—I left the lodestone lying on my commode by the basin of water in which I washed. No, I did not wear the lodestone at all. Could it be that my hands were magnetized?" Franz spread them out on his knees and gazed at them in bewilderment.

The sound of the door cut short Franz's musings. There were patients waiting. Franz used the magnets on them. All that day and the next Franz worked with the magnets, but he knew that he was only postponing the time of reckoning. Finally he sent Karl to the home of Fraulein Weber with a note inquiring as to the state of her health. Karl returned with a favorable report from the Fraulein and expressions of gratitude from her mother. It appeared that the Fraulein had been similarly afflicted on other occasions and that her pain had endured for days. The Webers were delighted to testify as to the efficacy of magnetic treatments.

But Franz had not used magnets on the Fraulein! He dared not tell even Karl.

Late that night Franz sat in his laboratory going over the case histories which Karl had so carefully compiled. He found the records of several young women whose symptoms had been similar to those of the Fraulein. In each case a cure had been effected, but the treatments had varied—and always he had used the magnets. "How extensively did I use my hands to check these women for pneumonia?" Franz couldn't remember, and Karl's notes did not say. Karl was never present in the examining room with lady patients. His information came from a relative or parent who usually accompanied each young female patient.

It must have been almost morning before Franz gave up demanding an answer from himself. He knelt in prayer. Before he rose, the answer came:

"Go now, right now, leaving your magnets behind. The stars are waning before the dawn, but pain does not fade with the stars. The sick are in your own courtyard. They await your coming."

Franz rushed to the courtyard. He found it filled with the

poor and ill, in huddled groups. Had they waited since yesterday? Had they come in the night? He did not know. Some were blood-stained and cancerous; some were burning with fever; and there were the cripples. Franz walked among them. He placed his hands upon them. To some he spoke reassuringly, others he massaged, and a few he simply held firmly between the palms of his hands while he mentally willed the healing force to flow into their bodies. Each patient responded in his own way. Some cried, others laughed hysterically, and there were many who swooned.

By sunup, the courtyard was empty. Franz could not possibly have cured them all, but even the incurables had found release from pain.

As he stood alone to face the rising sun, dew-soaked trees laughed and sparkled their delight in the coming day, and birds chirped a welcome to a world born again. But Franz could not share their joy, for his heart was as a stone in his chest. This new discovery was overwhelming.

Franz walked along the early-morning streets. A few of the faithful were on their way to mass. He joined them. He said his beads—but only with his lips. He could not gain possession of his mind. It darted about in a frenzy of meaningless activity.

After the services Franz remained sitting in a pew of the great, quiet cathedral. He wanted to reach a decision and plan a course of action, but his problems were beyond quick solutions. Acting on his theories, dedicated doctors were using magnets for healing. And now he had discovered that the magnets themselves did not contain the healing force. The enormity of it fought in his brain. "What would happen if I should declare the magnetic treatment useless? What of the doctors—and what of the patients? I have betrayed their trust in me—unknowingly, unwittingly, yes—yet I have betrayed them."

"What can I do? What can I do?" Franz lifted his eyes to the serene figure of the Christ, but there was no answer within his heart. He clenched his fists and dropped to his knees again. Finally tears came.

Some time later Franz felt a warm sense of comfort stealing over his body. "The problem is still with me, but I know that something . . . some action . . . will be revealed to me. . . ." He was sure of it without knowing how.

He left the cathedral and walked towards the woods. "Perhaps the trees will hold the answer." He walked for several hours, but no answer came.

It was late afternoon when Franz returned to No. 261 Landstrasse. Wolfgang Mozart awaited him, and he had brought friends—Herr von Paradis and his blind daughter Maria Theresa. The girl was a talented musician. She had played in the Mesmer home and Franz had heard her a number of times at Court. As a matter of fact, the child had been renamed for Empress Maria Theresa, who had become her patron many years before.

"I have told Theresa that you can cure her sight," said Wolfgang, his faith shining in his eyes.

"And Theresa believes that you can," added the father.

Their avowals of faith wounded Franz afresh. He thanked both young people but shook his head.

"Herr von Paradis, I am called out of town. I shall be away for several weeks. I'll get in touch with you when I get back." Franz was astounded as the words fell from his lips. He had no trip in mind. Furthermore, less than a month had passed since he had sat watching Theresa play and wished he might try the magnets on her. Doctor von Stoerk believed that her optic nerve was healthy and intact. "This sensitive, delicately beautiful creature should respond well to magnetism—if, of course, there is such a thing as magnetism."

But Franz could not bring himself to the point of promising to take her as a patient. He had to reconcile this new development in magnetism before he could experiment in such a challenging case. He excused himself and left the guests to Marie Anna. Not until he reached his rooms, and until he had read the afternoon post, did he decide where he would go on this trip which he had used as an excuse. A letter from an ailing Councillor Osterwald lay on the desk. Would Dr. Mesmer come to Munich and treat him, the Councillor begged. Franz went, grateful for every minute of the time he was able to spend in thought as the carriage rolled along the road. Karl was too busy to drive him, and he felt free to ask his new driver to sit on the outside seat so that he might have time alone.

Franz found Herr Peter van Osterwald to be a man of fifty-seven who suffered from a variety of ailments. He was almost blind. He had stomach trouble, hemorrhoids, and a bad hernia, and his legs were practically paralyzed. For a man of the Councillor's interests—he loved his land and his stock of highbred horses—such illnesses were particularly distressing. In spite of his physical disabilities, Councillor Osterwald was uncommonly alert in his mind. Franz was immediately drawn to this man of fine sensibilities and superior education.

Since Franz had brought his magnets, he used them; but he explained to the Councillor that he had recently come to the conclusion that these pieces of lifeless metal did not account for the cures.

"This is all experimental, sir, but we do get definite results, even though we don't know why." Franz was explaining as much to himself as to the Councillor, for he was feeling his way through a maze of questions. The Councillor appeared to be interested, and Franz continued.

"I believe magnetism has a two-fold nature. Henceforth, I shall refer to it as the mineral magnetism present in metal, and the animal magnetism present in the human body. Some persons are endowed with unusual amounts of animal magnetism. This animal magnetism issues from their fingertips in such quantity that it can be sent as a healing force into afflicted parts of other human bodies."

In four days Councillor Osterwald was walking slowly about his rooms. In eight days his sight was almost normal. In twelve days his hernia had disappeared, so that he could remove the bandages. Franz continued treatment until the Councillor could walk for an hour without feeling tired.

The Councillor was well pleased over what he considered to be his miraculous cure. To honor Franz's work, he invited a number of influential people for an evening of dinner, dancing, and music. At the height of the festivities he made a public declaration, testifying to the efficacy of the animal magnetism treatment.

But this was only the beginning of his generous overtures in Franz's behalf. He prevailed upon the Council of the Augsburg Academy to issue a report on Mesmer's work.

Franz read the report with humility and pride. The Council's statement read:

"What Dr. Mesmer has achieved in the way of curing the

most diverse of maladies leads us to suppose that he has discovered one of nature's mysterious motive energies."

Franz felt a certain reluctance to accept this acclaim in the midst of his uncertainty. "I must know . . . I must. . . ." he whispered.

The Councillor himself wrote a graphic report of his miserable condition before the magnetic treatments. He wrote in detail of the number of physicians who had treated him and the variety of cures he had tried in previous years. He made an emphatic statement, "*Should anyone be found to declare that the history of my case is a figment of the imagination, I am nonetheless satisfied with the result, and I shall not expect any doctor in the world to believe more than I imagine myself to have recovered perfect health.*"

Franz was made a member of the Academy of Sciences of Electoral Bavaria. His citation read, "*It is undeniable that the activities of so outstanding a personality, who has won to fame by special and incontrovertible experiments and whose erudition and discoveries are as unexpected as they are useful, must add luster to our institution.*"

"How good is praise—and how difficult to accept humbly," Franz said as he thanked the Councillor. The Councillor waved away Franz's thanks but settled back in his chair for conversation.

"Dr. Mesmer, do you recall ever hearing of a Father Gassner, who has the reputation of being a deliverer of possessed people. . . ." The Councillor paused to smile his nonpartisanship in such a belief before adding, "He casts out devils!"

Franz immediately remembered the journey he had made with Father Emmanuel, and the distaste he had felt *even when he saw something happen to that poor woman.*

"Yes . . . yes, I know of his work." Franz hoped the Councillor wouldn't wish to pursue the subject.

"What do you think?" the Councillor asked eagerly.

"Well, I don't know enough to think anything . . . much. . . ."

"Dr. Mesmer, I hope this will not disturb you," the Councillor's voice had grown soft and confidential, "but Maximilian Joseph has sent for Gassner and I have a note from the Elector here asking that I bring you to the Palace that you might question Gassner."

Franz was dumbfounded. He searched for words to refuse, but how could he refuse Elector Maximilian Joseph III of Bavaria?

"You will go?" the Councillor's voice prodded him.

"I shall be delighted to do anything to show my appreciation to you, to the Council, and to your worthy leader."

"Good!" The Councillor was pleased.

Franz found Father Gassner a simple man who gave simple answers to Franz's questions.

"I just command in Jesus' name that the pain become acute. If nothing happens, then I know that the illness is a natural one and I can do nothing to help. But if the pain becomes violent, I know that the illness is one of possession and I perform the *rite of exorcism*."

When the Elector dismissed Father Gassner, he turned to Franz.

"What do you think, doctor?" Franz hesitated.

"Speak up, doctor . . . no one will ever know . . . except us . . . how you feel. . . ." Maximilian Joseph smiled warmly.

"It's to protect our people," the Councillor added.

"Well, certainly Gassner has no scientific knowledge . . ." Franz acquiesced to himself. He cleared his throat and said, "So far as I can judge, I see no reason to believe that Father Gassner is making use of anything other than superstition."

"What do you advise?"

Franz longed to be done with this judging of another man. What could he say? The Elector and Councillor were waiting, looking at him with questioning eyes.

He took a deep breath and reluctantly voiced his decision, "I advise you to put a stop to this casting out of devils."

Maximilian Joseph had broken the Jesuit censorship of the press. It would not be difficult for him to impose a ban on healing by priests. Franz knew this. He felt the kindly admiration of these two men of Bavaria as he bade them good-bye and left for Vienna. But all the way home Franz felt uneasy when he thought of Father Gassner. A verse of scripture kept repeating itself in his brain—

"What reason ye in your hearts? Whether it is easier to say thy sins be forgiven thee; or to say Rise up and walk?"

In spite of the interest aroused in Bavaria, Franz wasn't happy. The acclaim and the citations—even the Councillor's cure—failed to erase the fact that something unusual had happened in the healing of Fraulein Weber. True, the Councillor had accepted Franz's explanation of animal and mineral magnetism . . . "but will my own medical staff be so easily convinced? Especially since I do not know myself what happened. And there in the courtyard that night . . . all those people . . . all made comfortable . . . some made well . . . I've got to face the awful truth that I'm going to have to tell my staff that the power to heal might reside in each of of them, independent of magnets, lodestones, and baquets." Franz closed his eyes.

"God help me not to say the wrong thing. I can't destroy . . . there is something. . . ." His hands clutched his beads.

CHAPTER X

THE FIRST thing Franz did upon returning to his hospital was to call a staff meeting. As undramatically as possible, he told them of his findings. He was surprised that they greeted the news as an avenue opening up to them. They were interested and excited and came up with many stimulating questions. Franz breathed thanks. Their enthusiasm was so great that Franz began to enjoy a delayed appreciation for his reception in Bavaria, plus, too, the fact that many foreign doctors were clamoring for entrance to his hospital. At last he knew that the time had come to request permission of the van Swieten group to present his theories and demonstrate animal magnetism. He was confident and enthusiastic as he made his formal request. He waited for several days in joyous anticipation. . . . "These men are my close boyhood friends; I want to share with them, above all." As he thought of his classmates, a mist filled his eyes and great tenderness stirred his heart.

At last he saw the letter lying on his desk.

"Ah, now we shall see." He laughed deep in his chest and pulled the letter open.

His request was denied. . . . Franz's legs refused to support him. Ripples of disappointment spread over his body. He sat at his desk, rereading the short, curt note with the van Swieten signature. "Why?" he asked over and over in his bewildered heartsickness.

Franz sat at his desk until a cold rebellion replaced his disappointment. His eyes fell on a journal carrying the story of the American rebellion against tyranny. He felt a sudden sympathy and kinship with these sturdy people. "I, too, will
"Dr. von Stoerk is a staunch member of the van Swieten
fight! I will somehow, someway, bring my case before the world!
group, as well as personal physician to the Empress. There is not a better-known eye doctor in Vienna, but lovely Theresa von Paradis remains blind in spite of his attentions. This is my chance.

"I'll show them! I'll cure her!"

Franz had never been so determined. He asked Wolfgang to bring Theresa to his office. He examined her with fear and trembling, praying all the time that von Stoerck's diagnosis of functional ailment was correct. At last the tension left his body. He relaxed and smiled happily. "The girl's eye tissue is healthy; this is a functional ailment," he told himself. "She will be cured!"

Franz placed his hands on her head and turned her face toward him. She surprised him by reaching up and covering his hands with hers, pressing them tightly against her cheeks.

"Your hands feel so good. I like them to touch and hold me." She sighed, and as artlessly as the child she was she placed Franz's hands in her lap and caressed them.

"Child? . . . This girl must be twenty—I remember some one saying she has been blind for sixteen years." But there was a winning, childlike quality in her personality—an innocent kind of coquetry which one sometimes sees in a little girl of four.

And she had said, "your hands." Shades of the Baron who took me to Lisa, Franz thought in flushed-faced excitement. Would he never forget the remark about his hands? Twenty-six years ago, and still a chance remark about his hands had power to disturb him.

Franz took a deep breath and rose from his chair, gently disengaging Theresa's clinging fingers. He placed one hand firmly over her eyes, the other against the back of her head, and spoke to her with conviction. "You shall see, Theresa. One day your eyes will behold all the beauty of the world. Your music tells me that you know that beauty already, but one day you shall see it all again with your eyes."

For the next week Theresa came to Franz's office every day, accompanied either by her father or by Wolfgang Mozart. He treated her, but he had no feeling that she was responding. "She is aloof, almost as if she is holding back, as if she did not wish to see." Franz was perplexed.

He spoke to her again of the beauties of the world. "Beauties, ha," she retorted with a sarcastic little half-laugh.

"What do you mean, my dear?" She shrugged and her expression grew cold.

Franz knew then that he must spend more time with her. Somehow he must gain her complete confidence and trust, so that he might get at the part of her thinking which separated them.

"One cannot be a doctor and fail to realize the tremendous power of thought upon the functioning of the human body. A patient is in good health only when all the various elements of which he is composed have the opportunity to perform their functions," Franz said to Gluck thoughtfully, as they set out for their evening walk.

"What of moral causes?" asked the interested Gluck.

"Yes, to the physical causes of disease must be added moral causes," agreed Franz. "Pride, ambition, and all the vile passions of the human mind interfere with perfect body performance."

"But, Franz, Theresa is very young . . . I can't imagine any moral conflict," Gluck protested.

"Yes . . . she's young . . . I've thought of that . . . but there is something troubling her . . . no matter its name."

The next day Franz asked Herr von Paradis if Theresa might be permitted to live in his home for a while.

"Our hospital is full; but on occasions we have taken patients into our home for special treatment, even when we had room in the hospital," Franz explained.

"Why, I think this is a splendid thing . . . yes, splendid, Herr Doctor." Von Paradis' voice was pompous as he gave his consent.

Franz put Theresa in a room large enough to accommodate her piano. From the first she seemed delighted, and her pleasure in her new surroundings seemed to increase as Franz spent more and more time with her. Often they sat at the piano together.

"I shall play you cold weather," she would say. She could dash off crisp little airs that spoke plainly of crackling ice and sleigh bells. Franz was enchanted.

"Now you play me a summer song." She placed his hands on the keyboard. He would make his tune lazy and languorous, and she would clap her hands in appreciation.

"Now, doctor, listen to the carriage bearing a princess to her prince." Franz saw that she had an uncanny aptitude for using the piano to express her thoughts and daydreams.

He studied her as she sat there at the piano, a newborn thought taking shape in his mind. "Can the piano serve to give me an insight into her thinking?" "Play me Karl," he requested.

She responded with a short, stiff marching tune which broke cadence only once to interpose a few deep chords and a soft bass run. Her face was solemn for a moment and then she twinkled, "You do me Wolfgang."

Franz described Wolfgang with a short, jubilant song. Then he said, "Let me hear Frau Mesmer."

She arranged her fingers precisely on the keys, paused for effect, and came forth with an intricate, overly-contrived melody.

"Next you must do my Papa."

Franz did Herr von Paradis, emulating on the keyboard his way of talking in jerky sentences.

"Now, Theresa, do your Mama." Franz was full of anticipation. "This is my master stroke," he thought.

She did a run, then a few sparkling measures, and followed them with a short series of discords ending in a crash. Franz realized that she was trembling, but he was unprepared for the violent sobs which came as she turned and threw herself into his arms.

Franz held her quietly, but he knew he must not question and she made no attempt to explain. It was a week later before he plucked a rose one morning and carried it to her room.

"Let's play our game again, Theresa," Franz said, "only this time let's make our people in words instead of in music." He placed the rose in her hand. "This is you. You have the beauty and the softness of the rose. Feel its petals." He wrapped an outer petal about her finger. "See how delicate, how yielding and soft to the touch. Yes, you are a rose."

"Oh, thank you, doctor," she said gravely, but her face flushed. Franz pretended not to notice.

"You are welcome, my dear. Now, would you like to describe someone?"

"Could I? May I try you?"

"You may, indeed. I should like to know how I look to you." Franz smiled to himself and straightened his cravat.

"Oh, doctor, you are the big soft bed that holds me. Your face is the pillow I embrace each night."

Her innocence made Franz flush, but so grave she had been that he thanked her and said, "Now it is your turn to do Wolfgang."

"Wolfgang is a dance done to a Requiem Mass," and she caught her breath sharply. "Why did I say that? Oh, doctor, what a sad thought; and yet it is lovely, too."

"It is a true thought, Theresa, and truth is both beautiful and sad at the same time. Yes, deep within Wolfgang there is a strong current of mourning. He would not like our seeing it. Let's try Frau Mesmer."

"Frau Mesmer is a gilded staircase in an opera."

This observation from a sightless child! Franz caught his breath. She must have taken his silence to mean disapproval, for she murmured an apology.

"Do not apologize, Theresa. I shall never disapprove of your thoughts . . . and now, would you like me to do your Papa? He is . . . he is a kettle singing on a very hot stove."

She laughed merrily, then suddenly she sobered. "Now, you want me to do Mama next. Mama is. . . ." Her face grew grim and she started again. "Mama is . . ." but her voice was drowned out in the flood of tears. Again she threw herself into Franz's arms.

This time he held her tenderly and talked as if she were a small child, "You are safe with me. Peace, my dear, you are safe." He stroked her head, her slender back, and her shaking hands. Gradually she quieted.

Franz put his hands firmly on her shoulders and held her away from him. "Theresa, I have no wish to hurt you, but there are some questions I must ask." His voice was somewhat stern.

She drew a deep, sobbing breath but made no attempt to pull away from his grasp.

"Now you shall tell me, dear Theresa—how long have you feared your mother?" "I've got to know if I help her at all," Franz thought to himself.

"Always."

"Why?" He was relentless.

"She was mean to me."

"What did she do?"

"She hit me."

"When?"

"When I was four. It was my birthday. Papa brought me an Easter egg with a beautiful window to look through. It had a picture in it. Papa told Mama he had spent many ducats for it."

"Why did he tell her?"

"Because she asked him."

"And she was angry?"

"She grabbed my egg and broke it."

"And what did you do?" His voice was soft.

"I fell on the floor and kicked and cried."

"And what did Mama do?"

"She hit me and hit me and hit me." He tightened his hands on her slim body.

"What did your Papa do?" he asked.

"He tried to pull her away, but she hit him in the face; and then she grabbed me up and she hit me in the face and he shouted at her to stop because she would blind me—and she did, doctor; oh, she did it." Theresa was sobbing again.

Franz put his arms around her and repeated, "You are safe now, Theresa, you are safe." His next question was spoken into the softness of her hair. "Did she ever hit you again?"

"Yes, whenever she is angry."

"And what does Papa do now?"

"He tells me to forgive her, that she is sick."

Neither of them spoke again. Franz sat and held Theresa as if she were still a hurt four-year-old. Finally, she dropped off to sleep. Gently he picked her up and laid her on her bed. She roused only enough to smile as Franz tiptoed from the room.

Gluck was waiting in the drawing room. "Are you ready for our evening stroll?" he asked. Franz pulled on his cloak and they started out. "What news?" Gluck asked.

"Of late I have been pondering over the curative effects of sleep. A few of my regular patients no longer experience the painful crisis type of reaction to magnetic treatment. Instead, they have begun dropping off to sleep." Franz reasoned that in previous treatment these patients had received the maximum amount of animal magnetism, and that the sleep state had occurred when animal magnetism pervaded the body fluidum and brought it into the perfect balance of regular ebb and flow.

"Sleep has always been one of life's great mysteries, but I do not consider it a negative condition—not merely the simple absence of the waking state. Things happen in sleep. The human faculties are not entirely at rest. On the contrary, they are just as active as during the waking state."

Franz and Gluck continued walking, Gluck providing the necessary audience of one.

"It's a shame you can't discuss this with men of your profession," Gluck said.

"Yes, I would have liked to discuss some of my observations on sleep with the older University physicians," Franz said thoughtfully, "but they have long since consigned me to medical limbo."

"Have you given up going to the medical meetings?" asked Gluck.

"The van Swieten group made my presence an embarrassment for the few who sympathized with or even listened to my views. I had to stop." Franz hoped he didn't sound pitiful to Gluck.

"I am frustrated by it all," he continued, "I know there are some Vienna doctors who would enjoy having me dismissed from the Society; but because of my excellent training and my many degrees, they dare not attack me openly. I am no Father Hell, to be elbowed out of practice." He tried not to sound bitter. "But they write papers, and contrive stories."

"Why don't you make some answer to these assaults?" asked Gluck.

Finally, Franz sent a letter to the paper, declaring: "At present I have no intention of trying to convince anyone of my theories. I shall not waste time with controversial pamphlets. Instead I shall investigate these discoveries, from which the human race can expect to derive important and fundamental benefits."

The paper displayed it well but brought no results.

At tea time Franz showed the paper to Marie Anna. "How nice for you, dear Franz," she murmured. She seemed preoccupied. She settled her cup into its saucer and announced, "I believe Junge and Franzl are falling in love."

Franz laughed at her. "You arrange even your son's love life," he chided.

"No, Franz, I do not; but had I done so, I could not have made a more admirable choice."

The next week the young couple announced their intentions, and Marie Anna launched the family into a frenzy of social events. Franz found it difficult to avoid any of the gala affairs in honor of his stepson and his wife's best friend.

"You are always going to parties," Theresa complained. "Why don't they hurry and get married?"

Franz laughed and asked her to play the Wedding March; she played it like a dirge and they laughed together.

"All things end, dear Theresa," Franz told her some days later, "and today at high noon the marriage will be solemnized."

Theresa held his hands and her voice was wistful. "Then I'll see you again."

Epilepsy interested Franz. This interest had started with a sixteen-year-old epileptic girl who was brought to him by her parents. She had suffered terrible attacks daily for almost two years.

Franz was delighted when she responded easily to animal magnetism—so easily, in fact, that he needed only to point his finger at her and she would quickly and quietly swoon. Each time she came out of a faint, she declared herself to be vastly improved. Within a very short time she had completely recovered.

The parents of the girl were extremely poor. He could not . . . would not . . . charge them; before they came to him they had exhausted their funds in a vain search for medical help for their child. In appreciation of Franz's services, they appeared to take upon themselves the chore of searching out most of the epileptics of Vienna and sending them to Franz's door. Franz felt deeply for these new patients. Most of them were unusually tender-hearted, shy, frightened people—yet they were quite intelligent as a rule. He worked hard at winning their confidence, for by this time he knew that a doctor must establish a rapport with his patient before he could cure. He was thankful that most of his epileptic patients responded to animal magnetism.

As for the few who did not respond, he felt that they must have some type of organic malfunction which was a barrier to cure. "Try as I will, I cannot instill into them my energy, my life force, my will to be." Sadness filled Franz as he admitted this to Karl.

Dr. de Haen must have heard of this work, for he sent Franz a patient with convulsive pains in his throat. This came as a surprise to Franz, for Doctor de Haen was one of the shining lights of the van Swieten group. His surprise was not long-lived, however, for the patient, Baron Horecky de Horka, explained the referral:

"Dr. de Haen says that, since none of the physicians can cure me, I might as well try your animal magnetism."

"So de Haen no longer classes me as a physician." Franz frowned as he took the Baron's history. The Baron had gone from one doctor to another all his life. What a feather it would be in Franz's cap to cure this sickly, thirty-year-old man. Franz knew what a challenge it was. He agreed to attend the Baron for one week at his ancestral estate near Vienna.

Franz found Horecky de Horka's wife the hysterical type. She gushed, first one way and then another. She knew Franz could cure her husband, but then she declared he was killing him. She would coo sweet things to Franz one day, then call him a witch the next. She demanded her right to stay in the room when Franz treated the Baron, but she screamed and cried when he tried to help the poor man arrive at a crisis.

In spite of the atmosphere of madness in which Franz worked, Horecky showed improvement. As a matter of fact, he felt so well that he insisted upon going to the Baroness' apartment one night. "I feel better than I have since I was a lad," he boasted.

Franz hoped that the Baroness would be pleased and placated—and she did seem so the next morning—but with evening she announced, "Doctor Mesmer, I trust you will forgive me. I have sent for Doctor Ungerhoffer, who referred us to Doctor de Haen."

"Why, Baroness?" Franz was puzzled.

She pouted, "I am afraid your treatment is too severe for darling Horecky."

"But look at him! See how well he appears," Franz protested.

The Baron walked in as Franz said this. "I not only appear well, my dear, I am well. I'm hungry. Think of it—hungry!" The Baron swaggered around the room.

Franz accompanied the two of them into the great dining room for dinner. The Baron pushed aside the cream soup and chicken dainties which had been especially prepared for him. "Give me a slice of that roast beef," he demanded.

Before the meal was finished, Doctor Ungerhoffer arrived. The Baroness' note which summoned him must have suggested an emergency, for the doctor rushed into the dining hall in his greatcoat. He was obviously agitated at the sight of the Baron at the table. "What is the meaning of this?" he shouted. "You are risking your life sitting here in this drafty room. You should be in bed. And look at that food—why, food like that is for a working man, not an invalid." Then the doctor's voice dropped to a confidential, bedside tone. "My good Baron, my friend, I want you to take better care of yourself. I cannot permit you to risk your health so foolishly."

"But I feel great," protested the Baron.

"Oh, no, you don't. It's all your imagination. This . . . this . . ." and he looked at Franz, who knew he was wondering whether he dared call him a charlatan; he didn't. "This fellow has only made you imagine that you feel well. You are a sick man."

He bundled the mildly protesting Baron off to his rooms. A few minutes later Franz heard Doctor Ungerhoffer in the corridor explaining to the Baroness that his patient was in grave danger and that Franz must be dismissed at once.

Franz put his hand into his pocket; he touched his rosary and whispered, "Father."

He finished his dinner—the food was excellent—and rose to go back to town. The Baron summoned him.

"Doctor Mesmer, we must settle your fee."

"Fee? No, Baron, I do not charge a fee unless I am able to cure my patient." Franz's voice made a finality of any discussion.

The look of chagrin on the Baroness' face at this moment was worth more to Franz than several fees. He regretted that he would not see Doctor Ungerhoffer's face when this matter was reported to him.

"It is not unusual for me to refuse a fee. I often do so when treatment has not been entirely satisfactory, or when the patient does not appear able to pay. But I've never enjoyed refusing one so much," and Franz chuckled to himself.

Word of his presence at Baron Horecky de Horka's estate had spread to the country people in the vicinity. They had brought their sick to the Baron's courtyard. There, in the gathering darkness, they waited beside an open fire which they had built on the cobblestones. Franz treated them before he left for home.

One fine-looking young peasant, Franz found, was especially interesting. Six weeks previously he had lost his hearing in a violent thunderstorm. Franz placed his hands over the boy's ears and stood thus for about thirty minutes. Franz spoke no word. He simply looked into the lad's eyes and willed the healing force into his body. When he dropped his hands and stepped back, he spoke to the boy for the first time. "What do you hear, son?" he asked and watched.

The firelight flickered over tears which gathered in the boy's eyes as he whispered, "I hear; oh, I hear." Then, turning to his parents, he spoke aloud, "Mama, Papa, I hear!" All three of them cried and kissed Franz's hands.

"What matter the fretful Baroness and supercilious Ungerhoffers of this world, when one can behold such joyous cures as this?" And Franz felt well paid.

Franz knew that his treatments and methods of cure were watched by many people who had no scientific background or training. Magnetic treatment and animal magnetism seemed so simple and easy that the whole country broke out in a rash of magnetic healers. No doubt these practitioners had only the best of intentions, but they were so entirely ignorant of the harm they might cause that Franz published a warning:

Magnetism is so closely connected with the science of medicine that only qualified physicians should be allowed to practice it.

CHAPTER XI

THE GUIDING light of the old Vienna medical school dimmed briefly and then went out. Van Swieten was dead. "My good teacher, my esteemed colleague, and my arch enemy lies silent in the regal splendor of death." Franz found it difficult to realize.

"Here lies what is left of a truly noble man," he thought, as he gazed upon the empty edifice of the body. "A truly noble man, loyal to his traditions. That he was not receptive to new ideas was a fault of his vision, not of his heart." Franz blinked against tears.

The cathedral service was lengthy and pompous. All the doctors of the school were honorary pallbearers. They were gowned and hooded for the occasion. Perhaps because this outward garb was a symbol of fraternity, it served as a bond; for certainly Franz felt sympathy in the greetings of his fellow doctors when he joined them in the small anteroom. "Or perhaps the hand of death humbles us all and catches us together in a common yet holy fear," Franz thought to himself as he took his place in line. "So often in the presence of death we feel the touch of Our Lord. Why is it that we cannot experience Him daily in the presence of Life?"

After the services were over, Franz found his carriage and Karl. In the sadness he felt was a sense of contentment. Somehow he had buried his bitterness with the body of this fine old man. Perhaps his going marked the passing of an era. Certainly the hostility of his colleagues had abated. Dared he hope that they, too, were experiencing a release from old school ties? Had their resistance to change been laid to rest with their leader?

Franz spoke of these things to Karl as they rode along. Karl was silent for some time and then answered, "It is hard for me to bring myself to speak to you, sir, at this time. I know that you have suffered from the indifference of your brother doctors...."

"Indifference, Karl? Did you say 'indifference'?" Franz smiled. "What is it you wish to tell me?"

"Oh, sir, the van Swieten group, God rest the departed doctor's soul . . ." and here Karl crossed himself routinely.

"Yes," Franz prompted.

"They have sent a paper to Baron Horecky de Horka and asked him to sign it."

"What kind of paper?" Franz asked incredulously.

"One saying that you endangered his life with the improper practice of medicine and that you should be dismissed from the Academy of Sciences and prevented from practicing as a qualified physician."

"No!" The word exploded like a shot. Pain and anger flooded Franz—he realized he was shaking violently. "This can't be, Karl—it just can't be."

"I hated to tell you, sir . . . but you had to know."

Still shaking, even though the anger had subsided into numbness, Franz went to Theresa's quarters. Karl brought him a belated meal. She played while Franz ate. One haunting little melody he especially liked and told her so.

"What is it?" he asked, seeking diversion from the black thoughts that were crowding his mind.

"It is my 'missing-you' music, dear doctor." She left the piano and came over to sit beside him. "I'm so lonely when you are away," she pouted like a spoiled child. "You do not even play games with me any more."

"Perhaps I have treated you too much like a child, Theresa. You are not a child, you know; you are a very charming and talented young lady."

Theresa grew flushed-faced and silent.

"Theresa," Franz began again, "I want your help."

Immediately he had her attention. Her face sobered as she turned it toward him and asked, "What may I do for you, doctor?"

Though it was difficult, Franz tried to talk to Theresa as if he were addressing a person his own age. "There are many doctors, my dear, who do not have confidence in my unusual methods of healing. I would like you to help me prove to them that there is great value in magnetic treatment. If they could see your eyes healed, and if the Empress could see your eyes healed. . . . Maybe, maybe, then, the doctors. . . ."

Theresa interrupted Franz with a grave little cry of delight. Clasping her hands together, she said, "Oh, I do understand, dear doctor. I do understand. Let's start right away."

Franz rose and stood behind Theresa. Placing his hands over her eyes, he talked to her in a confidential manner of the beautiful world which she would soon behold: ". . . the moon slipping in and out of the puffy clouds like a mischievous child tumbling in feather pillows. Moonlight, dear, is magic; under its gentle touch the whole world becomes a fairyland. Yes, the moon is gentle, but it has power, too. When it is full and round, it is a great magician under whose spell even the homeliest woman becomes glorious and the weakest man as splendid as a king. Moonlight, dear, is God in a tender moment."

"Sunlight," Franz continued, "is different. In sunlight we see reality. We see the sharp angles, the ugly gashes, the disfiguring scars. But these are things which we wish to see. Life reveals itself to us in diverse ways. If we would be whole, we must examine all. We are not afraid of seeing life, no matter the form in which it presents itself to us. We do not refuse to look; instead, we pull aside any curtain that would keep us from God's revelations."

For twenty or thirty minutes Franz stood thus with his hands over Theresa's eyes. When he released her, he walked around and up and down in front of her—asking her to open her eyes and make them follow him around the room. She performed this exercise well. They had, of course, used this discipline many times before. Theresa had long ago ceased rolling her eyes about in their sockets, as is the unpleasant practice of many blind patients.

"This evening, Theresa, we are going to try something new. I am going to put a bandage over your eyes. I have brought a silk scarf to bind them, so. . . ." He began wrapping the strip of silk about her head, securing it firmly. "And I want you to leave this bandage on—day and night—until your soul is ready to see. Do you know what I mean?"

She thought for a moment. "Yes, doctor, I know. You wish me to be unafraid . . . unafraid of anything . . . of blindness . . . of Mama . . do you think . . . ?" and her voice trailed off uncertainly.

"I do not just think so, Theresa—I'm quite sure. Now you must make ready for bed." Franz leaned over to kiss her on the cheek but changed his mind and lifted her hand to his lips as he said good-night.

He shut the door as he left; then on an impulse he reopened it and called back, "Remember the Empress!"

She laughed softly and called to him, "Remember the Empress!"

This phrase became their slogan in the weeks that followed. Franz spent every moment that he could spare with Theresa, treating her and talking with her. In addition to increasing the magnetic flow, he wished to make her eager to look upon the earth. The will of both doctor and patient is involved in successful healing, and Franz's will was ironclad. . . . And for the first time in his practice of medicine, he was thinking more of himself than of his patient.

He bought her a shepherd dog. She felt the dog all over, as was her custom with anything new, and then buried her face in the soft hair on his neck.

"Oh, how beautiful he is. I love him, I love him."

"You should look upon his face. You would know by the expression in his eyes that he loves you, too." Franz felt good, seeing Theresa happy.

And the shaggy animal did love Theresa. He walked with her daily in the garden. He lay at her feet while she practiced on the piano. At night he slept under her bed. His devotion touched Theresa's heart, and she was consumed with longing to look upon her pet.

One day she asked Franz to remove the bandage, which she still wore constantly. He tested her and found that she could tell whether the curtains were opened or closed. With the curtains drawn, she could locate sources of artificial light— the glow of lamps which he placed about the room. Franz was satisfied that the time had come.

"Tomorrow I shall have tea with you, Theresa. We must make this a festive occasion for just the two of us, for after tea I shall remove the bandage and you will be able to see."

They had tea, and then he began the treatment. Never had he tried so hard to bring all of his will and his powers of concentration to bear upon a patient. He was anxious, and he knew that he must overcome not only his own anxiety but that of Theresa's as well. So strong was his desire that after a few minutes he seemed to feel the healing fluidum flowing from his fingers into the soft skin at Theresa's temples.

"Now I am ready to remove the scarf, Theresa. You are relaxed . . . and confident . . . for soon you shall see."

The scarf dropped away. Her eyes were closed. Franz brushed his fingers lightly across her lids and commanded—

"Theresa, open your eyes and look at me!"

Slowly the lids parted and she lifted her head to stare full into his face. Disappointment and dismay wrote a message across her face.

Her dog barked sharply and she fell on her knees, her hands on his head. She regarded him for a moment and exclaimed, "This is the way I thought you'd look . . . he is so sweet!"

Relief, delight, and a strong sense of triumph flooded Franz's soul.

"My dearest, oh, my dearest Theresa," he cried out as he grasped her roughly by the arms and pulled her upright in front of him. Slowly she raised one arm from his grasp and reached her hand up to touch his face. She closed her eyes. Gently her soft fingers explored his eyes, his nose, his mouth.

"Yes, you feel like you"—She opened her eyes and looked into his; deep and long she looked. He lowered his head to hers. Slowly her lips sought his.

Their first kiss was a long one, and then he led her over to the sofa. He had sat with her in his arms at other times— but this was different. She twisted about so that her hard, young breasts dug into his chest and her eager mouth reached up to his. Finally she pulled away and looked at him.

"Does seeing you make this difference, doctor?" she whispered. "I see you, you know. Does that make me want to kiss you? I never kissed anyone like this before—not even Papa. I feel so good . . . so good." And she nestled back into his arms.

Franz's own need was great. He did not realize how great until he felt the response in the body of this child-woman. Again she pulled away from his lips to speak.

"I want something more, doctor, something more. What do I want?"

Franz knew a brief but luxurious moment, and then he came to his senses.

"You want to rest now, dearest, and to sleep. I must leave you to rest. Let me bandage your eyes again."

He rose and walked deliberately across the room to get Theresa's bandage, but his hands were still shaking when he returned with it to bind her eyes again.

She sighed, "If you wish, I'll try to rest . . . maybe that is what I want . . . but I do feel so tingly."

"Yes, dear, that is natural. You have had a most unusual experience. You have found a new world this afternoon. But now you must rest and quiet yourself."

He brought her pillows to the sofa; then he went over and sat down at the piano. The storm of their passion played itself out in his music. When it was spent, Franz felt his fingers drifting into a soft lullaby.

She slept.

Franz stole out of her room to walk for hours under the stars. "There is no way," he told himself, "no way at all. I am a married man . . . married in the Church. She is young . . . and in need of love . . . but I cannot . . . I dare not. I am too much older than she . . . oh, my lovely child-woman, I am almost a quarter of a century older than you . . . I cannot." But even as he talked, the fever of desire ached again within him.

The next day Theresa greeted Franz as gaily and as unaffectedly as a winsome child. She held his hand while she chattered happily about how they would astonish the Empress. ". . . and I must have a beautiful new dress," she said. "Oh, I must have the most beautiful dress in the world to wear the day you take me to the Empress."

Not by word or deed did she betray any recollection of their love-making of the evening before—not even when Franz followed her treatment with the command, "Theresa, open your eyes and look at me." He felt disappointed, and embarrassed at his disappointment.

Again he bandaged her eyes. "We must not tire you with too much light," he explained, "but tomorrow evening I shall take you out into the garden in the moonlight. There you can look and look to your heart's content. Shall I ask your Papa to be present?"

"Yes, yes," and then her face clouded, "but he will bring Mama." Her chin lifted defiantly. "I am not afraid. Ask the whole world."

And so it was that a large group, including Marie Anna and Herr and Frau Paradis, witnessed this dramatic event. Theresa and Franz stood a little apart from the guests. The air was clean and warm and the full moon shone brightly in the spring sky. The little fountain sent its tinkle of music to their ears, and the whole garden seemed blessed with a special kind of radiance.

"This is the time, Theresa, for you to see. You will see. See now." Franz slipped the bandage from her eyes.

She lifted her face to the moonlit heavens. The guests pressed closer and closer. They and the breathless night seemed to be waiting for her response.

"Oh," she whispered, "oh, how beautiful." Slowly and dramatically she lifted her arms wide and high to the sky and stood there in a pose of silent gratitude with her arms still upstretched. She declared in a hushed voice—

"Nothing . . . no, nothing in all this world can appear as magnificent as this. Can I ever feel closer to God than now?"

Slowly she lowered her arms, closed her eyes, and turned back to Franz.

"Please, my bandage—and may I go back to my room?"

Several of the guests wept quietly, but Frau Paradis rushed forward and grabbed Theresa. "Oh, my poor darling, don't you want to look upon your mother's face?" she demanded dramatically.

"Not tonight, Mama." Theresa's voice was tired but firm.

Franz motioned Theresa's mother away and took the girl to her room.

"Hold me close, doctor," she said as the door closed behind them. "Just hold me close so that I can be brave tomorrow."

"You were brave tonight, Theresa."

"No. I was afraid to look at Mama. Even in the moonlight I was afraid to look at her."

"Theresa, reality is beautiful, even when it is painful. Anger, hate, and cruelty have their counterparts in nature—hail, harsh winds, and destructive lightning. But each is an instrument of movement; movement is life; we revere life—and look at it." His voice was gentle but firm.

Frau Paradis must have babbled incessantly about Theresa's cure, for within a few days all of Vienna seemed to be gossiping about her. Many of the curious called at the Mesmer home, but Franz gave orders that Theresa was to admit only her father to her room and that she would see other guests only in the evening when Franz was present.

Herr von Paradis was deeply concerned because Theresa had discontinued her piano practice. "I find it difficult to strike the right notes when I am looking at the keyboard. My hands get in the way," she said in explanation.

"Close your eyes," Herr Paradis advised.

"Oh, no, Papa. Doctor Mesmer says for me to keep my eyes open." And she looked at Franz for verification.

He tried to reassure Theresa's father. "Be patient. Give her time. She will work this out as her eyes grow stronger and as she becomes more accustomed to using them."

But Theresa did not accustom herself easily to her new world of vision. She was often disappointed in the appearance of people; and as candidly as a child, she said so in front of them. Noses were especially disconcerting to her. "Your nose looks as if it is jumping out of your face," she said to a friend of her father's.

"Is that a hat," she asked, pointing at an enormous French creation on the head of a lady caller. Frau Paradis was present, and she rebuked Theresa sharply; but Theresa defended herself. "Mama, you know that's not a pretty thing. Who would think a lady would wear such a heap of dead birds on her head?"

The caller was offended, as were several others who came under Theresa's critical gaze. Theresa was sensitive to the unpleasant feelings her remarks provoked, and she became reluctant to appear among guests with her eyes unbandaged. But even with the bandage in place she was nervous, for she was beginning to depend upon her eyesight in finding her way about. In rooms where she once had walked swiftly and surely, she now groped her way about when her eyes were covered with the silk scarf.

All in all, Theresa was not a happy girl. Franz could see that she was nervous and irritable. Now that her music no longer served as an outlet for such feelings, she had become outspoken and given to temper tantrums. One evening her parents called with guests, and they pressed Theresa to play for them. Theresa refused.

"Young lady," said her mother, "if you don't mind me, I'll take you right home and teach you some manners again."

"I'll never go home again," screamed Theresa. "I'll never, never leave Doctor Mesmer." She burst into tears and ran from the room.

Herr Paradis rose to follow his daughter, but Marie Anna dissuaded him. Frau Paradis spoke loudly and complainingly of her selfish worries—

"Theresa's musicianship is ruined. Friends have advised us to put a stop to these treatments, lest the Empress lose interest in Theresa when she is no longer blind nor a talented performer. I don't know what we would do without Theresa's allowance from the Empress. Perhaps we should take her home right now."

"Absolutely not," Franz stated emphatically. "Theresa's music will improve with her eyesight. She may even become a composer of renown, if you can manage to be patient with her through this difficult period. Now is a critical time. She must not be crossed. Her every whim must be satisfied."

As soon as the parents subsided, Franz excused himself with the plea of hospital calls to make. Thoughts of Theresa occupied most of his mind as he made his rounds. When he returned to the house, he went on past the music room where the guests were being entertained. He rapped softly, and then he opened Theresa's door.

She was in nightdress, lying on her bed. Never had she

looked more appealing. She had been crying softly, and her flushed cheeks were still damp with tears. Her anger was gone, and in its place had come a gentle, childlike remorse.

"I am so sorry, doctor."

"Why, Theresa?"

"Oh, I don't care what all those other people think; truly, I don't care. But I do want to please you. I feel ashamed when I act ugly in front of you."

"Why are you unhappy, Theresa?"

"Don't you know?"

"I want you to tell me, my dear."

There was a long silence between them. Finally Franz asked, "Is it your eyes?" She shook her head and he continued, "Your music?" She shook her head again.

Franz felt an excitement beginning within him, mounting, making him vulnerable. Dared he probe further—yet, he must remain the physician. "Then what?" he finally asked.

Theresa looked at him. She seemed to be puzzling over the words she must say. "You know about wedded people.... ?"

"What about them?" Franz asked.

"Well . . . they kiss . . . and things . . . don't they?"

"Yes. Some of them do."

"Like I kissed you the other night . . . like I never kissed Papa."

"Yes, Theresa."

"Do you kiss Frau Mesmer like that?"

The wonder of it. Oh, the precious, agonizing wonder of it. This beautiful child-woman was jealous. "Darling," Franz leaned over and whispered against her cheek, "I have never kissed anyone like that."

"Oh," she sighed as her hand reached up to hold his face to hers. Then, still holding him, she asked in a whisper, "There are other things, too, with wedded people . . . do you?"

Her innocence made her question a just one.

Franz sat up and looked at her as he answered gently, "No, dear, I do not. Frau Mesmer and I are only friends."

"Oh," she sighed again.

"Do you feel better now?" Franz felt his heart pounding.

"So much better," she replied.

He stood up. "Where are you going?" she asked quickly. "Oh, you must not go now. Don't leave me; please, don't leave me," she cried out as she jumped from her bed and stood before him.

Her frilly little nightdress was of sheer kerchief linen. It prettied her lovely body, yet revealed it completely. Franz held out his arms. She walked into them.

Ruffles, tucks, laces, perfume, and warmth—all the dearness of her he held close as they lay together on her bed. "Come closer to me," she whispered as they kissed.

Tenderly he caressed her hair, her soft shoulders, and her flawless breasts. Her body moved eagerly under his hand. "I'll not leave you tonight, Theresa," he promised, "but I cannot be to you all that you wish."

"Why not?" she asked. And for the first time in his life he heard from a woman's lips, "I love you." His heart beat a rhapsody.

"I know. I know, my dearest, and I am grateful to you. But you are young and beautiful, so very young, my sweet. Some day another man will hold you this way. A man who is free to marry you—"

"Oh, no, doctor. No, I love only you."

"Yes, Theresa. One day there will be another who is free to give you his life, his children . . . I am not free to do this. Trust me to do only what is right for both of us. You do trust me?"

She nodded as her mouth sought his. Deeper and longer were their kisses. Passion burned within his soul and he longed for relief; but he restrained himself, denying his need to give to her. She followed his suggestions, slowly at first and then with growing abandon. Though their bodies did not meet, he felt her total surrender when it finally came.

At last she lay limp and quiescent in his arms. Her hand patted his bare shoulder intermittently. "How do you feel now, Theresa?" he asked tenderly.

"I feel as if I can see to the ends of the earth," she sighed, "and yet I feel as if I could sleep forever in your arms."

With her words came the pent-up dew of his own pleasure to cool the fires of his body. They slept.

The east was coloring for a new day when Franz slipped from her room. He found Karl asleep in a big chair in the hall just outside her door. His presence caught Franz by surprise, and he was probably gruff as he awakened Karl and asked the meaning of this vigil.

"Guarding you, that's what I'm doing," Karl answered sharply. "Frau Paradis came earlier in the evening. I saw her just before she opened the door. I told her that you were giving her daughter a very delicate treatment and must not be disturbed."

Franz was much taken aback. Previously, Frau Paradis had not dared to come to Theresa's room without asking permission. "Thank you, Karl," Franz said, altering his tone considerably.

"That is not all, doctor. Frau Mesmer came much later."

"In the name of saints, why?"

"I did not ask her, sir. I told her that you had just left and had placed me on guard."

"I do not deserve such a friend as you, Karl."

"It was a small thing, sir. I was uneasy about the gossip."

"What gossip, Karl?"

"They have seen her face when you walk in the room, sir. They have been saying for some time that you are her lover."

"Who is 'they,' Karl?"

"The servants, and some of the guests."

"And you, Karl, what do you say?"

"I do not say, sir. I know you to be an honorable man, and I trust you to do what is right for the poor girl. She cannot have known much happiness before she came here."

CHAPTER XII

LATE THAT afternoon a delegation from the Vienna School of Medicine came to see Franz. The men were doctors. They demanded to see Theresa and to question her for themselves. Franz sent for her.

When Theresa entered the room, she was as radiantly beautiful as she had been the evening before in his arms. Her glance barely touched Franz and her greeting was light; but as she turned to the waiting delegation she smiled with such warmth and spoke with such grace that the men rose immediately to their feet.

Franz presented each of the doctors to her in turn. For a few breathless seconds he watched them succumb to her charm. Perhaps they would leave without examining her and he and Theresa would then be free to go directly to the Empress, but Theresa's newly-won confidence deserted her in the face of this battery of masculine stares. She stepped back from the group suddenly and clutched Franz's arm. Lifting her chin defiantly, she said, "So you don't believe. Then question me."

Doctor von Stoerk was the first to speak. "What is this?" he asked as he touched his nose.

"Don't you know, my dear doctor; that is your nose," she replied sharply.

Doctor von Stoerk colored and two of his colleagues laughed nervously.

Theresa made an effort to cover the awkward situation by explaining, "Perhaps you have not heard; at first I was frightened by noses. They seemed to be jumping out of people's faces." Then she added, "Of course, I still think most noses rather absurd."

Professor Barth picked up a coal scuttle from the fireplace and asked, "What is this?"

Theresa looked at it. "Why, I don't know," she replied, "it rattles like a bucket, but I don't know."

Piece by piece he picked up the other items of fireplace

equipment, inquiring rapidly, "What is this—and this—and this?"

Each time Teresa shook her head. "I don't know. I've never been told their names."

Then another doctor took over. Walking about the room he touched a wall tapestry, a cornice board, and various pieces of bric-a-brac that would never have interested Theresa. In each case, she did not know the name of the item indicated and replied negatively.

"This is very bad," said the physician.

Immediately Theresa's temper flared. "You are mean, hateful men," she cried. "You don't care if I am cured. You only want to prove that Doctor Mesmer is wrong." She burst into tears and ran sobbing from the room, stumbling against a table in her haste and confusion.

"Too bad we upset her."

"Yes, poor child, it is not her fault that she only thinks she can see."

"Yes, it is very evident that she does not recognize even the simplest household items."

"Gentlemen," Franz protested, "the girl can see. You merely asked her to name items which she did not recognize. Remember her vision is new."

One lone member of the delegation seemed inclined to accept Franz's explanation.

"Her eyes look fine to me," he said, "and she found her way about the room easily at first."

"But she fell into a table on the way out," reminded another. "It must be presumed that she is still blind."

"Shall we go, gentlemen?" said Doctor von Stoerk. They departed. Franz felt his world crumbling about him.

"They don't want to understand." His clenched fist touched the rosary in his pocket.

Within an hour, Herr von Paradis and his wife were at the door demanding that Theresa leave Franz's care at once. He tried to reason with them, to quiet their fears; but Frau Paradis was hysterical. She pushed her way past Franz and screamed, "You evil man! You have betrayed us all. The doctors said so. Theresa! Theresa, where are you?"

Franz tried to prevent Frau Paradis from searching out her daughter, or to detain her while Theresa found time to hide. He caught the lady by a sleeve; her sleeve and bodice ripped; and Herr Paradis drew a sword.

"Paradis, be reasonable!" Franz shouted at the distraught man, releasing Paradis' wife and picking up a small chair with which to fend off his advances.

"Reasonable! Reasonable, when you have ruined my daughter's talent and taken her love from me," and he lunged at Franz again with the sword.

At this moment Frau Paradis came back into the room, dragging the terrified Theresa. "I won't leave, I won't leave," sobbed Theresa. She broke from her mother's grasp and ran to Franz.

He held the child close and tried to quiet her, but Frau Paradis was in a frenzy. She kicked at his shins and pulled Theresa's hair. Then both parents literally tore Theresa from Franz's arms and dragged her out the door.

"Help me," she cried at the door as their eyes met briefly. The hopelessness of their situation must have shown on Franz's face, for she called only this once before her eyes rolled back into her head until only the whites showed. She went limp. Her parents carried her to the waiting carriage.

The next day, the second of May, Franz was handed a letter from Doctor von Stoerk. His committee had decided against Franz's "so-called animal magnetism" treatment of patients. He was requested to resign from the Society and to cease his practice in Vienna.

Franz had a brief talk with Marie Anna. She was cool and preoccupied, as always.

"Of course, dear Franz, it will be impossible for me to go into exile with you . . . you know dear Franzl is with child . . . I must be here."

Franz kissed her hand in farewell. As he left the room, he heard her say to the housekeeper, "We shall use the Bavarian china for the guests tonight."

An alien numbness possessed Franz. His feelings seemed to be in a state of suspension, and his brain refused to function.

Fortunately, his financial affairs were in good order. He needed only to turn over the hospital to his associates and pack a few personal belongings. Karl helped him. He had not asked Karl to go with him, nor had Karl requested permission to do so; he simply packed their things into the carriage and crawled over them to the driver's seat.

They were well along the road before Franz asked, "Where are we headed, Karl?"

"Dillingen, sir. I have written Father Emmanuel to expect us."

"Thank you, Karl. I seem to have moved through this past week in a daze. Did you inquire about Theresa before we left?"

"Yes, doctor. She is blind again. They say she does not eat except when her father forces her to do so."

"Thank you—for asking." Franz forced the words, wondering why he couldn't feel concern.

Being expelled from the medical fraternity, having his practice ruined, and insults from every side only increased Franz's dedication to his research. . . . This he knew in some partially-opened cell of his brain, but he didn't have the fortitude to formulate any plan for the future; all he wished for was the sanctuary of Dillingen and Father Emmanuel's wisdom and grace.

Franz had been at Dillingen for several days, but he couldn't find a thing to talk to Father Emmanuel about. He spent much time in the chapel—not in communion or prayer. He sat there empty and vacant. His eyes would travel over the well-loved figures of the saints in the niches, or linger on the compassionate face of the Blessed Lord. But nothing responded deep within him.

"I don't have the mental energy to demand of myself."

Father Emmanuel contrived to get Franz to a piano, on the pretext that it was a new one and that he would like a verdict as to its worth.

Franz tried a sonata of Wolfgang's. The keyboard action was magnificent. He found himself responding to the voice of music. Gluck and Haydn, his dear friends, also spoke to him through his own fingers. Then he heard Theresa's lovely voice commanding, "Play me a summer song."

He re-improvised the song he had played for her. As he

played, his heart cried out in longing for the youth, laughter, and love of her whom he had known, for her dependence on him, for the wistful, clinging, womanly charm of her. Oh, that last tragic moment when they had been torn apart. Time would take care of academic honors. There would be other patients, but a thing of immaculate beauty had perished from Franz's life.

"It is dead; I will know it no more." Tears fell upon Franz's hands and the keyboard, and yet he played on. He felt that this was his darkest night . . . his appointment with the Cross.

At last, Father Emmanuel stopped him by offering a glass of wine. Tactfully Father drew out the story Franz needed to tell. Father listened to it all—never at any moment did he interrupt. When Franz finished, Father arose, refilled his glass, and resumed his seat. Still he didn't speak. Franz finished his drink and waited.

"How old are you, Franz?" This was the last question Franz had expected.

"Forty-four, Father, this month." Franz smiled ruefully. "According to astrologers, momentous things happen on one's birth date."

"Forty-four . . . hm-m-m, prime of life. Youthful, yet mature. What you worried about, lad?" The God-given wisdom of the saintly man restored Franz's sanity with this simple question.

"What you worried about, lad?"—Franz would ask himself this question in all the years to come.

Franz remained on at Dillingen for a few weeks longer. He slept well, walked a lot, heard Father Emmanuel holding classes, and then enjoyed the evening discussions—just the two of them —Father Emmanuel and Franz.

"These men, these doctor associates of yours—have they not observed your cures?" Father questioned.

"Oh, surely, yes, Father, and I've invited them over and over to experiment with me. Some have done so, with results the same as mine, but the group in power—"

"But seeing is believing, Franz. How can they deny evidence?"

"They call it imagination; 'The patient only believes himself well'; they say I stimulate the patient's imagination . . . a sort of medicinal witchcraft."

Franz walked about the room and continued, "Father, they are right about my trying to stimulate a patient's imagination."

Father looked at Franz, a slight frown between his eyes, and Franz hastened on.

"A painter imagines his canvas filled with the picture he has in his mind. He blocks it off and makes ready. This is for here," Franz walked over to a painting on Father's wall and pointed to a tree, "and this for here,"—a stream of water—"this landscape was visualized and imagined before it became alive on canvas. Music is the same. Everything—*everything*, Father, comes into being in this manner."

Father Emmanuel tilted his head slightly but didn't comment.

"Why not picture our bodies as we wish them? Why not paint our canvas well?"

Father Emmanuel laughed.

"Well, Franz, that does sound pretty far-fetched to me . . . but it's good listening." He stood up to say good-night.

Before Franz left, he had to speak of Theresa. He thought of ways to lead up to it, but the words couldn't pass his lips.

Father Emmanuel again anticipated Franz's need and asked, "The young blind girl, Franz, you loved her?"

"Deeply, Father," Franz was grateful to confess.

"But not enough, Franz."

Franz gasped. "How much more could I have borne? Not enough?"

"No, Franz." Father's voice was cold, the first time Franz had ever heard ice in it. "Had you loved her enough, you would have provided a way."

"How, Father? Tell me how."

Father waved the question aside. "You, with your intelligence and ingenuity, asking me how. For shame, Franz—don't lie to yourself, lad, ever; this to me is the greatest sin man commits against himself."

"I don't follow you, Father." Franz couldn't see his reasoning.

"You were entrusted with her care; you gained her confidence; she had been carefully guarded all her life; yet you played upon her emotions, awakened desire in her, aroused her passions, and worst of all created within her a false sense of security.

Her parents failed her because of their love for the money she provided them, but you failed her for the self-love and self-gratification you indulged in—you exploited her for the thrill of your own lustful flesh."

Then he gave Franz the worst blow of all.

"Poor little girl-child—no wonder she closed her eyes against a false world."

Franz mumbled, "What could I have done?"

"Again you ask me, a priest. . . . Listen, Franz, and I'll tell you. If you had loved her enough you would have kept her and protected her, even though you had to go to the ends of the earth to do so. See, you are leaving your past behind and soon you'll be starting a new life in medicine some place else. Had you loved the child, she would be by your side. Stop your comic-opera dramatics and be realistic. You didn't love her; you lusted for her—and furthermore, you enjoy being crushed by the pain of losing her."

"Father," Franz implored him, but Father continued.

"You failed her in three ways. First, she was not of your generation or learning. You overwhelmed her. Second, she was your ward and you violated your guardianship. Third, you sinned against her and the church in your love play."

"But, Father, I didn't deliberately do any of these things. They just happened."

"Sin always just happens; remember this, son, the church frowns upon sin—even when it just happens."

But something in Father's voice gave Franz his hope for absolution.

CHAPTER XIII

As Franz left Dillingen, he felt a vague uneasiness about his parents.

"We'll stop there first, Karl. Then I'll enjoy making an extended tour through Switzerland, and possibly Bavaria, before we make any final decisions about our medical future."

As soon as he arrived, Franz was thankful that he had gone directly to his parents, for he found both of them ailing. Evidently Mama had had fainting spells for some time. Franz immediately suspected her heart; and after an examination of Papa, he knew that Papa was only sick over Mama's condition.

Mama tried to be her old self. "See, Franz, I can still make the best fondue in Switzerland."

In only a few weeks, though, Mama was no longer leaving her bed, and Papa never left Mama.

Karl cooked the meals and helped out as best he could.

Franz did everything to make the loving old couple happy, but he knew it couldn't be long before one would leave and the other follow.

"They have been together too long and too close, Karl . . . God will not separate them."

Karl wiped his eyes and had no words to say.

Franz was gentle and loving, his whole being wrapped up in helping his parents make a safe journey over. He felt that he was in a different dimension than he had known before. His finger was on Mama's pulse when it gave a last feeble beat, and Mama was with God.

Six weeks later Papa joined her.

Franz, sad and lonely, driven by the faithful Karl, traveled for a time in Bavaria and Switzerland before he made the definite decision to go to Paris. Perhaps the stars, in their remote splendor, formed a pattern for Franz to follow—or perhaps it was a note from Gluck that beckoned him to France. At any rate, he sent Karl back to Vienna to gather his medical equipment, books, and personal belongings and he left by stagecoach for Paris in February of 1778. He took a cab straight to Gluck's apartment.

Gluck's welcome was warm. They had not been together in a long while and talked far into the night.

"You will find Paris quite different from Vienna," Gluck said. "There is tension here and an excitement in the air. The political situation is bad, but the court is very gay."

"Ah, yes, Marie Antoinette. I knew her as a child."

"Then you will not find her much changed. She is a playful, fun-loving Queen. Hers is a gentle heart, but she seems to be totally unconcerned with social reform. She is quite unlike her mother, our Empress Maria Theresa."

"And Louis XVI has not yet followed his grandfather into the extramarital fields of amour?"

Gluck shook his head. "It appears a happy union."

"What of Du Barry?"

"She is here—well-endowed financially and not without political influence. You see, Franz, there is a live-and-let-live attitude among wealthy Parisians. They are an emotional people," here Gluck grinned slyly, "and they are not critical of any kind of emotional display."

"Which means, of course, that they accept your artistic tantrums."

Gluck laughed aloud. "Yes, and I love them for it."

Franz shook his head. Time after time he had warned Gluck that his temperamental explosions were a danger to his health.

"And Rousseau?"

"He is here, too," said Gluck. "He agreed to write nothing against the government or religion; nevertheless, I fear him. He is supported by many of the aristocracy; yet these are the very people whom his doctrines would reduce to the lowest common denominator. The man is dangerous, Franz."

Franz was surprised at Gluck's change of heart. Rousseau had been his greatest supporter in the matter of reform opera. Franz almost questioned this . . . then thought better of it. Gluck loved to talk politics and the subject held little charm for Franz.

Voltaire, too, was back in Paris. His was a scientific and

practical turn of mind, so Franz changed the subject to the writings of Voltaire. He had published several fine papers on Newton's theories of matter.

"Newton was derided when he first stated his law of gravitation, but time and research have vindicated his work. Fancy anyone doubting gravity! To me, animal magnetism is as sure and certain a thing as gravity—and equally invisible." Franz enjoyed expounding to Gluck again. "Somehow, someway, I will presuade the French government to test and validate my findings in animal magnetism. This is my sole mission in France," he assured Gluck.

Franz's first move was to call upon Le Roy, president of the Academy of Sciences. Gluck provided the introduction, and the three of them spent a whole evening discussing animal magnetism. Doctor Le Roy was encouraging and urged Franz to open a clinic where he could demonstrate his techniques. He promised to send out personal invitations to all members of the Academy when Franz was ready to launch his campaign.

At Creteil, on the outskirts of Paris, Franz found a suitable building for a temporary hospital. A few repairs were needed, and he ordered these made while he awaited Karl and the medical equipment which Karl was bringing from Vienna.

"Meantime, Franz, you have much to do in a social way," said Gluck. "To Parisians, *who* you know is far more important than *what* you know."

"I have no wish to trade on your success, my friend. If I can get an unbiased hearing, my discoveries will stand on their own merit."

"Franz, Franz—the important matter is that of presenting your discoveries to the world in the interest of all humanity. Put your pride in your pocket. In the name of humanity, accept whatever help is offered you."

And so Franz did, with difficulty at first but with growing awareness that the course of affairs in France was set in the fashionable salons, not in sober conferences at court.

During the first few weeks, Franz saw only the gay side of Paris. The salons were colorful and filled to overflowing with a never-ending stream of the world's great intellectuals and artists. French women were clothed in a way that made beauties of them all. Their headdresses, silken fabrics, and perfumes made any social gathering a feast for the senses.

And Parisian aristocrats vied with each other in their efforts to live the ultramodern philosophy of religious skepticism. They flaunted convention, reached out with open arms to anyone who promised excitement, and accepted with delight all manner of peculiar entertainment in an effort to fill the void left by a loss of religious conviction.

Gluck and Franz attended a tea at the home of the Comtesse de St. Brisson. To replace the musical entertainment usually offered at such affairs, the Comtesse had built an elaborate puppet stage in her ballroom and hired a full troop of puppeteers to perform continuously for her guests. There were brilliant sallies of wit in the lines spoken by the puppets, but the over-all tinge of eroticism and the frequent risqué remarks were something of an embarrassment to the unsophisticated Franz in the company of ladies. He excused himself and started back to the tea table in the dining hall.

"Franz," a voice halted him in the corridor. He turned to look. It was Count Mercy, Empress Maria Theresa's ambassador to the Court of France.

"How good to see you again," he said. "I heard you were in town, and I planned to call on you this evening."

A weight lifted from Franz's heart. His countryman still held him in esteem, in spite of the gossip from Vienna.

"I'm glad to see you," Franz said, "even more pleased to see you than you know."

"I understand," Count Mercy laughed. "I watched your face during some of the puppet show. Paris society is quite unlike that of Vienna, but you will become accustomed to it. You do plan to stay in Paris?"

"If I am able to establish a practice here and gain recognition of my methods of healing. I assume you know what happened in Vienna."

"I have heard nothing officially, if that is what you mean. Emperor Joseph is not a man to take sides where professional jealousies are involved, and I must doubt that the Empress permits a word of gossip to be spoken in her presence. But I must warn you, Franz, the doctors of Paris, too, can be a stuffy lot."

"Then this French freedom of expression does not extend to the professions?"

"Professional men, Franz, tend to regard themselves as the defenders of established institutions . . . rightly so, I think . . . yet this attitude is all too often a hindrance to progress."

"Nevertheless, Count, it is the professional scientists whom I must interest in animal magnetism. How I long to draw the scientific faculties into recognition and investigation of my system!"

"Then let me help where I can. Whom have you met so far?"

"Le Roy, president of the Academy of Sciences."

"Good. He is a social man. Bring him for dinner Sunday evening, and Gluck, too. I'll send them both notes in the morning."

Count Mercy was a skilled diplomat. By the time the sumptuous meal was finished, he had Le Roy agreeing that Franz had discovered something very important and utterly new in the field of science.

"We can continue our talk and have our coffee and liqueur in the library," the Count suggested. "Perhaps Gluck will play for us later."

The men crossed the marble hall and entered a small room which smelled of old books and fine tobacco. A wave of nostalgia swept over Franz as he sank into one of the big leather chairs drawn up before the open fire. This was the first truly masculine room he had seen in Paris. Would he ever learn to live comfortably in this city ruled by women?

The Count bade the men make themselves comfortable. He had just leaned back and opened his snuffbox when there came a loud crash in the hall. The crash was followed by the thud of a body hitting the floor and then some additional sounds of threshing about. All four of the men jumped to their feet and rushed out to see.

There on the floor, in the final agonies of a seizure, lay the young lad who had assisted in serving dinner. About him were fragments of brandy glasses and demitasse cups. The silver service was scattered, and coffee and brandy ran in little streams across the polished floor.

Count Mercy's manservant arrived on the scene just then. He bent over the boy and stroked his hair before he turned to Count Mercy and his guests. "I'm sorry, sirs. I shall bring more coffee right away."

Le Roy and Franz looked at one another. "Epilepsy?" Le Roy questioned. Franz nodded. The horror in Le Roy's eyes only served to increase Franz's sympathy for the lad on the floor.

Franz hesitated only a moment before he addressed the manservant. "The lad has these seizures often?"

"Yes, sir. He is my son, sir, and the Count was so good as to—"

Here Count Mercy interrupted, "Pieter's wife died while the lad was serving as drummer-boy in our Empress' own regiment. He came back from the wars like this. We brought him to France, hoping a change of scenery—but it has not helped."

"Would you like me to treat him?"

"I had planned to ask you to do so, Franz, but not under these circumstances. Thank God his seizure is over, but now he will be in a stupor for several days. Pieter can take him to his room and bring our coffee. The lad won't move or speak before noon tomorrow."

"What is his name?" Franz asked.

"Andreas," the father answered.

Franz knelt beside the boy and took his head in his hands, holding it firmly and quietly until he felt the healing fluidum passing from his body into the boy's. Then he began to speak gentle, soothing words to him, "You are safe here . . . we are your friends and you are safe . . . your papa is here to watch after you . . . and I am here to cure your ills . . . you will awaken soon and feel well . . . soon you will feel well and strong . . . awaken, Andreas, and feel well and strong."

Franz rose and stepped away from the boy, just as he opened his eyes. He had some difficulty getting up from the floor, but once on his feet he bowed to the men with dignity and spoke calmly, "I'm sorry, sirs." Immediately he set about gathering up the broken china and scattered silver. The father watched with tears in his eyes.

Only a few minutes later the lad brought coffee and liqueur into the library. Much impressed, Le Roy repeated his offer to bring his colleagues to observe Franz's work.

Franz's hand slipped into his pocket and touched his rosary.

Because of Count Mercy's warm welcome, Franz now felt free to pay his respects to the Queen. She received him the first time he called.

Marie Antoinette was lovelier in maturity than she had been as a girl. Her gay manner was infectious, and Franz found himself chatting with her easily and lightly. They were certainly in rapport. As he left she bade him call often.

It was at one of the Queen's morning *levées* that Franz met Monique Montarre. "My friend from the New World," Marie Antoinette whispered to him.

The moment Franz first saw Monique, something shifted in his life. Like snow upon a mountain side, he felt it move. She was beautiful. Her gown showed an able body, her smile was warm and quick, and her dark eyes were large and intelligent; but more than this, she loved life. There was an intoxicating awareness about her—a deep, quiet vitality.

"Doctor Mesmer," she said, acknowledging their introduction. "Your fame has spread across the ocean to my home in New Orleans. I understand that you are a student of Paracelsus."

"When I was a child," Franz told her, "I lived on the shores of Lake Constance. It was there that I learned to love the stars—and Paracelsus. He was Swiss, you know."

She nodded gravely. "We earthlings have much need of stardust, doctor. We are grateful for that which you bring us. But walking as you do with your head in the stars, how is it that you have the look of a man who is one with the earth?"

"I seek neither the earth nor the stars, but the harmony which lies between the two. My work is not concerned with secret remedies, but with the invisible ebb and flow of . . ." and Franz found himself talking freely of his theories to this lovely woman whom he had known for only a few minutes.

Many French women were intellectual in a hard, brittle way. Their sharp tongues and rapier wit drew Franz's interest, but not his admiration. He could not feel at ease with them—but with Monique it was different. Definitely, she was an intellectual; yet she used her mind to nourish a conversation rather than to dissect it.

Franz left the Queen's *levée* a rejuvenated man. And a good thing it was, too, for he arrived at Gluck's quarters to find that Karl had come from Vienna with four lorries full of his belongings and medical equipment. That same day, they set to work furnishing the place in Creteil.

In the combined music room and drawing room, Franz bowed to French fashion with satin draperies and gilded chairs; the musical glasses went well with this décor, but in the rest of the house he kept to the plainer furnishings which were more to his taste. Karl had brought the old baquet. They installed it in a centrally-located room off of which smaller rooms opened. These smaller rooms were suitable for patients who might experience violent spasms after treatment. His own bedroom was in the same wing, with the medical office, but the arrangement of the house permitted no alternative.

It was mid-March when Karl hung out the newly-painted sign, and patients began arriving right away. Franz had been at work for a week when Karl opened the door early one morning to admit Wolfgang Mozart.

"Have you room for an old patient, doctor?" he asked.

"Never have you been more welcome," Franz assured him, "and I hope you brought your whole family."

"Papa and Nannerl are in Salzburg," he answered. "Papa could not get away, but he sent Mama with me to look after my food and money." He smiled happily. This musical genius was still a little boy in the heart of his family.

"Then go and bring her in, Wolfgang."

"Oh, no, doctor, she is not with me today. We have rooms in the city and Mama is busy setting them straight. I slipped away to consult with you."

They chatted for a few minutes and then Wolfgang said, "I shall bring Mama and come spend an evening with you soon, but today—today I should like to consult with you as a doctor—that is, I need help with a physical problem and—"

"Then come," and Franz led the way to his office.

Through the years Wolfgang had paid Franz office visits with an assortment of ailments—toothache, earache, sore throat, and once a bruised heel. Boyhood ills, they had been. But as he sat facing Franz today, Franz knew that something of a different nature troubled him. His thin, handsome face showed concern and determination.

"And where is the pain, Wolfgang?" Franz smiled, for he could not imagine it to be serious. In spite of his delicate build, Wolfgang had always possessed an abundance of healthy energy.

"Well . . ." and Wolfgang fidgeted with his chair. Finally he moved it up to Franz's desk, resettled himself, and reached for a quill and a blank of paper.

"There's something bothering me," he said as he began to draw lines on the paper. "And now that I am in Paris, I know it will bother me more and more." He drew a clef across the lines.

"Yes," Franz prompted, keenly interested.

"Do you know my age?" Wolfgang demanded, looking up from his drawing.

"About twenty-two," Franz said quietly, for he could see now that Wolfgang was truly disturbed.

"Just past twenty-two . . . I've written my father about this matter . . . I'm a man . . . but this is not easy to talk about . . . I don't know how to tell you . . ." and he drew musical notes on the paper as he felt for words.

Franz jumped to a conclusion. "Wolfgang, do you have a girl in trouble?"

He looked up, startled, and colored deeply, "Why, no . . . that's the trouble. . . ."

"Trouble?" And then it dawned on Franz. "Now I see; you are longing for a girl."

Wolfgang's legs wrapped around the chair. "Yes, as I wrote my father, I'm a man."

"And what did your father reply?"

"He said I must remember that I am a good Catholic." Here he unwound his legs from the chair and resumed his drawing with the quill. "He says that I am in no financial condition to marry."

"Such advice helps somewhat?"

"Not much," and he shook his head slowly and solemnly as he sighed. "Even when I am working . . . I can be lost in the movement of the music, hungering with my whole soul to hear the last notes of a sonata . . . and suddenly feel this pull of nature which levels me with the earth and leaves me shaken and empty."

Franz waited.

"When I was younger, I could go to the kitchen and feed upon sweetmeats or some other forbidden food, but now. . . ."

"Now?" Franz wanted him to word his difficulty.

Wolfgang wrote a few more notes before he laid down the quill and looked at Franz. "After Paris concerts, some of the fellows, the single ones, go to see girls . . . strumpets, that is. . . ."

"Yes," Franz waited again.

"I can't; I just can't."

"Why not?"

"I feel a horror and a sense of disgust for that sort of thing . . . then, too, the fear of disease. Some of the fellows have—" He shuddered.

Franz nodded his head in sympathy. "But innocent girls?" Franz asked.

"Why I would never seduce an innocent girl," Wolfgang said, appalled.

"I'm not suggesting it," Franz corrected hastily, "I'm just asking if you have a sweetheart—a chosen one whom you can consider marrying as you build your future?"

Wolfgang smiled. "Well, there are the Weber sisters. Aloysia sings like an angel. She has sung in some of my operas. I write her daily about music and I advise with her about improving her work." Wolfgang's mood was lifting.

"Don't I recall a few other young ladies you have found pleasing," Franz smiled, "so it seems to me that your problem is one of coping with your sexual nature until the right woman comes along."

"Not exactly, doctor. My problem is that of coping with my sexual nature when any woman comes along." Both of them laughed.

"Seriously, Wolfgang, I wish I could help you; but I cannot add much to your father's advice. Remember the teachings of the church and work hard—not only to relieve the pressure you feel, but also to establish yourself financially so that you can marry when you do find the girl of your heart."

Wolfgang stood up. "I'm sure you are right. It's just that sometimes. . . ." and here his voice trailed off. He was looking at the sheets of notepaper on which he had scribbled while he talked to Franz. He picked them up and began to hum the tune.

It was an arresting air. Franz moved around the desk to look at the notes. "B-flat minor," and Franz hummed a few bars with Wolfgang.

"This is the part I'm missing in my piano concerto," Wolfgang said excitedly. "It's the beginning of the adagio movement." He thanked Franz hurriedly and rushed away.

CHAPTER XIV

FRANZ HAD planned to call on Monique soon after meeting her, but Karl's arrival from Vienna plunged him into the duties of establishing his offices; his social life would have to wait.

Karl brought news of Theresa.

"I arranged for her to have the big dog, sir," said Karl. "Herr Paradis' feeling toward you has softened considerably, and he explained to the girl that the animal was a gift from you. She was delighted."

"Thank you, Karl. I wish there were some way I could make Theresa the gift of her eyesight."

"She is playing again, doctor. Perhaps her music is more important to her than her eyesight. Frau Mesmer says tell you not to worry about the girl."

"How odd that Marie Anna should concern herself with my worries—or has the advent of a grandchild called out the maternal tenderness in her nature?" In a burst of gratitude for her comforting message, Franz wrote Limoges and ordered for her a collection of the miniature porcelain flowers which French ladies were using as decoration on their gowns.

Franz had much opportunity to observe ladies' gowns. Possibly because the Queen received him so cordially, he immediately began receiving medical calls from the ladies of Paris.

It was late in the afternoon when he arrived at the home of Nina la Julienne in response to her note requesting his professional services. Franz had met this beautiful woman at a concert the week before. He could understand why she was looked upon as one of the darlings of Paris society in spite of the fact that her alliance with the wealthy merchant, François Chevez, was a matter of common gossip.

"What could be ailing the scintillating Mademoiselle Julienne?" he wondered, as he followed her manservant up the thickly-carpeted stairs and to her boudoir door, which stood open.

The servant departed and Franz stood watching the lovely

lady. She was in negligee, seated before the three large mirrors of her dressing table. Intently she studied her reflection, reaching up a finger to smooth a tiny furrow here, to lift the chin or jaw line there. Finally, she picked up a hand mirror and carefully observed her profile—all the while taking no notice of his presence.

At last Franz shook the door knob and, pretending to have just entered the room, he spoke, "Ah, most gracious lady, you do me honor by asking me to attend you."

She turned to him quickly, and for a moment her face was radiant with a welcoming smile.

"What is troubling you?" Franz asked gently; then he assumed his medical voice, "Tell me everything." (*"You must instill confidence, right from the very first; you can do it with your voice, your demeanor. . . ."* Van Swieten's instructions had a way of coming back to Franz at odd times.)

Mademoiselle Julienne turned back to her reflection. She lifted her chin slightly and their eyes met and held in the mirror as an expression of fear came over her features. Her shoulders drooped, her body sagged, and she answered him in tones of tragedy. "Doctor Mesmer, my protector is leaving me. Monsieur Chevez is bored with me."

"Another woman, younger perhaps?" Franz asked. So this was the reason for the mirrored scrutiny.

"How did you know? There has been no gossip." Her nervous hand reached for a bottle of scent.

"You really love him?"

"He has been the only man, doctor." Not justification here—just the simple truth.

"For how long?"

"Since I was sixteen. I am now forty-five. That is a long time."

"You no doubt felt secure."

"Like a wife. He is sixty, you know. Wouldn't you think—?"

Franz shook his head. "No, my dear. He is an old grey goose trying to be a gosling. Now, do tell me the young woman is sixteen. This will make the picture complete."

For a brief moment her reflection showed a smile. "Oh,

doctor, how delightful that you understand." Then the light went from her face as she added soberly, "He is an old grey goose, but I love him." Tears overflowed her eyes.

"My dear," Franz said as he placed his hands on her shoulders and looked into her mirrored eyes, "you are fifteen years younger than this man. You are the light of Paris now, and yours is a beauty which will charm men when you are seventy. You love many people, and you are loved by many people. Life is a joyous passage for you. The music of your laughter heals where medicine cannot reach. Let the grey goose fly his course—you must dance yours. Life is beautiful for you, my dear, you love and you are loved. . . ."

Their eyes held and Franz saw a look of peace cross her unhappy face. Then slowly her lids drooped. Could it be? Franz was surprised. Then he knew it was so—the fluidum had flowed from him to the mirror, which had reflected it back into her troubled soul. He carried her to the chaise lounge and left her sleeping.

On the way home he made plans for the installation of additional mirrors in the treatment room at Creteil.

Franz's medical practice expanded rapidly, in spite of the fact that he was receiving no referrals from Paris physicians. About the first of May, Franz drove into the city to inquire of Le Roy about this matter and to remind Le Roy of his promise to invite the members of the Academy of Sciences to his clinic.

"In accordance with the rules of procedure," Le Roy said, "I placed your invitation on the agenda of the last meeting of the Academy. I'm sorry, doctor, very sorry that there was little response. We do feel, of course, that animal magnetism should be investigated."

"What method of investigation do you suggest?" Franz inquired.

"Well . . . that is hard to say. The Academy members are rather busy these days . . . perhaps if you wrote a paper. . . ." Le Roy was vague.

The same day Franz applied for membership in the newly-formed Academy of Medicine. He did not expect to be welcomed; but inasmuch as his credentials were in order, he knew that this organization of physicians could not refuse him.

Within a week he was notified of his acceptance and invited to attend a meeting. He went—and took the opportunity to invite his colleagues to Creteil.

"I am not asking you," Franz said, "to accept my theories, but I do entreat you to experiment with me. I am humbly grateful and proud that I trained in the Vienna school. I honor the memory of the great Girard van Swieten, for without his guidance our modern eighteenth-century medicine would lack both luster and system. I am a product of his guidance—and you are my brothers. Together, standing as we do on the firm foundation of medicine, we can reach out and examine a new and fertile scientific discovery—animal magnetism. I beg and implore of you—experiment with me. Visit my surgery hours at Creteil." Franz sat down.

Ominous silence was the only reply to his plea for help and recognition. Could Gluck have been right when he advised— "Establish yourself first in the social realm."

Franz took a morning from his work and attended another of the Queen's *levées*. Monique was there.

"I hear that you have opened a hospital at Creteil," she said.

"Madame, you observe that which the Paris doctors overlook."

"Ah," she said, "I am as jealous as the Paris doctors, but my jealousy is of a different order."

"I do not understand."

"Then I must explain to you, doctor. Shall I begin at dinner tomorrow evening? At my home, please, nine o'clock."

Monique's invitation was almost a command; yet so candid and so affectionate was her manner—not coquettish, in the way of some French women, but openly cordial and warm—that Franz accepted; but he was puzzled and a bit apprehensive. He sought out Gluck.

How Gluck laughed! "My dear Franz, by all means, go. She is a delightful person. And as for her intentions, I can only tell you that she has been in and out of Paris for several years now and not a breath of scandal has touched her. She is a widow, you know."

"I was not sure. She was introduced as Madame. . . ."

"So that is what was bothering you! In Paris, Franz, women quite often hold salons and give dinner parties at which their husbands are not present. Do not hesitate to accept an invitation simply because you have not met the husband. The present King is a much more moral man than was his grandfather, but his views have made little impression on Paris social customs."

Franz's carriage rolled into Monique's drive promptly at nine o'clock, but there were guests who had arrived ahead of him. He was glad to see the two vehicles already in the courtyard—and in the same breath he chided himself for his temerity in thinking it might be otherwise.

"Fool that I am," he said to himself as Monique gave him her hand in greeting, "to imagine this beautiful creature has more than a friendly interest in me."

She led him across the drawing room. "Madame d'Eslon," she said as Franz gazed into the first placid female face he had seen in all of Paris, "may I present Doctor Franz Mesmer."

"Doctor Mesmer." Madame d'Eslon's gracious, gentle tone went well with her face.

Monique turned next to the gentlemen who stood waiting to be introduced, "Doctor d'Eslon, Count Puységur, and our beloved Diderot."

"Diderot—the famous compilor of the *Encyclopédie?*" Franz inquired, his enthusiasm mounting.

"Perhaps infamous is the word, doctor," Diderot answered with wry humor.

"Do savor our great man's moment of modesty, Doctor Mesmer," said Monique. "Before the evening is over, he will be boasting of his accomplishment—as well he should."

The friendly laughter of the group brought a feeling of easy camaraderie to the room. These people were at home with one another, and they welcomed Franz into their midst.

"Doctor Charles d'Eslon is a practicing physician, Doctor Mesmer," said Monique. "We are expecting that you and he will discuss animal magnetism healing this evening."

"I can't do much discussing," said d'Eslon, "but I look forward to listening—and if I may, to questioning you about your findings. Sorry I missed the meeting of the Academy the day you spoke there."

His words were balm, and the casual, friendly talk flowed about Franz like the waters of a healing spring. He contributed little to the conversation, even when it turned to medicinal herbs and spices as they sat at the dinner table. Count Puységur seemed especially interested in herbs. Finally Franz inquired the reason for this interest.

"My father instilled in me a love of the land," Puységur said. "He always felt that French soil would grow many of the crops which we import at such great cost and effort. I traveled a great deal when my father was alive, and always I brought home to him cuttings and seeds from interesting plants. He developed an apothecary garden which I have maintained since his death. Monique brought me several plants from the New World."

"Monique did?"

"Have you not seen her herb gardens?"

"Diderot," said Monique, "will you change the subject? I am having trouble charming Doctor Mesmer and I may want to mix him a secret potion. He must not know yet that I am skilled in such things."

"Monique, my sweet," the aging Diderot replied, "with me at your feet, what do you want with all these other men?"

More easy laughter—and Franz reveled in it. But he enjoyed more the after-dinner talk when d'Eslon drew him out on the subject of animal magnetism. D'Eslon's questions were penetrating, and his interest was obviously sincere.

"I cannot come tomorrow with Le Roy and the others," said d'Eslon, "but would you permit me to visit next week?"

"I should be honored to have you at any time," Franz said with his lips while his mind busied itself with this revelation. "Le Roy and the others! So, they are planning to visit my clinic —but unannounced."

How grateful Franz felt toward Monique. This had been a singularly rewarding evening.

The next morning Franz arose early to make his rounds, but Karl was in the clinic ahead of him. Franz had several operations scheduled for the day, and Karl was preparing the theatre. This preparation was a daily ritual with him. He scorned the French servants' lack of cleanliness and personally carried on the battle against soil in this room which was used for surgery and emergencies.

Franz explained to Karl about the guests they might expect. Karl had just finished placing chairs in the theatre when the men arrived—Le Roy and four colleagues. Le Roy introduced the men as doctors, but Franz had no way of ascertaining whether they were physicians or scientists from other fields.

He invited the members of the delegation to make themselves comfortable in the chairs, but to feel free to step up to the table at any time they wished a closer look. They sat talking in short, excited sentences, as French people do—watching while Franz scoured his hands and arms and donned the apron which he used for surgery.

Franz's two young assistants brought in the first patient, a peasant by the name of Denis. The man was unable to walk. Franz had examined him the day before and found a highly developed scirrhus of the left testis. So massive was it that the scrotum had grown to the size of a child's head. Its dark-blue mass pressed against the urinary system so that the man screamed in pain when his kidneys acted.

"I treated him yesterday with animal magnetism," Franz explained to the visiting doctors, "and he fell into a deep sleep. This morning early I repeated the magnetic treatment. Again I shall repeat it, so that he will feel no pain when I do the necessary surgery."

The man lay in a mild stupor. Franz placed his hands on the man's shoulders and spoke to him. "As the fluidum permeates your whole being, you shall feel its ebb and flow . . . ebb and flow. . . . then will come sleep. . . . Rest and sleep, Denis, rest and sleep." Franz repeated these assurances over and over as he slowly moved his hands over the man's body. Denis was asleep.

"Now turn him on his side and remove the dressings," Franz directed his assistants.

They did so; and as they pulled away the sanies-laden coverings, the vile odor of cancer filled the room. The accumulations of the night covered the whole area. "Wash him," Franz directed as he turned to the doctors again.

"Beloved colleagues," he said, "as you can readily see, this man's condition is such that only an operation can relieve his tumor for any appreciable length of time. He is fortunate that the urinary passages have not entirely closed. His is a case of ulcerated cancer."

"My esteemed professor, Doctor van Swieten, advised us to leave most cancers alone. He believed that to cut into the acrid field only released the sanies to spill into healthy tissues of the body, bringing about a more rapid demise of the patient. In fact, he averred that the less done the better, except in cases such as this—when the mass presses against other vital organs to such a degree that necessary body functions are distorted or threatened with stoppage."

Franz turned back to his patient with reassuring words. "Hold his leg, so," he said to one of his assistants as he demonstrated how to lift the limb.

"Now, gentlemen." And the doctors pressed forward as Franz incised the taut skin at the base of the scrotum and laid bare the evil-smelling mass of the tumor.

That his knife did not slip was a wonder, for at that very moment one of the doctors lurched against the table and fell to the floor in a faint. Franz continued with his work as a colleague lifted the visitor from the room; but when neither returned, Franz knew the answer—those two were not physicians!

Quickly he cut, while his assistant mopped away the discharge. The distended bladder emptied even before he had finished tying off the wound.

"Your patient," Franz said to the remaining doctors.

They counted his pulse and raised his eyelids to peer at the pupils of his eyes. They felt his abdomen and counted his heartbeat; then they nodded to one another and stepped away. The whole procedure had taken slightly less than an hour.

While Franz washed, he explained to the men, "He will live for a while, but only God knows how long. The cancer may or may not return. We can hope, and we can keep him comfortable while he recovers from the operation. In two days he will be walking."

Karl made a paper fire in the brazier to clear the air of the cancerous stench. Then he set about stripping the table and covering it with fresh linens.

The next surgery case had to be postponed, for one of the assistants entered the room with a girl-child of about five years in his arms. She was in a faint. He laid her on Karl's freshly-prepared table and said apologetically, "She is very sick, Doctor Mesmer."

As Franz approached her, he remarked to one of his distinguished visitors, "We always attend to the children as quickly as possible. This was not scheduled."

The child's pulse was so weak that he had difficulty finding it. Her eyes were rolled back and set. She felt cold to the touch and was as white as death. Her middle-class parents stood at the door in mute despair. Their eyes pleaded with Franz. He smiled reassurance as he inquired, "What seems to have brought this about?"

The mother came forward. "Oh, doctor, my little one had the congestion of the lungs. The fever was burning the life out of her."

"And what did you do for her?" Franz tried to speak patiently and gently.

Reassured, the mother lifted the child's garments and pointed. There in the center of the tiny chest clung a leech measuring a full three inches. On the concave little belly was another of the loathsome worms. "She was afraid of them, but it was all I knew to do for the fever."

Franz motioned to his assistant for a jar. With tweezers he loosened the things from the child's body and dropped them into the jar. But for the regard of his observers, he would have flung them into Karl's brazier. His offense against institutionalism was great enough without affronting these physicians who believed in the use of leeches—as did the van Swieten group of Vienna. Franz felt a sudden anger sweep over him. "Poor fools . . . poor fools."

He applied a cleansing agent and a healing powder to the leech sores; he asked his aide to get a sugared brandy and warm water drink for the child.

"Look on her back, too, doctor," said the mother.

Franz turned the child over. There were more leeches. He repeated his plucking and treatment of the sores.

"Poor little tyke." His tender feeling enfolded her as he sat on the edge of the table and lifted her to an upright position against his shoulder. He talked to her as he offered her the brandy from a spoon. "Now you are better. Now you are safe. Sip just a spoonful of this. Good, that is good."

He was not consciously using animal magnetism. He was only consoling a weakened little child. He was surprised when she opened her eyes wide and reached for the glass. She drained it, and the color began to return to her face. Within a few moments she was smiling and chattering like a magpie.

"Feed her plenty of good rich broth and keep her warm," he admonished the delighted parents as they carried the child into Karl's small office to settle the fee for treatment.

The third patient of the morning was Captain Honoré Jaques Watteau of the Queen's own regiment. He was a handsome gallant, a cousin to the painter Antoine Watteau and himself given to the ancient arts of tilting and amour. He strode into the theatre—as splendid in nightdress as he was in uniform. Swinging himself up on the table with his good left arm, he flippantly demanded, "Start your show, horse doctor."

"And what manner of animal can this be?" Franz joked back.

There had been a rapport between them since the day Marie Antoinette had sent Watteau to Franz, his right arm badly damaged by a lance point. Treatment over a period of three weeks had proved ineffectual, and Franz had decided to operate.

The assistant carefully took the Captain's arm from its sling and laid bare the wound. Franz called the visiting doctors forward to see the arm and to be introduced to the Captain. He winced when one of the visitors gently touched the flesh surrounding the festering cut.

"The Captain responds quickly to animal magnetism, gentlemen," Franz said. "We have used it frequently to relieve the pain of dressing his wound. For some reason, however, the tissue has not healed with treatment. Today we shall discover and remove the source of irritation."

Franz motioned the doctors back a few paces and looked squarely into Watteau's eyes. Slowly he reached out his hands to Watteau's shoulders as he spoke. "You are filling with the flow . . . you are relaxing . . . you will lie back slowly now . . . giving yourself into the fluidum you will sleep . . . your eyelids are heavy with sleep . . . you are sleeping now . . . you will feel no pain . . . no pain . . . no pain. . . ."

Franz picked up a blade and made a long incision. He motioned the doctors close. "I suspect this is a necrosis of the upper third of the humerus. I propose to incise all the way to the bone. If the bone was bruised at the time of injury and has become diseased as a result, then I shall remove the deterioration, clean out the unhealthy flesh, arrange for drainage, and sew up the wound." Franz worked as he talked.

It was a long operation and a tedious one, for Franz avoided cutting muscles wherever he could. "I cannot let this knight lose his tilting arm," Franz smiled to his attentive audience.

At last the bone lay bare. A small section was honeycombed. He carefully scraped out this unhealthy segment, trimmed the wound, and sewed loosely, as van Sweiten had taught him. He knew there would be drainage and it must have room to escape.

The patient had not moved. Franz did not try to awaken him but had him carried to his room, where he knew he would sleep until the strength of the fluidum had been used up in the healing process.

"Shall we stop for lunch, gentlemen?" Franz asked. "I should be honored to have you as my guests and we can talk about the morning's work."

"We must go," said one of the doctors, as his colleague nodded agreement. "Le Roy promised to have us back in our offices by mid-day."

These men had neither admired nor criticized Franz's surgery. Doctors, however, are often noncommittal and may be especially so when confronted with unusual medical situations. At any rate, Franz thought of Le Roy as the spokesman for the group and was overjoyed when Le Roy said:

"Doctor Mesmer, this has been a great honor. Surely the medical profession of France will profit by this day's work. We thank you. I shall be in touch with you."

Recognition at last. Franz felt such elation that he could hardly wait to see the rest of his patients—to complete the day's work and drive in to share the good news with his two real friends in Paris, Gluck and Monique. Of course, there was Wolfgang—but Gluck and Monique were the ones who would truly understand.

Gluck was not at home. He went to Monique's place. She was there, and she was alone. They talked far into the night.

In the same elated mood Franz worked through the following week. D'Eslon sent word that he was leaving town and must postpone his visit to the clinic until September, but Franz was not dismayed. Soon his discovery would receive recognition from the Academy—he felt sure of it. He and Monique celebrated with an evening at the opera. And then they celebrated again with dinner and a concert.

Two weeks passed before he began to wonder—and to worry. He called on Le Roy.

"This is difficult to explain, Doctor Mesmer," Le Roy said, fumbling with the paperweight on his desk. "My colleagues feel that if they had been granted an opportunity to examine your patients carefully . . . that is, they feel that you, not they, made the diagnosis. Of course, soldiers are hardened to pain—and the other man. . . ."

"What exactly is the trouble, Le Roy?"

"Well, you know, your colleagues in Vienna. . . ." He looked up at last.

"They have written letters?"

"Perhaps. One can't be too sure about these things. . . ."

Le Roy was vague, but Franz could understand his position. Once again Vienna had arranged for a door to be slammed in his face.

"Perhaps if you could summarize your theories in a paper for me to read to the Academy . . ." Le Roy suggested.

"Perhaps . . ." and Franz departed.

It was to Monique that he turned in his heartbreak.

"Then write the paper, Franz." She was emphatic.

"I am accused of ambiguous behavior because I do not make known the theory upon which my system is based," Franz sighed. "I answer the accusations so, Monique: 'It is impossible

147

for me to make this theory known. I long to be able to give systematic, clear, and definite proofs of my doctrine; but I cannot find the proper phrases to describe them.' " He shook his head in despair.

"Try, Franz. Try now and never stop trying. That which is in the mind of man must have expression."

"I express what I know in action. Why must I express it in words? Why can't they see?" he demanded.

"Because words are a part of the eternal trinity—thought, word, action."

Franz felt over-tired. He heard Monique, but her philosophy did not come clear. Too much was happening too fast, and his mind could not sort out the changes that were occurring in his soul. Even as Monique voiced her philosophy, he felt the old longing return. "Does my body cry out for a woman—or is my soul in search of God? And, what of my profession? Thought, word, action—the trinity—what of it?" He sighed and got to his feet abruptly.

"Forgive me, Monique; I must go."

Franz departed, but even on the drive home his mood did not lift. He yearned, yet he knew not for what. The horses' hooves hit the ground in a cadence—thought, word, action—thought, word, action—he heard Monique's words in rhythm, but their meaning would not take form.

It was a week before Franz saw Monique again. She opened the door herself that evening, and this sudden, unexpected sight of her took his breath away.

"I came by to tell you that I'm leaving town to write the paper." He stopped abruptly, looking at her; he knew he didn't want to leave.

"How wonderful; oh, how wonderful," she exclaimed. "When do you leave?"

"I shall leave Monday."

"Good. When will you be back?" Her voice was reserved, almost cold, or did he imagine it?

"Not until I've formulated my theories into words."

"Good." Her approval pushed him on, but he wished she had shown more reluctance to have him go.

◆ CHAPTER XV ◆

FRANZ LEFT Paris at four in the morning. The stagecoach was as drafty and uncomfortable as Karl insisted it would be. Karl had been certain that all manner of evil would befall Franz if he didn't take the new carriage and the span of dappled horses which were his pride. Karl had wanted to drive them, of course. At last Franz had convinced Karl that the future of medicine rested on Karl's presence at the hospital during his absence.

Franz had to leave Paris to write his paper and he had to go alone. He knew deep down that he must return to nature and become one with her before he could voice his theories.

He leaned back in his seat and his eyes found the morning star. Something of the strain was already leaving him. He could feel the muscles in the back of his neck loosening. A few miles more and dawn began to break. Like the gradual swell of symphonic music building to a crescendo, light mounted from the horizon and moved up to fill the sky—then lo, the sun burst forth in all its splendor.

A rooster jumped to the ground and stretched his night-cramped wings. He ran his proud head up as far as it would go on his sleek neck and poured forth his trumpet blast—a fowl's rhapsody to the new day. A simple thing, yet Franz's own heart echoed the joyous song.

A wind so soft that it might have been a fairy's breath ruffled the roadside flowers. They waved hail and farewell to Franz as the coach rolled past.

He leaned forward in his seat to greet the flowers. It seemed years since he had seen them growing wild and free in the fields like this. Elegant, artificial Paris had done something to him. It had cut him away from his roots in the past and had cast him into an ocean of new people and new experiences. He had reveled in the change—the excitement, the intrigue, even the falsity and glitter of Paris—but this simple pastoral landscape which came to life under the hand of God had power to restore his mind to reality. It made him one with himself.

In the late afternoon, he left the coach at a small village. He walked through the little town and down a cart trail until he came to the farmhouse of a middle-class couple. Would they board him for a few weeks?

They would. The blessed aloneness of the following days. He walked miles down the rows of cultivated fields and through the pastures of wild grasses. Occasionally he came upon shallow streams of water which gave forth music like that of his childhood brooklet. "What do I believe? What is my theory of animal magnetism?" He would query himself as he walked.

"Why, indeed, can't I write a paper or construct a list of propositions to explain my discovery? Why are my methods suspected when my colleagues are willing to use other medical aids which have been handed down to them from what was veritable witchcraft—witness the disgusting use of leeches from the time of the Druids.

"And the tar water treatment. Berkeley, the English philosopher, gave us that treatment. He found it somewhere in the New World. A quart of resinous tar mixed with a quart of water; shake together in a jar; allow to settle, and drink the water as treatment for smallpox. Vary the ingredients to make the solution stronger or weaker, if you wish—no precise formula. Even the van Swieten group used tar water." Franz kicked at a clod.

"Yes, I can enumerate practice after medical practice which has no scientific explanation or background—but of what use?" He picked up a rock and threw it across the field.

After two weeks of such conversations with nature and of daily prayer in the little country chapel, his mind began to heal and to reach out toward words that would formulate his methods. A series of propositions—he decided—each building upon the other to describe the fluidum, its ebb and flow, and the body's susceptibility to the presence of the flow.

Not with ease, perhaps not with clarity, but certainly with all the sincerity of his medically-trained mind, he set down the first of his propositions.

1. A responsive influence exists between the heavenly bodies, the earth, and all animated bodies.

2. A fluid universally diffused, so continuous as to admit no vacuum, incomparably subtle and naturally susceptible of receiving, spreading, and communicating all motor disturbances, is the means of this influence.

3. This reciprocal action is subject to mechanical laws with which we are not as yet familiar.

Day after day he worked on, adding to the list until at last he wrote:

4. Alternative effects result from this action, which may be considered to be an ebb and flow.

5. This reflux is more or less general, more or less special, more or less compound, according to the nature of the causes behind it.

6. It is by this action, the most universal in nature, that the exercise of active relations takes place between the heavenly bodies, the earth, and its constituent parts.

7. The properties of matter and of organic substance depend on this action.

8. The animal body experiences the alternative effects of this agent, and is directly affected by its insinuation into the substance of the nerves.

9. Properties are displayed, analogous to those of the magnet, particularly in the human body, in which diverse and opposite poles are likewise to be distinguished, and these may be communicated, altered, destroyed, and reinforced. Even the phenomenon of declination may be observed.

10. This property of the human body which renders it susceptible to the influence of the heavenly bodies, and of the reciprocal action of those which environ it, manifests its analogy with the magnet, and this has decided me to adopt the term of animal magnetism.

11. The action and virtue of animal magnetism thus characterized may be communicated to others, animate or inanimate

bodies. Both types of bodies, however, vary in their susceptibility.

12. This action and virtue may be strengthened and diffused by such bodies.

13. Experiments show that there is a diffusion of matter, subtle enough to penetrate all bodies without any considerable loss of energy.

14. Its action takes place at a remote distance without the aid of any intermediary substance.

15. It is, like light, increased and reflected by mirrors.

16. It is communicated, spread, and increased by sound.

17. This magnetic virtue may be accumulated, concentrated, and transported.

18. I have said that animated bodies are not all equally susceptible; in a few instances they have such an opposite property that their presence is enough to destroy all the effects of magnetism upon other bodies.

19. This opposite virtue likewise penetrates all bodies; it also may be communicated, spread, accumulated, concentrated, and transported, reflected by mirrors, and spread by sound. This does not merely constitute a negative, but a positive, opposite virtue.

20. The magnet, whether natural or artificial, is like other bodies susceptible of animal magnetism, and even of the opposite virtue: in neither case does its action on fire and on the needle suffer any change, and this shows that the principle of animal magnetism differs fundamentally from that of mineral magnetism.

21. This system sheds new light upon the nature of fire and of light, as well as on the theory of attraction, of flux and reflux, of the magnet and of electricity.

22. It teaches us that the magnet and artificial electricity have, with respect to diseases, properties common to many other

agents presented to us by nature, and that if the use of these has achieved some useful results, they are due to animal magnetism.

23. These facts show, in accordance with the practical rules I am about to establish, that this principle will cure nervous diseases directly.

24. By its aid the physician is enlightened as to the use of medicine and may render its action more perfect, and he can provoke and direct salutary crises so as to control them completely.

25. In communicating my method, I shall, by a new theory of matter, demonstrate the universal usefulness of the principle I seek to establish.

26. With this knowledge, the physician may judge with certainty the origin, nature, and progress of diseases, however complicated they may be; he may hinder their progress and accomplish their cure without exposing the patient to dangerous and troublesome consequences, irrespective of age, temperament and sex. Even a woman in a stage of pregnancy, and during parturition, may reap the same advantage.

27. This doctrine will, finally, enable the physician to decide upon the health of every individual, and upon the presence of the diseases to which he may be exposed. In this way the art of healing may be brought to absolute perfection.

He sighed, content, "Now, they will listen; now they will help me experiment." In thanksgiving he touched the rosary in his pocket.

CHAPTER XVI

In mid-July Franz returned to Paris with the paper for Le Roy—his twenty-seven propositions.

"I'll arrange a meeting of the Academy of Sciences." He nodded. "Perhaps the wise thing would be to have you appear as guest speaker and read your paper."

Well content, Franz went from Le Roy's office to call on Gluck. Wolfgang sat drooping in a corner.

"What has happened?" Franz demanded.

"I lost my mother while you were away, doctor," and his eyes filled with tears.

Franz embraced his young friend. "I'm sorry. Can you tell me about it?"

"It was a sudden thing. She had every care and we did all we could—but as I wrote Papa, our time is really in God's hands. When our hour of death is come, no good fortune or gift of chance can add one hour to our span of life."

"God's will is good, Wolfgang."

"Yes, and it is done."

Gluck and Franz exchanged glances. The Mozarts were a close family—how touching was a faith which could sustain its unity even under the shattering hand of death.

"Come and stay with me," Franz invited Wolfgang.

"Thank you, doctor, but I am comfortable in Paris—and busy. I'm working on a ballet, *Les Petits Reines*. When it is finished, I go to Munich. But if I could come for a day occasionally. . . ."

"Any time at all, Wolfgang. My home is yours."

Wolfgang's thin, white fingers, lost without the keyboard, tapped his wine glass and finally reached for a string to worry with. Franz smiled at him. "Wolfgang will never completely grow up . . . I hope . . ." he thought to himself in a sudden thrust of nostalgia for the early days of Wolfgang.

"I regret Vienna, sir." Wolfgang's fingers held the string

taut. "You were a part of all of that life for me, 261 Landstrasse is desolate without you."

"Thank you, Wolfgang."

"And here, Paris is kinder?"

"No, it's the same." Franz regretted his sigh and tried to make his voice lighter. "Science is afraid of being unscientific . . . I am not the first man—nor will I be the last man—to suffer because he has a revelation to share."

"No one shares your views?"

"Yes, a few—a mere handful—and some of them are afraid to speak of their convictions."

Wolfgang leaned forward, listening. Franz looked at him earnestly as he continued, "Conviction used to be coupled with so much courage that men were willing to become martyrs."

"Oh, yes," Wolfgang broke in, "men died for their belief."

"And nowadays men are unwilling to subject themselves to the slightest ridicule."

Gluck refilled Franz's glass. Franz nodded his thanks and added, "Formerly men considered the strength to resist attack as their greatest glory; now they fear nothing so much as to be considered credulous."

"Bravo!" Gluck lifted his glass.

"Please tell us more," asked Wolfgang.

"Formerly, superstitious aberrations of thought did not prevent people from acknowledging strange facts, the cause of which mankind was too ignorant to recognize; one gave these facts the consideration due them; and even if one was deceived by the principles behind the facts, one did not deny the visible effects. Now people tend to repudiate the visible facts so firmly that they remain as ignorant of them as they are of the unknown causes."

"But in spite of this, Herr Doctor has an excellent practice." Gluck was refilling glasses again. "Rich and poor alike seek him."

"Medicine is much the same as Vienna?" inquired Wolfgang.

"No, Wolfgang, it isn't. The profession here is much more social and money-conscious. In Vienna a patient was a sick person to be treated; here there is a scale."

"A 'scale'? Do, re, mi?" laughed Wolfgang.

"Ach, hardly . . . but do tell him, Franz."

"It takes at least four middle-class patients to equal a Count in importance of cure."

"Oh, I see, then I can presume it would take four healed Counts to equal one Duke?" Wolfgang's eyes sparkled.

"So precisely right you are, lad, and one has truly arrived when he heals a prince!" Gluck's voice bespoke grandeurs beyond compare. The men laughed together.

"And the fees for services?"

"In like manner, Wolfgang, Madame de Barry paid me a hundred louis to install a baquet in her apartment, but I placed one in my cook's mother's home because she needed it. That's life, Wolfgang."

They had visited longer than Franz had intended, and it was late afternoon before he was free to see Monique.

"She is still in the garden, sir. I'll call her," said the maid.

Monique appeared immediately. Her hair was in disarray and tiny little tendrils curled damply over her beautiful forehead. A smudge of dirt ran across her cheek and disappeared under the left ear lobe. She wiped her hands on her apron as she hurried toward Franz, laughing.

"I must look terrible, but I couldn't wait to see you."

"You are lovely." And with sudden clarity Franz knew that she was more than lovely—she was utterly and completely herself. No sham, no pretense, no affectation marred the beauty of the spirit which dwelt in this woman. He caught both her hands in his and carried them to his lips. They smelled of the earth.

"Monique . . ." and then he caught himself.

She looked at him quizzically—then bade him be seated.

The moment passed and he found himself telling her of the paper, of his hope that it would be well received, of his plan to move his hospital into the heart of the city. He talked for an hour before he said:

"Forgive me, please. You may have plans for the evening and I have overstayed my visit. I must go."

"Not until you have had tea. Excuse me for just a few moments." Monique left the room quickly, but she returned within ten minutes. Her hair was smoothed and she had on a fresh dress.

"Shall we go into the library, Franz? It is quite cool there."

She led the way through the dining hall and across the corridor to a door which stood ajar. At first Franz did not notice the furnishings of the room, so attracted was he to the small, walled garden that lay just outside the long, open windows of the library. An astounding array of both medicinal and cooking herbs grew in disciplined abundance almost at their feet.

"This takes me all the way back to my medical school days," Franz said, adding the jingle:

> Take the ones with the flower. Watch out for the burr—
> Crosswort, moneywort, mignonette and myrrh,
> Catchfly, sea lavender and the potent sloe,
> Yellow flag, foxglove and wild indigo.

"But, of course," she answered, smiling, "you did have to recall."

The room was not large, and the chairs were drawn up around the open windows as furniture is sometimes grouped about a

"I don't need the wine now," he said. "The sight and scents learn them in medical school."

"All of them and their uses. We made rhymes to ease the drudgery of so much memory work. Later, of course, when we actually put the herbs to use, we found them quite easy to of this garden are comfort enough."

fireplace. Monique handed Franz a glass of wine and indicated a chair.

But he took the wine and settled into the chair. Monique's library chairs were as big and as comfortable as his own. True, her chairs were covered in the silky damasks and brocades which were the fashion, but the colors were muted. The feel of the whole room was one of soft restfulness and simple elegance.

And the books—two walls were lined with books. One shelf held nothing but medical volumes and pharmacopoeias.

"Do you read them?" Franz asked, curious.

"They were my father's, Franz. He taught me from them."

"He was a doctor?"

"Oh, no, but our estate was large and we had many slaves to attend. Papa had to know. I'm a colonial."

"Then long live the colonists," Franz toasted as Monique's maid appeared with the tea.

Franz's glimpse into Monique's private life increased his respect and regard for her. He must be careful not to fall in love with this utterly charming and fascinating woman, but at the same time he wished with all his heart to keep her friendship. He must not offend her by assuming that her regard for him was more than friendly, yet he felt honor-bound to speak to her of his marital status. Remote though Marie Anna was to him, in the eyes of the church she was still his wife. "How can I tell Monique?" he kept wondering.

It was time for him to depart and he still had not found the words. He felt awkward and provincial as he stood at the door clutching her hand and fumbling for words. Finally he blurted out:

"I'll not see you again soon, Monique. I'm married, you know, and I really have no right to call upon you like this."

"She is coming to France to join you?"

"Oh, no . . . not at all . . . oh, no." His voice was vehement.

"You are parted by more than distance?" she asked.

"Oh, yes . . . for years . . . but my regard for you is such that I must not." And he fled with only a hastily added good-night.

The drive to Creteil was short, but he relived that scene a hundred times before he arrived home. "I'm Franz Mesmer, an educated man of mature stature, bumbling through a delicate relationship like a clumsy-footed boy of fourteen. What must she think of me? Or was I allowing her opinion to become too important?"

These painful questions came to his mind often in the days that followed. Even under the pressure of work he remembered Monique—but as he remembered, he reminded himslf, "I am married. I am a Catholic."

Karl and his aids had kept the baquet in operation during his absence from Paris. They had not attempted to diagnose, but had simply treated—or permitted the sick to treat themselves—with such magnetic force as issued from the baquet. Several serious cases awaited Franz's attention, and the little hospital was full of bedfast patients.

Death took two of his surgical cases that week. He redoubled his efforts with the remaining patients.

Ten days passed and he did not hear from Le Roy. He would not humble himself to call upon him again, but he longed to discuss his concern with someone. Monique? No, he could not presume upon her kindness further.

The next afternoon he entered the baquet room to find Monique seated with the several patients who had gathered about the magnetized equipment. These patients awaited the personal attention from him which would bring on their crisis. Most of them were here for treatment of nervous disorders—but surely this was not Monique's problem.

Franz looked at her closely. She did not raise her eyes from the steel baquet rod which she clasped in both hands. Was she pale, or did he imagine it? "Her mouth . . . her beautiful mouth . . . oh, my God, restore my senses . . . what manner of idiocy has come over me that I would permit such immoral thoughts!"

"She is my patient," he reminded himself. "I am a physician."

He began treatment of the others—soothing words here, a touch of the wand there, stroking down the shoulders and holding the hands of some. One by one the patients reached a crisis—each manifesting it in his or her own way. His aids began carrying the violent cases to separate rooms.

He completed the circle, coming last to Monique. Before he touched her, she swooned. She crumpled slowly; but even so, she almost touched the floor before he caught her.

Although he sees it daily, a doctor never becomes hardened to illness and suffering. His familiarity with disease can cause him to worry about all manner of complications when loved ones are affected. Franz thought of this, for it was the way he felt now with Monique.

He picked her up in his arms and carried her to his own suite. Gently he laid her down on his bed, pulling up extra pillows to support her head and shoulders. She lay absolutely quiet.

Her pulse . . . how could this be? It was regular and strong . . . perhaps a trifle fast. . . .

"Monique," he said.

She opened her eyes and looked at him. Her lips curved into a smile . . . and then she laughed.

"What is the meaning of this?" he demanded.

"Must I tell you, Franz?"

"Are you ill? How do you feel? Monique, are you all right?"

Her laughter rang out as her hands lifted to his face. "You poor darling old German. You look so solemn and distraught. Don't you know I'm never ill?" And then her voice softened, "Franz, my love. . . ."

How do these things happen so quickly? One moment Franz felt tender concern, and in the next moment he was crushing her to him with utter disregard for her needs or wishes. The madness raced in his veins and his body demanded appeasement.

Lightning struck, and not until the storm was subsiding did he realize that she, too, had given herself up completely to the torrent of the moment.

He had possessed her. She was his. Yet even as he had taken her, she had given of herself while taking all of him. Never before had he felt so accepted, so totally at one with himself and with another human being at the same time. Tenderness overwhelmed him.

He caressed her body, delighting in this sunset of passion, this heartbreaking beauty of the afterglow. He removed the pins from her hair and spread the dark abundance of it wide on the pillows. Her indulgent laughter was pianissimo, so soft and sweet was it.

"I'm sleepy," she whispered. And he held her close, quietly lest he disturb her dreams as she slept in his arms.

A sharp rap at the door. Karl's voice broke into paradise. "Dinner is served, sir," he called.

Monique kissed him sleepily, and then she arose and began putting on her things. "You go on, Franz. I'll let myself out."

"Stay for dinner, Monique. I can't let you go now."

"But I must."

"Why?"

"Just because, Franz," and she smiled.

"I'll drive you home."

"No," she said abruptly. She went into his dressing room and closed the door sharply.

Franz couldn't think. To be lifted to such heights and then dropped coldly into nothingness . . . he was staring blindly out the window when she returned to the room. She walked up behind him and put her arms about him, leaning her head against his back.

"Franz," she said, "I love you—no, do not turn around—and I am afraid. I have never loved anything or anybody in my life that I did not lose in one way or another.

"The government of Spain took my home—oh, they gave me money in return, of course—and death took my parents. Years ago there was a man I loved—and he turned out to be a scoundrel.

"I cannot bear children . . . a childhood illness took that hope from me.

"I love you Franz, but I must have some time tonight to think—and so must you."

Franz turned around at last and took her in his arms. He did not kiss her. He just held her quietly for a few moments, and then he excused himself and went into the dressing room. "Wait," he said.

She rapped lightly on the door while he was dressing. "Are you free tomorrow afternoon, Franz?"

"Yes, I am."

"Then I'll pick you up for tea—early—at half past three."

When he returned to the room, she was gone.

Franz dined alone. How he longed to look across the table and see her there. He had his coffee in the library. Was she doing the same at her home, and was she alone? He knew a pang of jealousy—and then he chided himself. He had no right . . . and then came the terrible thought—perhaps she wished to withdraw. "I can offer her nothing in a material way which she does not already have. Her social position is more secure than my own. It is even possible that I have offended her with my passionate exhibition. Have I hurt her, or caused her dismay?"

He heard a carriage in the courtyard. He went quickly to the door and out into the night. By the driver's dress he knew it to be a rented coach, but Monique might use a rented coach if she wished to return unobserved. Almost before the vehicle stopped, he was at its side. He swung open the door. There sat Wolfgang.

"Were you expecting someone else, Doctor Mesmer?"

"Yes . . . no . . . that is, sometimes there are emergencies," he finished lamely. "Come in, Wolfgang, get out and come in."

And it was good to see his young friend again. They talked for a while, and then they played—Wolfgang on the piano and Franz on his musical glasses. It was late when Franz showed Wolfgang to the upstairs bedroom and returned to his own.

The fragrance of Monique's perfume clung to his bedclothing and drifted through his dreams.

CHAPTER XVII

FRANZ WAS having breakfast the next morning when he heard Karl greet Wolfgang in the upstairs hall. "I trust you slept well."

Wolfgang's voice was young and hearty. "I slept like a dormouse and snored like a bear."

Franz heard Karl's laugh, and then the sound of Wolfgang's quick feet on the stairs as he descended in time with his chant, "Snored like a bear, a bear, a bare-headed bear, hair bare, bear hair."

It was good to have the noisy lad about again. Not until after lunch did Franz begin to wonder how he could slip away for tea without arousing Wolfgang's suspicions or being called upon to present him to Monique.

He went to his rooms, bathed, and dressed in his afternoon attire. Twice he changed his waistcoat. She would notice—his clothing must be just right. No doubt she was taking him to the home of one of her friends for tea. "Would this neckerchief do—or should I use the other? Or was the lace too elaborate? Which of the two hid the chin line the better?

"Perhaps I should have taken time for a massage." His fingers traced the lines between nose and mouth. Monique must be well out of her twenties . . . even so, he might look old to her. And if she compared him to Wolfgang. . . .

He opened his door to listen. Wolfgang was at the piano in the drawing room. Monique would surely find him attractive. He was young, famous, and not bad-looking. Guiltily he recalled the lecture he had read to Wolfgang about love out of wedlock.

He forced himself to walk into the drawing room and tell Wolfgang that he had an appointment. Wolfgang barely nodded at his words. His face had the glow of creation. Here was an artist in touch with infinity. Humbled, Franz moved on out the door to wait for Monique in the courtyard.

Several vehicles passed in the street. Five minutes—he looked at his watch—five more minutes to wait. The warmth of the afternoon sun poured down through the trees and splashed in dancing patterns of light on the cobblestones.

A light breeze ruffled the leaves. It blew aside the silken curtains of the handsome cabriolet which whirled into the drive. He stared in disbelief. The spirited horses were hitched to the little vehicle, and they were driven by Monique.

She brought the animals to a prancing stop before him and leaned forward to declare, "Ladies don't drive!"

"Oh, don't they?" Franz laughed in sudden joy—"She is here; she is my beloved" . . . he knew it in his heart.

She drew back the curtains and indicated that he was to sit beside her.

"Get in, Franz, and let's be off for tea."

"Her voice is light, but there is a pitch of excitement; suppressed, yes . . . but . . . the Blessed Saviour knows how excited I am," Franz thought as he climbed in and kissed her hand. She was dressed as a peasant maiden. This was the vogue of the moment in fashionable Paris. Her gown was made of a rich, luxurious fabric that only resembled that of the peasant's homespun.

"You are a picture, darling," Franz told her.

"Are you wondering where we are going . . . with me like this?" She touched her gown and braided hair, tied with ribbons.

"Anywhere with you, darling Monique." He kissed her hand with fervor and hoped Wolfgang was still busy at the pianoforte. She lifted the reins and the horses leapt at her command.

"I know a place . . . the right place for us . . . for this occasion." She glanced sidewise at Franz.

"You are a flirt, Monique, an incurable flirt," declared Franz, "You should be thrashed for making me feel young and carefree."

"Why shouldn't you feel young and carefree, dear? You are, you know."

"How about the tea you promised?" Franz asked, ignoring her compliment.

"I have it here." She motioned to a large hamper on the floor. Franz had not noticed it before. They were on a thoroughfare leading out of town.

"Are we going to Marie Antoinette's queenly shack?" Franz referred to the rustic playground the Queen had built after coming under the influence of the dynamic Rousseau. "Is this why you are gowned for a rural tryst?"

"It will be a rural tryst, but not at Marie Antoinette's," she smiled. "Why—don't you admire my driving?"

"I do—enormously."

"Why don't you ask where I learned?"

"Where did you?"

"In America—you know I'm an American?"

"The Queen told me, but it's hard to believe; you are so French."

"I'm American, all right; no French girl could drive horses," she bragged.

"That's true—now tell me, how did you learn?"

"My father taught me."

"He was an American?"

"Well, yes and no—he was born here."

"And your mother?"

"She, too, was French, but they went to America for religious freedom."

"Oh?"

"They were freethinkers."

"And you, dear, are you one, too?"

"Yes."

They drove for a time in silence.

"Freethinkers?" Franz tried to remember, to recall something of the philosophy of a freethinker.

"Freethinking doesn't mean license . . ." her voice broke in.

"I'm certain of that," Franz assured her with a smile.

"You are . . . ?"

"Catholic."

"Oh."

They rode again in silence. "Should I tell her about Marie Anna? What can I say?" Franz asked himself, all excitement gone.

"Marie Antoinette says your wife is a beautiful woman."

"Bless the Queen for telling her," was Franz's first thought, but his eyes flew to Monique's profile. "What does she think?"

"Is she?" demanded Monique.

"What?"

"Is she beautiful."

"Yes."

"As beautiful as I am?"

"In a different way . . . perhaps yes. . . ." His voice was indifferent.

"You love her?"

"She is not with me." Franz wondered why he felt no impatience with Monique.

"Why not?"

"She didn't choose to be."

"Did you want her?"

"No."

"Why?"

"Because I no longer love her."

"Did you ever?"

"I thought so. . . ."

"Oh—"

They rode in silence.

"When did you know?" she asked.

"Know what?"

"That you didn't love her."

"The night I married her."

"Oh. . . ."

There was silence again, but not for long.

"You mean . . . ?" She turned and looked at Franz, her hands tight on the reins. She looked into his eyes.

"Precisely."

She sighed, then laughed.

"This is the way a freethinker thinks, Franz; I must know the truth."

He reached for her hand and held it against his lips.

"You may ask me about me," she offered.

"Darling, I love every precious bone in your beautiful body; that's enough for me."

"Oh, Franz," she whispered tenderly and leaned to him for a hurried kiss, then returned to her driving.

"Franz, I've been married, too."

"Yes, you are Madame Montarre."

"But, I've been married twice."

It was Franz's turn to say, "Oh."

"My first husband was a dear friend of my father's. When Papa died, I turned to him. He was gentle and kind. He tried to be a husband, but the fire had died. I loved him quietly. We lived together four years; his death left me desolated but rich with worldly possessions."

"Where did you live, dear?" Franz felt an interest in all that concerned her.

"On a plantation near New Orleans. My people had gone there. That is where I was born." Franz watched her eloquent face brighten. "That's where I learned to drive. I can ride a saddle, too, like a man."

Franz smiled and made the proper response, but his mind was busy trying to frame the next question.

"Your second marriage?" he asked at last.

"Yes," her voice was cold and hard, "he was young, and a scoundrel; my father would have fought a duel with him had he been alive, but I divorced him."

"*Divorced?*" Franz instantly regretted that his voice betrayed his revulsion to the word. She turned to him.

"So you are shocked—that's why America is for freethinkers . . . for people unafraid." Franz felt her anger.

"You are lovely, and I love you. Why quarrel?" Franz noticed they were well out into the country. He held her hand and added, "Hail, America that produced you, beloved Monique. I know you would wade across the river Styx, slap the devil, and walk back to Paradise unafraid. If this is being a freethinker, darling, I'm for it."

Monique was in a good humor at once. She threw him a kiss and said, "We are nearing our journey's end. Soon we'll have tea." She turned into a little side road and drove a few paces before she found the desired place.

"This is a sylvan retreat—a green room for the gods—and my goddess." Franz helped her down. He made the horses comfortable and secure; then together they spread blankets and pillows on the soft grass.

Monique lit a little spirit lamp and soon they had tea.

"I will say I love you between every sip of tea." Monique lifted the cup to her lips and said, "I love you."

"Drink another cup," urged Franz. "No, the whole pot," he amended, and they laughed.

They cleared away the food and lay side by side in the aloneness of the forest. Franz kissed her hands, her arms, her throat, her lips. "My heart sings louder than the birds in the trees above us," he told Monique.

"Franz?"

"Beloved?"

"We do not follow the same religious path?"

"Probably not, dear one."

"You will respect mine?"

"I respect all religions—but especially anything you believe I will respect."

"Thank you."

He kissed her.

"Franz?" she questioned against his lips.

"Yes, dear?"

"What is marriage?"

"A contract." He kissed her forehead.

"Between two people?"

"Yes." His lips were feeling her words.

"In the presence of God?"

"Yes."

She pushed him back. She was gentle but firm, "Franz, I want to marry you."

"I want to marry you, too, Monique, but. . . ." He sought her mouth again.

"No, Franz, I mean out here." She sat up. "Out here in this cathedral . . . in the presence of these, our friends," she motioned to the trees, "and our musician," she pointed to a bird singing in a nearby tree.

Franz's thoughts turned back to a time when he had made much the same statement to Marie Anna and was rewarded with her scorn. Tenderly he pulled Monique into his arms—how well he knew her emotions. Holding her close, he arose to his feet, lifting her with him. They stood there a moment, holding on to each other other. Then Franz stepped back and took her hands.

"Monique, before God and all the Saints in Heaven, I ask

you to be my wife . . . I will love you and cherish you forever."

"Franz, as God is my witness, I become your wife . . . I swear by all that I hold sacred and divine to be yours alone forever. . . . Amen."

Franz reached in his pocket for his rosary and dropped to his knee. Monique hesitated but a moment, then knelt beside him. Franz held the cross in his hand, and together they prayed the Lord's Prayer. Franz wiped the tears from Monique's face and kissed her gently, too moved to talk.

They gathered the picnic equipment. They talked but little on the road back. They were content to be close.

"You are my precious wife," Franz whispered to her once.

Monique dropped Franz at his place. "You'll be over for dinner?" she asked.

"Darling, yes." He kissed her hand, with restraint.

Franz made his rounds of the patients and then went to his room to dress. Karl knocked.

"Young Herr Mozart went back to the city," Karl announced.

Franz flung open the door. "Karl," he answered in dismay, "I forgot all about him."

Karl's keen eyes searched his face. Slowly the line between his brows softened and his lips curved in a rare, kindly smile. "That's good, doctor. I'm very happy for you." His hand reached out and patted Franz gently on the shoulder—almost in benediction.

So Karl knew—and he approved. Franz's happiness was complete.

CHAPTER XVIII

FRANZ DID not hear from Le Roy that summer, but his practice expanded so rapidly that he scarcely had time to think of Le Roy and his associates during the day. Evenings and nights were filled with the blessed presence of Monique. With her he found the resting place between heaven and earth.

Monique kept her separate establishment. "Don't you see, Franz, you must maintain a public behavior absolutely above reproach. There must be no gossip about the life and love of the great Doctor Mesmer."

Always her thought was of Franz's well-being, his comfort—yet she had social activities in which he did not share. Occasionally he would be jealous, and how merrily she would laugh and tease him.

It was almost September when Le Roy's invitation came. "The French Academy of Sciences would be pleased to hear Doctor Franz Mesmer read his paper. . . ."

Franz accepted with pleasure and a feeling of confidence. Only four and a half years had passed since he had observed the first magnetic treatment with Father Hell. In the world of science he knew this to be only an eyelash flicker of time—yet he had packed this period with hours of serious thought and weeks of hard work. His knowledge of animal magnetism had expanded with every case. There were still many questions which he could not answer, but surely the Academy would see that the foundation work was done.

There was some minor business before the meeting. Le Roy disposed of it before he introduced Franz. Le Roy seemed to be clearing the way for a long discussion after Franz completed the reading of the propositions—for he knew that the paper was not lengthy. His introduction was brief, but enthusiastic. The friendly applause warmed Franz as he arose to speak to this distinguished company.

He read the first proposition slowly. "A responsive influence exists between the heavenly bodies, the earth, and all animated bodies." He could feel the interest of his audience.

He read the second proposition just as slowly. The doctors seemed to be with him and waiting.

The third proposition was short, "This reciprocal action is subject to mechanical laws with which we are not yet familiar." He heard several chairs scrape.

He read a bit faster—the fourth, the fifth—and by the time he reached the sixth proposition he realized that he had lost at least half of his audience. They did not leave the place physically, but they seemed to have departed mentally.

Perhaps he was reading too fast. He slowed his pace and tried to let his voice rise and fall in a musical cadence. By the time he reached the fifteenth proposition, every face in the audience was completely devoid of expression. Neither by the twitch of a muscle nor by the bat of an eye did they show approval or disapproval—interest or lack of it. They sat like men lost in their own private worlds.

He forced himself to read the remaining propositions. It was agony. He sat down in absolute quiet. There was no question, no remark. Finally he turned to Le Roy, "That is all, sir; thank you."

Le Roy seemed startled by his remark. He rose quickly to his feet and tipped over his chair. The unexpected noise in this unearthly quiet was like a cannon shot. Immediately the scientists rose and began to leave the hall. A few of them nodded politely to Franz. Others went as far as to wish him good-night. But not one—not a single one—expressed the slightest interest in the paper.

Sick with disappointment, he left the hall. He went straight to Monique. She did not question, nor did he explain.

It was one of his aristocratic patients from the city who finally told him the full bitter truth: the Academy of Sciences was calling him a sensation-seeking *gobe-mouches* whose defense of his own vague theories was absolutely incoherent.

"The d'Eslons are back in Paris," Monique announced near the end of September. "I have invited them for dinner next week."

"Did you tell the good doctor that your renegade physician friend might be present?" Franz questioned Monique bitterly.

"No," she answered serenely. "I didn't feel it necessary."

"Then I'd best not attend your party. I should not like to be an embarrassment to you."

"As a matter of fact, my cross lover, Doctor d'Eslon specifically requested that I invite you. He is still most anxious to visit your hospital at Creteil."

Franz stared at Monique.

"Franz, did you hear me?"

"Hear you, indeed I did. Monique, you precious idiot! But you're a darling, Darling," He held her close.

Doctor d'Eslon appeared at the hospital the next morning. "My apologies, Doctor Mesmer, for arriving unannounced. If my visit is inconvenient. . . ."

"I'm delighted to see you. Do be seated, doctor."

"Sir," said d'Eslon, "I know that you are a busy man. I shall not waste your time with pleasantries or with argument. With your permission, I shall state my mission briefly."

"By all means, doctor." They were both quite formal.

"There is much talk in Paris about animal magnetism."

Franz nodded.

"I prefer firsthand observation to garbled secondhand reports. I should like to spend the balance of this week watching you in your work. Will you permit me?"

Franz arose and bowed to d'Eslon. "I salute your courage, sir, and your integrity, and I extend to you a very warm welcome."

They smiled at their ridiculous little scene. Franz knew they were both out of character. In their shared amusement came one of those wonderful moments of complete rapport. It stretched over the busy hours of the whole day.

"See you in the morning, doctor." d'Eslon bowed his departure that first evening.

The second day was a busy one, too. Franz gave treatment after treatment and ended the day in surgery. A miller had caught his hand between the grinding stones. There was no hope of restoring the mangled appendage. He had to amputate. D'Eslon assisted.

On the third day d'Eslon asked if he might sit at the baquet for a few moments before they admitted patients. "I want to try it on myself," he said.

He sat for twenty minutes, alternately holding and rubbing the magnetized rods against various parts of his anatomy. "I feel nothing," he finally admitted.

"A man in good health is seldom affected," Franz explained. "There already exists within him a harmonious ebb and flow of the fluidum."

"Do you believe that I could effect cures such as I have seen you perform in the past two days?"

"I know you can. Work with the next baquet group."

Franz introduced d'Eslon to the patients as they arrived for their baquet appointments. They accepted him, and he treated them all successfully.

"I am convinced, Franz," he said at the end of this third day. "I am not without influence among the young doctors of Paris. Will you permit me to ask some of them to my home for dinner to meet you and discuss this great discovery with you?"

"Thank you, Charles. I should consider it an honor."

And so it was that Monique yielded the date set for her dinner party. "Madame d'Eslon and I have discussed it, Franz. We feel that professional problems take precedence. Madame d'Eslon will supervise the preparation of the dinner—she is a superb cook—but only men will be present."

Franz did not know how many doctors were invited. Three accepted. Franz thought it was well that Madame d'Eslon was not present to hear the medical talk that flowed over her justly famous cuisine.

The men questioned Franz about the greats of medicine in the Vienna School—De Haen, von Stoerk, and van Swieten. He provided suitable anecdotes. The French doctors listened with flattering attention.

"Do any of your professors subscribe to your theory of the necessity for a crisis?" asked one of them.

"Not in theory, perhaps," Franz answered, "but in practice

—yes. For example, they believe in the application of plasters for certain maladies."

"I use plasters," said another of the French doctors, "but I fail to see the relationship between a plaster and a convulsive crisis."

"Why do you apply a plaster?" Franz asked. He smiled to take away any sting.

"To create heat—and the heat pulls the inflammation from the humor, permitting it to subside."

"Exactly," Franz exclaimed. "As the stagnant blood is drawn up—or ebbs, shall we say—from the humor, new blood flows in and brings with it the healing force."

The first doctor spoke up, "Today I called on an old crone who had a plaster blister which covered the thoracic region and extended all the way down to the coccyx. She was in howling misery, but her coughing and vomiting had stopped."

"Was not her howling misery something in the nature of a crisis?"

"Touché," he conceded.

A number of stories followed this one, the first two of which were tragic to the point of tears. But the doctors were Frenchmen—their stories soon veered off to the erotic and then to the hilarious. Franz was enjoying himself enormously when d'Eslon broke into the laughter to announce:

"Gentlemen, we are wasting our time in revelry when we have as our honored guest tonight one of the greatest contributors to medicine this age has known. In my enthusiasm and pride, I predict that this man's discovery will lend brilliance to medical techniques in centuries as yet unborn. Science will one day point to him as a medical Moses. Gentlemen, I give you Doctor Franz Mesmer."

Applause—"Hear, hear!"—and a "Bravo." It was in this atmosphere of convivial acceptance that Franz began the second public reading of his propositions. In the beginning he felt the responsiveness of his small audience—but the withdrawal started on the fourth or fifth proposition. The men were not restless or yawning. On the contrary, they were too quiet—totally passive they seemed when he took a furtive look.

He finished reading in the blank silence of their indifference.

Even d'Eslon seemed submerged in a dream—worlds apart from Franz. Not until Franz cleared his throat at the end did d'Eslon respond in the slightest.

"Thank you, Doctor Mesmer, for . . . for this . . ." and his voice trailed off into nothingness. He squared his shoulders and breathed deeply. "Thank you, Doctor Mesmer, for this stimulating talk."

Franz was too disheartened to see the humor in the situation. Again he made his adieus and went to Monique.

One look at his face and she knew. "This time, Franz, you are going to tell me what happened." She led the way to her library.

Franz gave her a step-by-step account of the evening. "They are fine men," he said. "They cannot change their myopic perception any more than you or I can change our love of nature. They were nurtured in traditionalism. Their pattern is set and they cannot leave it."

"Franz, will you read your propositions to me?"

"Why, of course, Monique, but. . . ."

"Just read them," she demanded.

Franz took out his paper and began reading. With the fourth proposition, he saw a frown gather her brow. He read on through the seventh proposition before she interrupted.

"Franz, I can't concentrate; I'm going to sleep or something. Let me try reading them to myself." She reached for the paper.

She started at the beginning again, reading silently. Again she began to frown. She read through the second page. Abruptly she flipped the page back and started at the beginning again. This time she read through the third page; then she laid the paper in her lap and leaned back in her chair and closed her eyes.

"You find my paper restful?" Franz questioned in his hurt.

"Yes, Franz," she answered. "Do you realize what you have done?"

"Apparently not, my dear." He tried to keep from sounding cold.

"You have somehow infused these words with your animal magnetism. For all I know—or those doctors—this paper may perfectly describe your theories, but we cannot comprehend the theories because the cadence of the words lulls us. No, it is not cadence—I don't know what it is, Franz. Something in the words causes my mind to float off . . . it is bound to be animal magnetism! My thinking processes grasp the rhythm but lose the thought."

"It is my voice?" he asked. "Heaven forbid that the soothing tones I use with patients are becoming habitual with me."

She shook her head. "I wondered if it were your voice, since your voice is so melodious. That is why I asked to read them to myself. Your voice has tremendous power, Franz, and the same magic is in these words. They soothe me."

"You are trying to comfort me, Monique."

"No, Franz. It's a bitter truth I am telling you. You are not an orator or a writer—you are a healer."

"You mean I've failed?"

"No, Franz, no—you've succeeded—better than you know."

The next morning Franz caught Karl just as he finished preparing the rooms for the day.

"Karl, will you please be seated and read these propositions?" Franz handed Karl the list and turned to a stack of histories Karl had placed on his desk. Franz pretended to be reading, but he watched Karl—methodical, loyal, patient Karl was going to sleep after a good night's rest and this early in the morning!—"Yet, I've seen Karl read thick tomes of dry data and report the relevant part to me."

Franz took the list of propositions from Karl and released him to his chores. Franz continued to brood over this strange affair.

"These words are not lullaby words; they are definitely not poetry, nor music—then what?" Finally Franz slipped the sheets of paper into the bottom drawer of his desk.

CHAPTER XIX

SEVERAL DAYS later d'Eslon called at the hospital. He brought with him a patient, a sallow-faced young man.

"René de Maur," he introduced the smirking youth. "René has been my patient for nearly a year. We are getting nowhere with chemical treatment. His father requests that you examine the boy. Will you do so?"

The young man's pale skin clung closely to a bony structure that sagged from the domed skull downward. Only his eyes were alert. They darted about like frightened bees seeking escape from under a net, as the lad shambled into Franz's examining room and flopped down on the table. In spite of his noble birth and sumptuous clothing, the boy was repulsive to Franz. About him was an aura of psychic distress, spiritual illiteracy.

Narrow, sloping shoulders, shallow chest, concave belly—but the lungs were clear, the blood red. He had a record of chronic gleet which worsened at times.

"Any particular time?" Franz inquired of him.

"When a new interest has just taken hold of me," and he winked a knowing eye.

"And this happens often?"

"As often as I am ready," he smirked.

"You have examined him for venereal disease?" Franz asked d'Eslon.

"Yes," he replied. "He gives no evidence."

"I'm careful, doctor," said René. "I assure you the girl has to be clean or I will not touch her." He waved his hand airily.

Franz stared at the insolent pup, who was in no way perturbed.

"Yes," he continued, "my father says I get to all the little girls on our lands first—as soon as they reach puberty."

Franz longed to get his hands on the scruff of his neck and fling him from his office. If only he would fit in a jar—like the leeches.

Fighting for control, Franz turned to his pharmacopei shelf. "I'm giving you a bottle of white liquid with instructions for its use in a daily sitz bath," he said. "The black powder in the box is to be taken in wine three times a day for three days, then once daily for a month."

The boy had left the room when Franz explained to d'Eslon, "The liquid is merely an astringent. It may help the gleet. The powder is iron filings to build up his general health—so he can tear down the health of more little girls."

"Why didn't you use magnetism?" d'Eslon asked.

"Do you like that lad?" inquired Franz sharply.

"No, I don't. . . ." Then d'Eslon laughed, "But Franz, that isn't why I brought him to you—just to get rid of him."

Franz smiled, his anger gone.

"That boy is so revolting to me that the magnetism could not possibly flow from my body to his. I cannot focus on him. My vision of him is as blurred and distorted as would be my vision of a specimen under an unfocused microscope. I cannot see him as my ailing brother, or as a child of God. The failure is mine," Franz explained.

D'Eslon followed Franz into his office and they sat down.

"Does this non-focus—this lack of rapport—occur often, Franz?"

"Not often, Charles; yet when it does I am bitterly ashamed. Who am I to condemn, to judge? I have no right to permit my feelings to withhold treatment—yet I was unable to treat that boy."

"You feel an intimacy in treatment, don't you?"

Moans from the next room cut short their conversation. "Can you stay?" Franz asked d'Eslon.

"Yes," he replied. "My patient and I came in separate carriages."

Together they went on to see the woman in the next room. She lay on the high bed Franz used for childbirth cases, her wash-faded nightdress mounding strangely over her flatulent abdomen and falling into limp folds across her thin, small-boned thighs.

"She is forty-one," Franz told d'Eslon, "and has stillborne six babies. Her farmer husband brought her this morning. He walked her five miles in a wheelbarrow."

The woman's fright-filled eyes were upon Franz. "Save my baby, doctor. Oh, Mother of God, save my baby," she implored.

"Take my hands," Franz directed her, "and pray with me. 'Hail Mary, full of Grace, the Lord is with Thee. . . .'" By the time they finished the prayer, the woman's face was calm. Franz gave her another animal magnetism treatment. "She had the first treatment when she arrived," he explained to d'Eslon.

The patient lay quietly while Franz examined her. "Contractions strong," he reported to d'Eslon. "Four centimeters dilation—but unless I can turn the baby, it will be a footling-breech delivery. Her bag of waters has not broken."

He inserted one finger into the *os uteri* and caught the unborn child between this finger and his other hand, which pressed against the abdomen of the mother. Working between contractions, as firmly but as gently as possible, he pushed the presenting part of the child up and out of the pelvis—away from the birth canal. Massaging with the hand on the mother's abdomen, he turned the baby against his probing finger. Like a ball in a tight socket, the infant body moved round a bit—a little more—then one quick slip and the head was down.

He spoke soothing words to the mother. Her eyes were open, but her muscles were as relaxed as if she were asleep. She showed no evidence of pain.

A strong contraction—and the infant's head was engaged normally. She would deliver safely now. Franz washed his hands and waited, continuing his soothing words to the mother.

The distraught father burst through the door. In Franz's concern for the woman, he had forgotten the husband. He was crying. "Where are your beads, man?" Franz asked him. He produced them. "Now you sit down here and pray. Give thanks for the healthy man-child which you and your wife soon will have."

He examined the woman. Dilation ten centimeters. With the forceps he caught the baby's head firmly. As the contractions came, he pulled on the baby. It was delivered quickly—and it was a boy! A healthy, squalling boy.

Later d'Eslon asked, "Why did you predict a boy? Did you know?"

Franz laughed. "As Professor de Haen used to say, I had a fifty-fifty chance of being right."

"What do you think caused the stillbirth of that woman's other children?"

"That is hard to say, Charles. They, too, may have been feet-first presentations. They were delivered by midwives, possibly ignorant ones who could not turn the infants in the womb. As you know, such delivery is hard on both mother and baby—and fear increases the difficulty. Incidentally, I do not make a practice of praying with my patients. Generally that is best left to a priest—but in this case. . . ."

"I understand, Franz. The woman's great fear . . . and she was trying to pray."

"Yes."

They saw several more patients together before they had time to talk. They sat in the office again.

"I am a well-qualified physician," stated d'Eslon, his intelligent eyes serious.

"So," Franz smiled, thinking him about to question a point.

"I am a physician to Count d'Artois, the brother of the King."

"Yes, Monique told me. You are also quite popular in the social life of the court—you and your lovely, gentle wife."

"Thank you." He took a deep breath. "What I have seen here in this hospital convinces me that you have discovered one of the great laws of nature. I would like to work with you. Will you consider admitting me as a member of your staff?"

Franz stared at him in disbelief as the full impact of d'Eslon's words became real to him. He smiled with joy.

"My friend, you do me honor. I accept your offer with gratitude." They shook hands solemnly and Franz rang for wine, that they might drink to the occasion.

"I have a call to make in the city, Franz," d'Eslon said later. "Will you come with me?"

"I am due at Monique's place for dinner. Is there time?"

"Yes. This will not take long. Do you know the Marquis and Marquise de la Randeaux? They are leaders of the humanist group."

"Quite well. Followers of the Encyclopedist movement, too, are they not? Yes, their fetes and balls are as frequent as they are elaborate. Is one of them ill?"

"No," d'Eslon answered. "It is their little one—Fanya. I

saw her about noonday. She was going fast—typhus. There is not much I can do. This call . . ." he shrugged his shoulders.

Franz saw that Charles was quite right. The child was dying when they arrived. Both of them bent over her bed. Franz looked up first and caught the Marquis' eye, "Your priest?" he questioned softly.

The Marquis shook his head.

The Marquise broke into sobs. "My baby is dying. She is dying! We were *très chic*—no priest, no stale conventions, no religious fol-de-rol." She flung herself on the bed and gathered the wasted little body into her arms. Franz and d'Eslon did not remonstrate. The child was beyond hurt.

The mother stood up, lifting the child in her arms. "No altar in this house, no holy pictures, no prayerbook—only death, oh, God, only death."

She walked over and stood in front of de la Randeaux. "Where is your patron saint? Where is mine? How good is our reason now? What words of comfort can the Encyclopedists speak to us?"

Her hysteria mounted. She was like an animal goaded by pain beyond enduring. "This is your handiwork—and mine. God is punishing us. Our baby is dying."

The father sobbed openly. Tears blinded Franz's eyes as the mother turned to him. He held out his arms for the child.

"Oh, no, doctor, for a little while yet she is mine." Tenderly she put her cheek against the child's soft, blonde hair. The mother's voice was softer now. "Just for a little while Fanya is mine; but I have nowhere to pray, no priest to bless her."

"Come, my dear." Franz led the Marquise to the window and pulled the cord that slid back the heavy draperies to show the star-filled sky. He motioned to de la Randeaux to join them. The Marquis slipped his arm about his wife. Together they stood, holding their dying child.

"The stars," Franz said softly, "were the altar used by the Wise Men who sought and found their God. He is near to us, too. If we listen, He will speak to us in our hearts."

They stood thus for a long while—perhaps twenty minutes. The Marquise's sobs quieted to an occasional convulsively-caught breath. Her husband was quiet, too, his sports-browned hand holding the tiny feet that hung lifeless and still from under Fanya's frilled nightgown.

Franz did not formulate words of prayer, but his mind was in prayer and of prayer.

"Fanya is gone. My baby is dead," said the Marquise quietly. She walked over to the bed and laid the child gently on the ruffled pillow with the gay, pink bow.

D'Eslon and Franz were leaving the room when they saw the bereaved parents kneel together. The men did not speak, and once on the street they parted with only the fewest words.

Franz made his way to Monique. He told her most of the story while he drank the hot rum she prepared for him. He went to the piano. Between snatches of melody he told her the rest of the heartbreaking incident. She wept with him.

On and on he played. A long and intricately-fingered fugue absorbed some of his sorrow and he was able to speak again. "Tomorrow I shall arrange masses for the repose of her soul."

Monique did not answer. Franz continued playing. It was another hour before he came to the point of calm which music always brought him. He left the piano and found Monique sleeping on the sofa. Tenderly he aroused her. She sat up and he knelt beside her.

"How beautiful you are, how wonderful. I love you, Monique."

She put her hands on either side of his face and bent to him. With her lips barely touching his, she whispered, "When I go, do not pray for me. Say no masses for me as I wander through the vastness of purgatory—just talk to me."

Franz held her close. She spoke again, "Just talk to me."

CHAPTER XX

WITH D'ESLON's help, Franz could see more people than when he worked alone. They kept the baquet busy, treating patients in groups from early morning until late afternoon; yet one of them remained available for office or home calls.

D'Eslon was a dedicated man. Neither his social life nor his personal preferences interfered in the least with his profession. He shared Franz's belief that a physician should treat all who requested help—without regard for rank or ability to pay. He approved, also, of Franz's policy of leaving all money matters to a secretary—not knowing who had paid in full and who never paid. Karl audited the accounts and took full responsibility for the financial aspects of the hospital.

D'Eslon used animal magnetism as often and as successfully as Franz. He resented the Academy's refusal to accept their findings. Franz and d'Eslon talked long and often about this matter. D'Eslon's French temperament bubbled up and boiled over into a paper which was published daily in 1779. D'Eslon intended the paper as a clarification of Franz's propositions of the year before. He entitled it "Observations on Animal Magnetism."

And perhaps he did clarify the theories somewhat. He wrote: "Just as there is one nature, one life, and one health, there is only one illness, one treatment and one cure. When nature functions regularly, human beings are healthy. If these functions are confronted by any difficulties, nature makes an effort to overcome them. A convulsive crisis results which may be salubrious or harmful. Physicians have given each of these various crises a special name and explained them in terms of as many diseases. There are innumerable effects of a crisis, but the cause is always the same: all methods of treatment, no matter how different, have only the same effect, and cures can be performed only by creating a crisis in the disease. Cases of epilepsy, for instance, can only be cured by creating a crisis. The greatest advantage of animal magnetism is that this method hastens the crisis, without any dangerous effect on the patient. . . ."

Franz complimented d'Eslon on his paper. "I hope they will listen to you."

D'Eslon shrugged his shoulders cheerfully. "Who can say?"

But the physicians of Paris were not impressed with d'Eslon's paper. They began to avoid d'Eslon socially, for in his enthusiasm he had taken to cornering doctors in order to expound Franz's theories of animal magnetism. He even captured the floor in one of the medical meetings and outlined in graphic detail a harrowing case in which he had effected a salubrious crisis.

Such testimony should have aroused scientific curiosity—but the doctors of Paris were set against animal magnetism. They attacked d'Eslon, even as they had attacked Franz. Except for d'Eslon's position at court, they would have dismissed him from the medical faculty of the University—even as Franz had been dismissed in Vienna.

This was the year 1779. Puységur called on Franz one day and brought with him the hero of the New World, that glamorous and handsome young man-about-town—the Marquis de Lafayette. Between Franz and Lafayette there sprang up an instant friendship.

Lafayette asked to become a pupil of Franz. "Animal magnetism," he said, "could be of great help in America. Oh, my friend, had I known of it during that terrible winter at Valley Forge! But there will be need—perhaps greater need—in the years to come. Doctors are few in America. Teach me, I entreat you."

He spent days trailing Franz from patient to patient—from bed to bed. Franz saw that his was a keen and eager mind, and his heart was warm. "He draws out the best in me, and he encourages me to voice my personal philosophy as no other pupil has ever done," Franz thought as they were walking slowly through the hospital corridor.

"Should the magnetizer have any particular traits or talents?" Lafayette asked.

The question pinpointed a vague uneasiness which Franz had felt concerning this matter. Now he found himself answering with conviction. "Yes, a person who treats with animal magnetism must be well-centered within himself. He must be strong and vigorous, and he must have a will to do."

Lafayette caught Franz's arm. "Yes," he said eagerly, "and there must be more."

"What more?"

"Patience," he said smiling.

From the look on his face, Franz knew he spoke this as a compliment. "Thank you. Yes, patience is important; but it can be learned. There are other qualities—compassion, understanding. . . ."

They entered a room. Franz gave a treatment.

Back in the corridor, Franz continued, "There seems to be an actual transfer of awareness, a state of assumption. One almost becomes the patient, feels his inadequacies and delinquencies—then dispels them by ascending over the problem into the healthy state of being which is affirmative truth."

Franz stopped and looked at Lafayette. "Does this talk make sense to a military man—a soldier?" Franz asked.

"To sum it up, the magnetizers excite the reluctant will of the patient into a state of activity," Lafayette said.

"Precisely. How aptly you state it." Franz pushed open the door of his private office and waved Lafayette to a chair.

"And what of sidereal magnetism, sir?"

"Sidereal magnetism and animal magnetism attune perfectly. They are an ebb and flow of harmony—nature's prayer." Franz reached in a drawer to search for a quill.

"And do you pray, doctor?"

Franz looked at Lafayette sitting upright in his chair—at ease, yet every inch the well-disciplined soldier. And he spoke of prayer.

"Yes," Franz answered him, "I pray often. When we come into harmony with God, all things are made right with us. Harmony is the goal—the only goal."

Lafayette nodded his head and his expressive eyes agreed as Franz continued:

"Go to the piano and strike a harmonic chord. Add even one uncomplementary note to that chord and there is dissonance. Harmony is the principle of balance, of fitness, of belonging."

They sat in contemplative silence.

Lafayette's voice broke the quiet, "Why are some of us born into a pattern of harmony? Has this to do with the stars?"

"I have pondered this very question. Assuming that the planets do give off an invisible force, we arrive at a picture of the earth bathed in a magnetic mist which varies according to the positions of the heavenly bodies."

"Magnetic mist . . ." Lafayette repeated. "And—?"

"The skin of a newborn babe is translucent in its porosity. In its tenderness it is highly susceptible. Such a skin would easily absorb the magnetic mist, and thus the child would begin his life under the influence of the planet or combination of planets which dominated the mist—or fluidum—at the time of his birth."

"Do you think this sets his pattern?"

"I would not put it that strongly. Let us say this establishes his basic harmony—the key in which his life will be played. Let me remind you that with study and practice a musician can learn to find harmony in any key and can even make use of dissonance!"

"Ah—there is the goal again—harmony—and in any key! You know," Lafayette added thoughtfully, "this mention of the newborn babe's tender skin interests me. In America I saw Negro slaves delivered of their young. The infants are light at birth. It takes several hours for them to deepen to the ebony of the mother."

Lafayette had interesting bits of information to contribute to any conversation. He was observant, and his observations stimulated others to observe. His support brought Franz in closer contact with many who were near the throne—Madame de Lamballe, the Prince de Condé, the Duc de Bourbon. They became ardent supporters and personally escorted numerous patients to the hospital.

As the numbers of lay supporters grew, so grew the enmity of the professional scientists of Paris. D'Eslon was attacked openly in a medical meeting. A new member of the faculty, a young Dr. de Vauzesmes, launched a vituperative attack in which he referred to Franz as an impostor made all the more dangerous by the fact that he possessed the qualifications and training necessary to allow him to practice as an effectual member of the medical profession. He castigated d'Eslon for defending Franz and demanded that d'Eslon resign or recant.

D'Eslon's loyalty to Franz never wavered. He was cheerful, even in the face of disaster, and kept assuring Franz that they could count on their friends at court. But Franz was disgusted and soul-sick. He could see the events of Vienna repeating themselves. He announced his decision to leave Paris in the spring of the following year.

As Franz left the hospital, the little newsboys were shouting a story on the street corners. In bold, black letters the *Gazette* confirmed their cries: Empress Maria Theresa of Austria was dead. Marie Antoinette, Queen of France, had lost her beloved mother.

Franz felt a sense of personal loss, and he grieved for the young Queen. Well he knew that the old Empress's letters were a stabilizing influence on her light-hearted daughter, and thus upon the Court of France. The death of the Empress would be felt by many.

Franz called upon the Queen and left cards. He also called upon Count Mercy.

"You are having difficulty yourself, Franz. May I help? I may be leaving here soon, you know."

"Thank you, no," Franz replied. He had not the heart to tell Count Mercy of his troubles in the face of the Count's own grief. He had been devoted to the Empress.

Lafayette would leave again soon for America. In his charge were troops and guns to aid the struggling Colonists.

"You are made of strong fiber to be able to leave the luxury and glamor of Paris to fight in a strange country," Franz told him.

"Aren't you doing this very thing in the field of medicine?" Lafayette smiled.

"Touché."

"Any change in the attitude of the academicians?" Lafayette's voice was hopeful.

"Not that d'Eslon or I have noticed. However, I did hear that the King had questioned you about what General Washington might think of your becoming apprentice to the apothecary Monsieur Mesmer." Franz tried to keep his voice light, but there was bitterness in his heart. He saw the color stain Lafayette's face and wished that he hadn't spoken.

Lafayette coughed slightly but didn't comment on the King's question. Instead he said, "Speaking of General Washington, I wish your approval before I post this."

He handed Franz a letter to read. It was addressed to General Washington.

Franz read the paragraph Lafayette indicated:

Sir, a certain doctor here, by name Franz Anton Mesmer, has made the greatest possible discovery and has taken a few pupils, among whom I, your most humble servant, am one of the most enthusiastic. Before leaving for America I shall obtain his permission to reveal to you this secret which is a philosophical discovery of the first magnitude.

"Thank you, Lafayette, thank you." Franz's hand reached out to Lafayette. "May God reward your efforts."

CHAPTER XXI

MONIQUE, D'ESLON and Franz's patients protested his decision to leave Paris in the spring.

"You are loved by so many worthwhile people, Franz; why do you worry about those dreary old doctors?" Monique asked him.

"My dear one, those dreary old doctors represent the school I trained in, the oath I took, the discipline I've maintained and the medicine I practice . . . if they won't accept me here in Paris, I must find a spot where they will. . . ."

He walked about the room trying to suppress his anger. At last he stood in front of her. "I don't want to tolerate insults forever. . . ." His voice broke.

Monique slipped her arms about him and whispered, "Wherever you go, I'm going, too."

The next morning Karl handed Franz a calling card. Franz read aloud, "Jean Frédéric Phélypeaux de Maurepas—now that's a name, Karl!" He studied the card and repeated, "*de Maurepas*—Count de Maurepas—oh, yes, I remember, he's one of the King's ministers—the one Pompadour had Louis XV banish from court. Am I right, Karl?"

"You are, sir. But he is in high favor now. As minister of state, he has the wisdom to surround himself with the ablest men of France, Vergennes, Turgot, and Malesherbes." Karl dropped the names as manna from heaven, and Franz wondered anew how Karl could gather so much information.

But Karl was not finished. "He is doing everything he can to improve the financial condition of France, and he also supported the alliance with the American Colonies." Karl was filled with respectful awe.

"I think you should show him in, Karl, don't you?" Franz couldn't resist the temptation to tease. "Now tell me, Karl, shall I drop him a deep curtsy?"

"Sir," Karl almost snorted, "I'll show him in."

Count Jean Frédéric Phélypeaux de Maurepas was as officious as he was ornamental. He received Franz's greetings with an economical wave of the hand and came to the point.

"Our Queen thinks highly of you. She has appealed to the government to do something to keep you in our midst. After due deliberation, we have reached the decision to offer you an annual pension of twenty thousand livres, plus another ten thousand for lodging, if you will remain in Paris and furnish the State with three fully-trained pupils capable of demonstrating the powers of magnetism."

"What have I been doing in Paris for the past two years but demonstrating?" Franz protested, amazed. "Can't any of you understand that what I want is scientific help in investigating the potential of my discovery?"

De Maurepas shrugged. "You refuse?" he asked, astonished.

"I cannot sign a contract with the State until the correctness of my views and discoveries have been fully substantiated." Franz tried to put warmth into his words. He felt kindly toward de Maurepas. After all, it was a generous offer by de Maurepas' standards. "Yes, I refuse; but thank you."

Count Jean Phélypeaux de Maurepas rose on his small feet, gave Franz a courtly bow, and promenaded from the office. "Had he been preceded by an escort of twelve white horses and a regiment of footed soldiers, he could not have been more self-assured," Franz told Monique.

In spite of Franz's refusal of the offer, he was deeply touched by the Queen's concern. He wrote her:

Solely out of respect for Your Majesty, I am prolonging my stay in France until September 18th, and up to that date I shall continue to treat the patients now under my care . . . I am seeking a government, Your Majesty, which will be willing to recognize the need for spreading a truth throughout the world, not in a spirit of levity but seriously recognizing that it can exercise its influence upon the human body to good ends if at the outset its properties are studied and properly controlled and utilized to worthy ends. Monetary considerations are of minor importance where a matter of such vital moment to humanity is under discussion. . . .

D'Eslon was dismissed from the faculty at the University. He showed Franz the letter of dismissal.

Anger, like a flash fire, swept over Franz. "The fools, the stupid, pig-headed fools. You are worth more than the lot of them. Fools . . . bastards . . . we'll show them . . . we'll leave."

D'Eslon broke in, "No, oh, no, never. We can't ever flee in defeat."

"It is not defeat—not even retreat." Franz wanted d'Eslon to understand. Patiently, he explained again, "It is withdrawal in the face of superior enemy forces. Don't you see?"

D'Eslon shook his head, "No."

"But perhaps we can find another government—another place," Franz pleaded.

"No!"

In the end they quarreled violently. D'Eslon was as stubborn as Franz. Through his tears he kept saying, "I shall stay here and keep our practice going. I'll never leave."

They heard no more from the King's ministry. Franz decided he would go to Spa. He asked Karl to make the travel arrangements, and he busied himself in closing his private office. He embraced d'Eslon in farewell and invited, "Join me any time you wish."

Emotion-ridden, they laughed without mirth and embraced again.

Monique agreed to close her house and follow Franz. Now she was ready to travel. "I'll have my maid with me," she planned. "After we are well on the road, Karl can ride with her and I shall share your coach. Traveling with you will be such fun." Franz knew she was trying to cheer him. "Shall we leave early tomorrow?" she asked.

The sun was still clinging to the east when Franz and Karl climbed into the well-packed carriage. Monique and her maid were waiting in the carriage just behind them. Karl gave the driver the word and they were off. Franz looked back to see if all was well with Monique.

"I wish you would look, Karl."

Karl looked and exclaimed, "Your patient, Monsieur Goncourt, and his family, just behind the carriage of Madame. There are more, too."

"It looks like a procession, Karl."

"It does, sir. Isn't that Madame Maria Louisa de Compton?"

Franz leaned out and waved.

"They are seeing you out of town. Isn't that kind of them?"

Franz felt a glow in his heart. "It's good to have friends." He sighed, content.

At the city's edge, Franz had Karl order the driver to stop. "I shall bid our friends one last good-bye," Franz said.

The coaches had pulled up behind them, blocking the road for some distance. Franz walked back to speak to his friends and patients. There was the aged Countess Kantor—"You should be in bed," Franz said to her. "I explained to your son—"

"We are wasting time, doctor," she answered in her pert way. "We can talk about my bed at Spa."

"At Spa?"

"Young man," she said, "don't fret me about trifles. Just lead on."

"But your son. . . ."

She interrupted Franz again, ". . . is smarter than you are in some ways, doctor. He knows not to argue with me when my mind is made up."

"She is right, doctor," said Monsieur Goncourt, who had walked up behind Franz. "There is no use in protesting. We are all going with you. And there are others who will follow."

Franz was so deeply touched that words could not pass the tightness in his throat. He gave up trying to speak, but he walked to each carriage and touched the hands of his people. How humble he felt—and how grateful. This was not another Vienna. This time he had friends, real friends—and with them came hope. "We shall rest for a time; then, God willing, we will try again—perhaps in another country."

The sun broke through the leaden September sky to brighten the road and warm the travelers as they proceeded to Spa.

This resort town on the border of Germany was the site of famous mineral springs. Roman legionaries had once bathed in these waters, whose curative properties had been proclaimed for centuries. Franz wished to study the mineral springs.

Accommodations were good, in spite of the number of people attracted to the town by the luxurious gambling halls. Spa had become the most fashionable resort town in all of

Europe, too, and even the musical entertainment was superb.

Franz and his entourage were soon comfortably settled and enjoying all that Spa had to offer. Of course, he had no hospital, but he did set aside two rooms of his spacious hotel apartment for medical use. He arranged, too, for a private bathhouse for himself and his patients.

Monique reveled in Spa. She enjoyed the gambling halls, the amusements, the social life, and the theatre. She insisted that her already flawless skin had improved beyond belief and that she felt much more alive than she had ever felt in Paris. Franz ruled out her testimonial regarding the baths. "You are responding to the whole rather than any one phase of treatment," he teased.

And so was he. For one thing, he was with Monique more than he had ever been in Paris. He never ceased to wonder at her ability to extract the last drop of pleasure from her cup of life. Always she was able to fit her own mood to any situation in which she found herself; yet deep within her nature lay a serenity—a certain virginity of spirit—which totally encompassed yet remained untouched by any of the problems of living.

For three months the holiday lasted, and then Monique and Franz attended the theatre production of "Irene," Voltaire's last play. They had seen the play previously in Paris and afterwards had attended a party to honor the aged philosopher. Now Voltaire was dead. Seeing his play again filled Franz with a vague nostalgia—and a restlessness for which he had no name.

After the theatre, Monique and Franz walked along the streets. On and on they walked, beyond the happy throngs and out into the night. Finally they were in the country. Wordless, they blended with the night. They were one with its silence as they walked slowly along hand in hand. Thoughts came together in Franz's mind and made a picture. Voltaire and the pattern of his life—the way his enthusiasm carried him repeatedly into difficulty, and how he went back to his pen for the words that would resolve the difficulty. His busy pen bespoke the ebb and flow of life experience—back and forth, up and down, but never at rest.

"Why am I standing still?" Franz asked himself aloud.

"Franz," said Monique, "the play was not this moving."

"No, Monique, it was not—but the life of Voltaire was this moving."

"Then you are ready to start again?"

So—she had known all along. He caught her up in his arms. Her laughter bubbled out over the night.

A new energy filled Franz, and he began work with a new strength and a new respect for his beliefs. He determined that he would express these beliefs in words. He began afresh a paper on animal magnetism. He wrote, "Where once I had sought the Truth with tender affection, I now seek her with urgency."

Franz now spent most of his time writing on the history of magnetism.

Monique encouraged him. "Go to early mass, Franz, and then you'll have all morning to write."

He read parts of it to her and was rewarded by her thoughtful comments.

Karl copied chapters for him and saw that he stopped for meals.

He was hardly aware when Monique kissed him on the top of his head and slipped from the room.

Franz's history was almost complete when Count Puységur and Monsieur Bergasse arrived in Spa. Bergasse was a lawyer by profession, a learned man of very high reputation in Paris. Franz knew that he and Puységur had formed a group to press for the support of magnetism, but he had no idea of the extent of their work until now.

"Franz," said Puységur, "Paris eagerly awaits your return. Your admirers and patients are now organized in support of your cause. We call ourselves the 'Société de l'Harmonie.' One hundred of our members have pledged one hundred gold louis each—and we are prepared to furnish additional funds without limit until your system shall be established throughout the world."

Franz was astonished. "I knew these handsome, personable, and wealthy young men were concerned with my welfare and my work—but that they would go to such lengths! And ninety-eight others!" he exclaimed, amazed.

"There are more than ninety-eight others," said Bergasse. "We closed the list when we reached a hundred subscribers."

Franz looked in bewilderment from one to the other of the two as they went on to reveal their plan. "We shall establish a special academy of which you will be director. We shall take a large place in the heart of the city—large enough for your living quarters, clinic, lecture hall. You can train young doctors and assistants." Bergasse smiled and added, "d'Eslon is eager for your return." Bergasse's legal voice was in command.

Franz embraced his friends and thanked them for their interest. "Give me a few more weeks to think about this," he asked.

Puységur and Bergasse returned to Paris, and Franz talked with Monique. She listened and questioned, but she could not or would not help him come to a decision.

Franz longed to see Father Emmanuel. Father would listen and question, too, but he would understand and point the way to a decision. Perhaps Father would be able to come to Spa. In his last letter he had mentioned needing a vacation. Franz wrote him, telling him of his problems and asking him to come for a visit. Father's reply filled Franz's heart with sorrow. His script was light and uncertain. His handwriting had lost its bold dash, and the words failed to show any fire. He thanked Franz but declined the invitation. "My body is old, lad; and my mind is tired." He spoke of the beauty of his moss roses:

"They are unusually lovely this year; I sit here among them and drink in the spice of their perfume; I pull a stem closer for examination; why did the Blessed Lord cover the calyx and part of the stem with this tender, mossy growth? Are they loved more tenderly than their thorny sisters? I love them, I think, the best of all of my flowers. Does our Lord give some of us a protective covering and others the thorns that serve, but in such a different way? Such a different way, son."

His letter trailed off. Franz puzzled over this thing of the thorns, "What is he suggesting?" Perplexed, Franz reread the letter. "He's just growing old." He shook his head in sadness. "Father Emmanuel is slipping away—like Papa and Mama—he, too, will leave. . . ." Franz went to the Cathedral for comfort.

Franz soon realized that he longed to return to the fray. He was filled with apostolic zeal; yet to go over the heads of the French Academies, to ignore the protests of recognized scientists and take his discoveries directly to the people—this would not be ethical. Or would it?

Like a contrapuntal strain of music, the Hippocratic Oath wound through his pondering. "You do solemnly swear . . . that you will be loyal to the profession of medicine and just and generous to its members . . . that you will exercise your art solely for the cure of your patients. . . ."

If he let the discovery of magnetism drop—would this constitute loyalty to his profession? Perhaps not. Yet could he press in France for the acceptance of his discovery and remain just and generous to the doctors of Paris? Just and generous . . . d'Eslon was urging his return . . . what would be his answer if he willed to be just and generous toward this loyal member of his profession? And there were the German doctors who had supported him in Vienna. What did he owe them? "And then, too, what do I owe to myself . . . my generation . . . and generations yet to come?" Thoughtfully he fingered his beads, then decided, "I shall return."

The mail brought Franz a letter from Gluck, who wrote:

BELOVED FRATER:

You will be pleased to hear that Father Hervier of Bordeaux Cathedral took the dogma of animal magnetism as his text last Sunday. Those who heard him were tremendously impressed by his incisive knowledge of the subject and his heroic defense of your theories.

I do not know how we can further delay your return to Paris, for we are over-subscribed in membership of a new academy. We await your leadership. When will you return?

In Peace Profound, I remain your affectionate

Christoph Gluck

And there was a typical letter from Wolfgang. Franz smiled as he read:

DEAR FRIEND, BENEFACTOR, AND CONFESSOR, NOT TO MENTION PHYSICIAN:
I was told a letter would reach you in Spa. I am at present working on the opera I told you about—Idomeneo—and teaching the fat stupid daughter of a local brewer. She is hopeless. I talk to her, I demonstrate to her, I threaten her, and she giggles—yes, she just giggles. Her papa criticizes me constantly.

The other day I gave her a chord and asked her to improvise only a few simple measures—I even hummed a part for her—and she could not follow. Definitely my work with her is only depriving the world of a good barmaid—on second thought I speak hastily—a good barmaid would need brains—five times more brains.

I hear you are criticized, too. Criticize, magnetize, improvise, dramatize, sensitize, criticize.

I am going to have dinner with the Webers tonight. I look forward to it, for I am starved on my own cooking. My belly is as flat as piss on a platter.

Tell Monique I kiss her hand a thousand times and love her to distraction. Tell Karl to stay out of those mineral baths. They might be bad for his manhood.

Your devoted and obedient servant,
Wolfgang Mozart

P. S. Papa still grieves for Mama. He looks at her picture while he plays all her favorite airs on his violin and his cheeks stream with tears. I know that death is the desired end of each life—that death is a gift of priceless beauty—but to those of us who are left—Will you make a prayer for Papa? He is such a kind man.

P.s.s.s.s. I saw Haydn and copied his Stabat Mater for you. I shall send it along. It will take you "all the way."

❖ CHAPTER XXII ❖

IMMEDIATELY UPON Franz's decision to return to Paris, he seemed to lose all control of his affairs. Matters were settled before he had time to protest, and he was carried along by an adoring and powerful group that seemed intent upon lifting him to its shoulders and bearing him forth for the world to look upon as a new kind of idol. For the moment he was hemmed in, and there was nothing for him now but to endure.

Franz was touched by this tribute; yet its spectacular nature was offensive to him. Had he not been informed that Queen Marie Antoinette, the Princess de Lamballe, Prince de Condé, and the Duc de Bourbon would be among the official greeters, he would have ordered his driver to take a back road and slip into Paris quietly.

"The History of Animal Magnetism"—Monique had bound the pages of Franz's manuscript and lettered its title on the cover. Now it lay beside him on the carriage seat. Franz and his manuscript, his friends from Spa, his patients who had followed him into exile, and twenty-odd servants were entering the outskirts of Paris. Soon they would be met by members and friends of the Société de l'Harmonie—and like some triumphant oriental potentate, Franz would head the procession through the streets of Paris and up to the entrance of the hotel which the Society had taken in the Place Vendôme.

Franz looked at his manuscript. Before the year was out, perhaps he could add a new chapter; and with all his heart he prayed that it would be one which would add to the luster of his profession.

They reached the city streets before pandemonium broke loose. The sumptuous carriages of the Society members had attracted hordes of the Paris poor. Beggars, sick people, cripples, and gangs of little street urchins blocked the way. Someone went for the gendarmes, and soon their shouts were added to the confusion. Franz was heartsick at the débacle and numb with despair by the time they reached the Place Vendôme.

The massive stone building was hung with multicolored bunting. Flags fluttered in profusion. Floral offerings were banked against the walls, and a satin runner made a path up to the entrance. Franz, seeking for some reassurance, decided that the building was sturdy.

"It is not finished," said Bergasse in his legal voice as they made their way through the crowd and up to the entrance hall, "but we are quite proud of the décor and know that you will be pleased."

There were workmen's tools and ladders in the entrance hall. Bergasse led Franz past them and into the main salon. "The most elegant place in Paris," he said. Franz was speechless.

The entire ceiling of the huge room was draped in blue velvet. It rose from the walls in a dome-like effect of swags and pleats. From its misty heights descended—or floated—the signs of the zodiac. They seemed to be cut out of metal—or were they plaster—and gilded and set with jewels. They caught the light from the stained-glass windows and threw it back in sparkles of color.

Gluck arrived and Franz embraced him. Gluck pounded Franz heartily on the back. "Is it not beautiful, Franz? A palace worthy of your work—but we are not finished yet. There will be draperies and thick carpeting—and you must help me plan the music."

"And there will be perfume—incense—a carved mahogany baquet—" The room was filling with people, and they all seemed to be talking at once. In their enthusiasm they were bent on explaining to Franz every detail of the outrageous setting. "The lecture hall—and some of the doctors will wear—"

"What doctors?" Franz finally gasped.

"The young physicians who have applied for training," someone answered.

A glimmer of hope—a ray of pure light—broke through this garish display. "Tell me about the doctors," Franz insisted.

"We have a wonderful following, Franz. It has been most gratifying to see the young physicians of good medical background who are interested in your methods of treatment. Several have applied for training. And many able philosophers have applied, as well as a sprinkling of men trained in the allied sciences. You will lecture to all the great intellects of Paris." Bergasse beamed with pride.

"Gentlemen," Franz said, "I am overwhelmed." He thanked the stars that it was not necessary for him to say more.

They planned on and on, through the hectic reception, the board meeting that followed, and the days during which Franz witnessed the rapid assembling of all the theatrical trappings of the new academy.

The place was nearing completion when Gluck arrived at Monique's home for tea one afternoon. He had a tailor in tow. "The finest tailor in Europe," said Gluck, "and he is here to measure you for smocks, Franz."

"Smocks—for me?"

"Yes, we have decided that it will be far more impressive if you wear well-tailored smocks during your treatment hours— more impressive, that is, than a morning jacket or an afternoon coat."

The small, cat-like figure of the tailor was prowling around Franz as Gluck talked. Now the little man purred, "Big shoulders, big chest, long torso, big man."

Monique looked up from her tea service, "Observant, isn't he?" she said in German.

"Do not poke fun, Monique. We are fortunate to get this man on such short notice. If he were not vitally interested in the cause of animal magnetism—"

The tailor had opened his sample case and lifted out a piece of cerise satin. Now he flung the material over Franz's shoulder and leapt back with feline grace. "*C'est charmant!*" he exclaimed.

Franz felt like a fool. Monique reached out and stroked his hand. "*C'est beau,*" she cooed—and she collapsed on the sofa in a fit of laughter.

The little tailor shrugged and spread his hands as Franz flung the offensive fabric from his shoulders. "Oh, well," the tailor said, "It was a bargain and I could have made the smocks cheap."

Monique busied herself among the samples. Finally she pulled out a swatch of greyish-violet silk. It was soft in color and texture, but not shiny. "This will do nicely," she said to the tailor.

He was all agreement. *"C'est superbe,"* and he snatched up a crayon and pad and began to sketch.

Monique watched. "We do not want this to look like the King's lounging jacket," she objected and took the crayon. "It must be long . . . flowing lines but no drapery . . . there," and she handed the drawing to Gluck.

"Good," he said. "The neckband eliminates the need for a neckerchief. It has dignity."

The excited tailor was sidling between the two. Now he approached Franz, tape in hand. Franz fended him off. "This has gone quite far enough. I need no fancy dress for the practice of medicine. I am a doctor—not a sorcerer." Franz felt a flood of anger, rising and spreading.

"Franz," said Gluck firmly, "listen to me. Always you have gone quietly and unobtrusively about your work—cautious, reserved, fearful lest you offend your colleagues. What has been your reward? Have you furthered your cause among the scientists? Do they accept you or your discovery?"

Franz looked at Gluck. He looked at Monique.

"Franz," Monique said, "Christoph is right. You know it."

Franz looked back at Gluck. "Do you remember Prince Kaunitz?" Gluck asked.

Franz nodded. He saw the Prince as if he stood before him —the bizarre wig with its powder of many colors, the flamboyant cloaks which he affected, his air of being a procession—and after thirty years of such unorthodox staging, he remained one of Austria's most valuable statesmen. "Good theatre," Gluck had said of his behavior many years ago. And even Empress Marie Theresa had loved and respected Prince Kaunitz.

"Measure me," Franz said to the quivering little tailor.

It was late afternoon when Franz drove out into the country alone. He left the carriage and walked toward the setting sun. A grove of trees loomed against the brilliance of the sky. He slipped into this shadowed sanctuary. The moist, dank smell of the woods lent solemnity to the moment; as he walked he chanted the *Miserere*—"Have mercy upon me, oh God, after

Thy great goodness. . . ." At last he knelt for his personal *miserere*. He waited there in the stillness until the answer flooded through his heart and mind. "I must accept. If my discoveries are to survive, I must accept."

It was dark as he stumbled back across the rough terrain, knowledge deepening within him. "If I am to play a part in a theatrical production, then I shall be the greatest actor the profession of medicine has ever known."

Also, he decided on the way home, he would open a hospital for the poor. At the house he asked Karl to look for a location. Karl's eyes were weak now, but in some ways his perception had increased with age.

"Doctor," he said, "I have been looking around for another hospital site. The poor folk . . . yes . . . there is a place in the rue Montmartre. . . ."

They set up a simple hospital. Karl hired assistants and nurses. Soon the place was overcrowded. Franz touched his rosary in gratitude every time he entered the building.

"Here I am a doctor," he told Karl, "but not the other."

Hôtel de l'Harmonie—they named the place. "It's more like Madame Roussault's," Franz thought grimly.

On opening night the elaborate décor of the place was enhanced by lavish use of fragrant flowers. Sprayed perfumes blended with the aroma of the flowers and flowed over the assembled guests with the dulcet tones from the string orchestra.

The huge square of the Place Vendôme was packed with carriages, and still the guests arrived. Franz did not know how many people were present when Bergasse asked for their attention and said, "This evening is unique in both medical and social history. To explain this statement would be superfluous, but I do have another explanation to make. In just a few moments we wish to make the formal dedication of the Hôtel de l'Harmonie. In anticipation of this event, we have kept the doors of the baquet treatment room—heartbeat of our establishment—closed. Now we shall open the doors. We ask that members and friends of the Société de l'Harmonie enter this inner sanctum in absolute silence. Walking in single file, please form in circles about the baquet. Doctor Mesmer will address the assembly as soon as it has gathered."

The utter silence that fell over this large group of people impressed Franz. Quietly they began to move across the entrance hall and into the exotic atmosphere of the treatment room. "Bless my friends," he murmured as he went to the dressing room to don his robe.

The orchestra was playing a glorious Bach. Franz couldn't identify it, but he knew that everyone would respond to the spiritual quality of Bach's music.

Holding to his resolve to be the best actor in the medical profession, Franz took center stage and signaled the servants to part the curtains. The guests faced him, bathed in violet light from shaded candelabra. The music grew muted and Franz felt the excited expectations of the group. "Can I dispel this carnival air and change it to one of peace . . . and attunement to God?" he wondered.

His audience was waiting. Softly he began, "Beloved members of the Société de l'Harmonie, let us give thanks for the beauty of our establishment; let us join hands in gratitude to each other and pray that through our united efforts we can give our message to the world. Love and Peace abide here among us. Let us send that love out to every creature everywhere . . . Love and Peace."

For a moment there flashed in his mind's eye the little brooklet that became Lake Constance.

"All is harmony . . . all is peace. Let us take a deep breath," he instructed them. "Hold it . . . feel peace drifting through our bodies, slowly exhale . . . again a deep breath . . . hold . . . harmony . . . love . . . exhale . . . we are at peace in harmony and love . . . nothing can harm us . . . peace . . . love . . . harmony. . . ." Franz felt tranquility pouring over them; the music came as a mere whisper. Franz lowered his voice to say:

"The Lord is my Sheperd . . . I shall not want. . . ." When the Psalm was finished, he motioned for the curtains to be drawn. He slipped off his robe and made haste to greet his thoughtful guests as they reassembled in the outer rooms. For the moment Franz was at peace.

CHAPTER XXIII

CHARLES D'ESLON was Franz's good right arm. They arranged alternate office hours at the Hôtel de l'Harmonie, for both of them had a private practice elsewhere. Without the young doctors who came to them for training, they would have been swamped with patients.

Daily the crowds increased in front of the hotel in the Place Vendôme. Parisians accepted their decision to bar no one from treatment, but royalty and distinguished visitors from other places were sometimes aghast to find themselves seated at the baquet with prostitutes, priests, soldiers, duchesses, beggars, merchants, and peasants.

Many of the poor and some of the merchant class were reluctant to approach the elegant Place Vendôme. Gradually these people began to make their way to the hospital in rue Montmartre; and the wonder of animal magnetism was discussed in daily conversation by bootblacks as well as barons.

D'Eslon and Franz chose their assistants carefully. Their intelligence as well as their health, interests, and physical presence were factors which they considered. In addition to these carefully trained, handsome young men, they had numerous physicians from other towns and villages. As a rule, the physicians were accepted by twos and fours and worked in teams. Ultimately, however, Franz trained twenty-one fully-qualified doctors who practiced in the city of Paris.

He also trained a number of qualified scientists and philosophers, as well as a few members of the landed gentry who wished to be able to treat the peasants who worked their estates. Count Puységur was among the latter. Franz had known him as an admirable man; he found him an able student.

The popularity of animal magnetism spread like wildfire among the lay people of Paris. To Franz's horror, he often heard its practice referred to as Mesmerism.

"Magnetism is a natural law that we, as medical doctors,

can use." He put his hand on d'Eslon's shoulder. "We must not isolate it or name it as a thing apart from good medicine."

"I know, my friend, I know," d'Eslon sighed, "and in spite of your published warnings, I keep hearing reports of weird treatments masquerading under the name of animal magnetism or," d'Eslon sighed, "Mesmerism."

Franz fought his dismay. "We must keep on trying. Perhaps someday. . . ."

A small landowner by the name of François Rolette brought his wife to Franz. Although they arrived during the morning hours, she was dressed in ballroom attire. Upon her head she wore a silver filigree crown. She swept into Franz's office and in a haughty manner demanded, "Kneel before your Queen."

As gracefully as his middle-aged legs would permit, Franz knelt to her. "Arise," she said immediately, and she accepted the chair he offered.

"She has been like this," explained the husband, "since evening before last when we visited a neighbor and took part in a demonstration of animal magnetism. She threatens to have me beheaded if I touch her, and she hasn't made a bed or cooked a meal since she became queen. Oh, help me, doctor, help me get her out of this."

"Who magnetized her?" Franz asked.

"A peddler. He insisted that he had studied under you. We did not really believe him, doctor, but we thought it would be interesting to see his tricks. And now—" The poor husband dropped his head in his hands and groaned.

"What did the peddler say to her?"

"I cannot remember all of it, but he did talk to her about being warm and comfortable."

"What is her name?"

"Renée."

Franz knelt before this miserable man's queen. "Renée," he said, "look at me. You are warm and comfortable . . . warm and comfortable . . . warm and comfortable. . . . You are Renée beloved wife of François Rolette. You are warm and comfortable . . . go home and be Renée."

Slowly the woman turned her head from Franz and looked at her husband. Recognition came into her face—and then she began to cry. He put his arm about her and took her from the room.

The couple never returned. Later Franz wished that he had inquired as to the location of their lands, for he would like to have known if Renée ever again experienced this queenly personality which had come into her with the universal fluidum. D'Eslon and Franz pondered over the case, but they were never able to explain it.

Nor did they find a reasonable explanation for the case of the boy named Paul. He was with a group of high-spirited young students who in a moment of levity decided to experiment with animal magnetism. According to the other students, Paul declared himself to be a monkey. He climbed the university chapel tower, swung off on a vine toward a tree, but missed the tree and fell. He broke both legs. D'Eslon had him in the hospital for two months. Paul continued to deny any knowledge or remembrance of his antics previous to the accident.

There were many phases of animal magnetism which Franz longed to investigate, but there never seemed to be time. He and d'Eslon did continue to refine and revise their techniques until they could bring about violent crises or a swoon in a matter of seconds with many patients. They concluded definitely that ritual and litany played a decisive part in conditioning patients to receive the power of the fluidum.

In their daily practice they made less and less use of pharmacology. In spite of this, rumors reached them that certain physicians in Paris declared that their cures resulted from the copious administration of powder made from the seeds of the poppy.

One evening Monique greeted Franz in high spirits.

"My darling, the great St. Germain has invited us to his home for Thursday evening . . . I am excited."

She flung her arms about Franz. He returned her greeting with a kiss.

"My precious, I'm a little too skeptical to be as overjoyed as you. Can Gluck take you . . . I . . . I have a very ill patient," Franz finished lamely, under Monique's knowing eye.

"You tried, Franz—but, of course, it isn't true. Too sick patient, indeed!" Her voice was scornful.

"Monique, I just can't get ready to socialize with a man who claims to be beyond universal laws—who says he's had the same valet for five hundred years—and who speaks of having been among those who heard the Sermon on the Mount. Such a man is. . . ."

Franz knew Monique would have her way, but still he protested.

They attended the most lavish dinner they had ever beheld. Each lady's place at the long banquet table was marked by a small, gold-framed miniature of herself, done by St. Germain. Suspended upon it was a diamond-set lavaliere on a slender chain. The diamond, a single flawless stone, was large enough to cover a man's thumbnail. While the women shrilled their delight and donned their lavalieres, the men were holding up champagne glasses for inspection, for on each one was etched a profile likeness of the seated male guest, plus the date. St. Germain assured them he would have the glasses delivered to their residences the following morning.

St. Germain gave each person at the table an opportunity to express himself. His affable manner induced brilliance in some people Franz considered dull. They reassembled in the music room and the Count asked Franz to play. The piano was an excellent one; this, plus the glowing introduction he gave Franz, made the andante movement from one of Wolfgang's concertos a thing of joy and rare beauty.

Franz outdid himself, and knew it. All performers are aware of moments like this.

Then Franz asked St. Germain if he would honor them with a selection. Franz had heard of his musicianship.

St. Germain promptly lifted his violin from its case. "I was waiting for you to insist," he joked.

The melody was unfamiliar, but only a man close to God could have written it. Everyone was transported, lifted above the beauty of the tangible present—they soared into a mystical infinity.

"How can I question a man of this temperament and talent?" Franz thought, but the reports of his many idiosyncrasies had Franz wild with speculation. He eyed the diamond lavaliere blazing at Monique's throat. Surely it was worth the proverbial King's ransom—was it transmutation? No lesser person than Marie Antoinette had told Franz of the fabulous Count who had taken several of the King's diamonds containing small flaws and, holding them in the palm of his hand, had not only banished the flaws but had enlarged the size of the stones by several times.

Franz stepped back from the guests during this period of speculation. Everyone was pressing about St. Germain, praising him and questioning him about music, but soon he invited everyone to retire to the ballroom for dancing. As they left, he approached Franz.

"You have a question?" His eyes twinkled.

"How did you know?" Franz asked.

"You a doctor, a man of science, wondering about the stories they tell that I have never known death." His brilliant smile flashed and Franz heard the song of his brooklet. . . . There is no death.

"Why, of course. Now I understand, but the transmutation —the diamonds. . . ."

"All things are possible on the material plane—one man looks at a clod of dirt and sees only dirt. Another man takes the soil in his hand and, loving it, finds gold. These are laws." St. Germain moved a candle nearer the center of a small table, and picking a bit of the hot wax he began molding it in his fingers.

"Yes, doctor, these are laws. Sacred laws, that all men must come to know."

"Are we learning them?" Franz asked, fascinated.

"A man never grows on excitement, or while plotting another's downfall, or in a state of hatred."

"That is true, and Paris is exciting," Franz said.

"Oh, yes, and all of France is seething—the peasants are joining hands to become bold." St. Germain shook his head, and for the first time he appeared sad.

"They are pathetic in desperation, God's little people—half naked, always hungry, exploited by church and state, nowhere to turn except to each other."

"How well I know the truth of your words. I shudder daily for the serfdom in our enlightened age, for the exploitation of human flesh such as that which is being perpetuated in France."

St. Germain nodded, "Someone is responsible for their desperation. . . ." He paused. "It grieves me to find religion at such a low ebb."

Franz offered, "Ah, yes, churchman against churchman, Catholic and Protestant overlooking their allegiance to God Almighty, lining up in opposition to each other, forgetting completely the greatest commandment."

A servant appeared and offered them a glass of brandy. Franz took one, but St. Germain waved the man away and continued:

"A child queen romps her way through her duties, seeking to keep her husband only unto herself. She forgets that her first duty is to her subjects. The King, nurtured on inadequacy, gropes his way down the corridor of doom." He looked at Franz intently for a full moment, then added:

"We can deplore but not condemn—that is all. . . ." His mood changed. He held between his thumb and forefinger a perfect pearl—the small wax ball! Franz was confounded. St. Germain dropped the pearl in Franz's hand with the comment, "You, too, are misunderstood and misquoted. You, too, know laws you wish to share. . . . Welcome to the brotherhood," and he laughed his infectious laugh and moved on to the ballroom.

"Maybe that's what it is . . . after all . . . a brotherhood. . . ." Franz shook his head in his perplexity and examined the pearl.

CHAPTER XXIV

TIME PASSED and popular approval of animal magnetism grew. Hardly a home was without some member who had sat at one of the baquets and felt the life-giving power of the fluidum. For outrageous sums of money Franz installed private baquets in the homes of the wealthy.

They were besieged at every point by patients, but in the deeps of Franz he was beginning to despair of medical recognition. Constantly he was criticized by the faculties of the University and the Academy of Science. The Société de l'Harmonie had on its rolls some of the greatest names of France, but always the academicians spurned their overtures.

"In many ways I have a good life," Franz thought, trying to overcome his disappointment. "My work is rewarding, my music consoling, and my evenings alone with Monique precious beyond telling. There is joy in loving and joy in being loved—but when the two are combined, heart and body know peace."

A letter from Wolfgang told Franz that he, too, had found something of this peace. He had married Constanze, one of the Weber sisters.

Only occasionally did Franz feel disquiet at the turn his life had taken in France. One such instance occurred when Madame Helvetius brought the great American, Benjamin Franklin, to the baquet at the Place Vendôme.

The French people loved this great man who was now growing old in their midst. His quaint speech was quoted and misquoted at all the parties in Paris. Most of all, he endeared himself to the people by being so completely himself—the ridiculous fur cap above immaculate linens, the scintillating humor combined with a scholar's gravity. Franklin's picture was in every Paris shop—on a plate, a platter, or pressed on a snuff box.

Now he wandered about the Hôtel de l'Harmonie, expressing his admiration for the décor. In what seemed a sudden and penetrating grasp of the situation, he turned to Franz and asked, "You choose this rather than staid, medical professionalism?"

In a younger, less-gifted man the question would have been sheer affrontery. Even from Franklin, the query carried a sting that burned into Franz's soul.

He nodded. "I had no choice." Then a wave of gratitude swept over him and he added, "God gave me friends. In my hour of need they came to my rescue. They made the choice. I am grateful."

"Reminds me of a story," Franklin said.

"Once there was a two-headed snake which had only one body. All was well with him until one spring day he decided to go off his beaten path and run down to the river for a drink. He crawled along, enjoying all of his new adventures with both of his heads. Then he came to a tree. While the heads were trying to decide what to do, the body starved to death."

Franz did not laugh at the joke. The best he could manage was a smile. "Two-headed snake . . . that's what I've turned into," Franz thought bitterly to himself.

Shortly after this, Monique came to Franz's office with a letter written by Benjamin Franklin to Madame Helvetius.

"No doubt he composed it in a spirit of levity," said Monique, "and Madame Helvetius thought it so charming that she permitted some friends to make a copy. Numerous copies were ultimately made, some of which are being used by the spiritists to prove that the Honorable Benjamin Franklin conducts séances."

Franz laughed heartily. Apparently it was not too difficult for a snake to acquire two heads. Franz read the letter.

Mortified at the barbarous resolution pronounced by you so positively yesterday evening, that you would remain single the rest of your life as a compliment due to the memory of your husband, I retired to my chamber. Throwing myself upon my bed, I dreamt that I was dead, and was transported to the Elysian Fields.

I was asked whether I wished to see any person in particular; to which I replied, that I wished to see the philosophers. "There are two who live here at hand in this garden; they are good neighbors, and very friendly toward one another." "Who are they?" "Socrates and Helvetius." "I esteem them both highly; but let me see Helvetius first, because I understand a little French, but not a

word of Greek." I was conducted to him; he received me with much
courtesy, having known me, he said, by character, some time past.
He asked me a thousand questions relative to the war, the present
state of religion, of liberty, of the government in France. "You do
not inquire, then," said I, "after your dear friend, Madame Helvetius; yet she loves you exceedingly; I was in her company not more
than an hour ago." "Ah," said he, "you make me recur to my past
happiness, which ought to be forgotten in order to be happy here.
For many years I could think of nothing but her, though at length
I am consoled. I have taken another wife, the most like her that
I could find; she is not indeed altogether so handsome, but she has
a great fund of wit and good sense; and her whole study is to please
me. She is at this moment gone to fetch the best nectar and
ambrosia to regale me; stay home awhile and you will see her."
"I perceive," said I, "that your former friend is more faithful to
you than you are to her; she has had several good offers, but refused them all. I will confess to you that I loved her extremely; but
she was cruel to me, and rejected me peremptorily for your sake."
"I pity you sincerely," said he, "for she is an excellent woman,
handsome and amiable. But do not the Abbé de la Roche and the
Abbé Morellet visit her?" "Certainly they do; not one of your
friends has dropped her acquaintance." "If you had gained the
Abbé Morellet with a bribe of good coffee and cream, perhaps you
would have succeeded; for he is as deep a reasoner as Duns Scotus
or St. Thomas; he arranges and methodizes his arguments in such
a manner that they are almost irresistible. Or, if by a fine edition
of some old classic, you had gained the Abbé de la Roche to speak
against you, that would have been still better; as I always observed that when he recommended anything to her, she had a great
inclination to do directly the contrary." As he finished these words
the new Madame Helvetius entered with the nectar, and I recognized her immediately as my former American friend, Mrs. Franklin!
I reclaimed her, but she answered me coldly: "I was a good wife
to you for forty-nine years and four months, nearly half a century;
let that content you. I have formed a new connection here, which
will last to eternity."

Indignant at this refusal of my Eurydice, I immediately resolved to quit those ungrateful shades, and return to this good

world again, to behold the sun and you! Here I am; let us avenge ourselves!

Franz thought the letter charming and said so. "To discover Franklin such a nimble-witted lover would increase any man's respect for him. This should be published."

"But, Franz," protested Monique, "don't you see the use to which charlatans are putting this letter. Both your name and Franklin's are being bandied about to lend respectability to all manner of irresponsible witchcraft."

"If the names are used together, they will remain in good company," Franz laughed as he caught Monique to him.

Franz was leaving the Place Vendôme when a boy ran up with a note. "It is my sister; please come, doctor." The lad's face was streaked with tears.

Franz drove with the boy to a cottage on the outskirts of Paris. The boy's sister was in labor with her first child.

Jacques, the young husband, talked as Franz examined the girl. "Her water broke yesterday, doctor, and I called the midwife. The woman used mesmerism to hurry the baby. Something went wrong."

"Where is the midwife now?" Franz asked.

"She left when I said I was sending for you."

The patient was in a coma. Franz could not rouse her sufficiently to give ergot. The baby's head was engaged and there was some dilation, but the contractions were so feeble as to be of no effect.

"Her pains were severe yesterday when the midwife first used mesmerism," said the agitated young husband.

Franz had no way of knowing the girl's condition at the onset of labor, nor could he guess how or why the midwife had used animal magnetism. There was some show of blood and the patient's pulse was weak, so he took the only course open to him; he used forceps and delivered the child.

The baby's head was badly damaged, and he felt sure that it had been dead for several hours. The mother bled extensively now.

Franz sent the young brother for the priest. The mother died while the last rites were being administered.

Franz left the cottage burdened with sorrow for the bereaved husband and the sobbing little brother.

Monique had been right. His name was being used in connection with ignorant and unscrupulous practice. Animal magnetism was a powerful force. In the hands of the untrained, it was dangerous. He did not know how the midwife had misused magnetism; yet he felt in his heart that she had interfered in some way with the normal processes of labor. He felt a grievous responsibility. It was he who had released this new force upon the world. How many innocent persons had been victimized?

Again he published a warning about the indiscriminate use of animal magnetism.

Parisians love excitement. The natural verve with which they receive the new can be a hindrance to the orderly process of science. On the other hand, this fervor sometimes acts to promote discoveries which would die aborning in other lands, among more placid people.

Because of their inventiveness, the brothers Montgolfier (Michel and Jacques) had long been popular. Now, however, they had come forth with an invention which titillated the imagination of all Paris. The Montgolfiers had invented a balloon, an airtight bag of paper-lined cloth which they inflated with hot air and smoke.

On June 5, 1783, they had demonstrated their invention at Annonay. Now, three months later, they were prepared to send the huge bag aloft again—this time carrying a basket which would contain a sheep, a duck, and a rooster—and King Louis XVI would be on hand to watch.

Monique and Franz were among the royal guests gathered for the event. "I have not a full breath left in my body," said Monique when the balloon was finally inflated and tugging at the ropes which held it to earth.

Franz looked at her in surprise—and then he laughed. Without realizing it, all of them had been quietly puffing and blowing —as if their efforts might increase the force of the hot air which rose from the pan of charcoal burning beneath the slowly inflating balloon.

The Montgolfier brothers now removed the pan of charcoal and tied on the basket of animals. Then they released the balloon. Up it went—up and up—and the cheers followed it. For eight minutes the contraption floated; then it descended slowly and the animals came to earth unhurt.

The King was as enthusiastic as his wildly-cheering subjects. "Next time you shall have a man in the basket," he said to the brothers. "I shall provide you with a criminal who has already been sentenced to death. . . ."

"Sire," protested Pilâtre de Rozier, the King's historian, "to make such a flight would be an honor. Let me go."

Franz could understand Rozier's offer, as could many others present who had dreamed of flying.

They all gathered a month later to watch Rozier climb aboard and sail eighty-four feet into the air before he was stopped by the long tethers which remained attached to the balloon on this trip.

It was January of the following year before the Montgolfiers finally completed their big balloon. It carried seven passengers to a height of three thousand feet over the city of Lyons. By now the inventive brothers had perfected a method of keeping the balloon's air hot with a straw fire tended by the basket's occupants. The flyers also carried buckets of water and sponges, lest the fire get out of hand.

During this same period the Robert brothers were working with the great physicist Charles on the construction of hydrogen balloons. Their first balloon drifted away and came down in a field about fifteen miles from Paris. There it was promptly beaten to pieces by frightened peasants who thought it an evil spirit.

The future of ballooning was assured, however, when King Louis issued a royal proclamation describing balloons and explaining to his subjects that they need not be feared.

"Dare I hope that popular interest can ultimately gain such sanction for animal magnetism?" Franz asked Monique that evening as they talked over the proclamation in Monique's library.

"My dear, I wish you could be happy." Monique settled on a footstool by his knees and looked into his face. "Do you want to talk about it?" she asked.

Franz sighed and closed his eyes in weariness.

"Sometimes it all looks hopeless. I can't see how it will end . . . all this display . . . the excitement . . . it's not the medical way."

He opened his eyes and smiled at her. He reached down and lifted her onto his lap. "I don't deserve you, dearest; you are too patient with me."

"Franz, what do you really want from your profession?"

"Complete vindication . . . full acceptance . . . an invitation to join the faculties . . . and the moral support of all good medical men everywhere."

He sighed. Was he asking the impossible?

CHAPTER XXV

"We have not been to the theatre in weeks, Franz."

"I know, Monique. Would you like me to get tickets and ask Gluck to escort you?"

"You do not wish to go?"

"If you can find me a proper disguise."

Monique laughed merrily. "Oh, you precious, stuffy, old German. Why can't you enjoy being the rage of Paris. I simply adore being seen with a gentleman who leaves a wake of swooning women behind him."

"Aren't you joking; surely you jest, Monique? Weren't you embarrassed last week when Madame Gestault fainted and fell into the tea service? You saw the look her husband gave me. Did you know that I lost a perfectly good cloak only yesterday? The crowd in the rue Montmartre literally ripped it from my back and tore it to shreds for souvenirs. This isn't medicine, dear; it isn't!" Franz felt like a caged animal. "All I want is the freedom to practice good medicine."

"But they love you, Franz, and their reverence increases daily," Monique protested.

"Reverence is not the word, Monique. I'm a rage. You said it correctly the first time."

"Perhaps, but why not enjoy it?"

"Dear Monique, how sweet you are in spite of my quarreling. I suppose that deep in my heart I am grateful for the adulation of the people. I only wish their enthusiasm were shared by the academies." Franz dropped his face in his hands.

"If I recanted," he whispered to himself, "they would accept me." He shuddered and pushed the thought away.

But the next week an academician did appear at the hotel in the Place Vendôme. It was Jean Sylvan Bailly, the eminent astronomer, writer, and political figure. He seemed pleased when Franz stopped to speak to him in the corridor one day after his baquet treatment.

"This luxurious setting," he said, "has no counterpart in Paris. And I admire your use of music. It is indeed unique."

"Thank you," and Franz opened his mouth to explain the theory which underlay his use of music in treatment, but a lovely young woman walked past at that moment. Bailly's head swiveled like a weathervane caught in a sudden breeze. Franz knew this was not the time to speak to him of the soul's response to soothing music.

A few days later, a young student doctor came to Franz complaining that Bailly opened his office door and peered in while he—the doctor—was examining a young lady. Franz suggested that the intrusion could have been unintentional. His suspicions were aroused, however, when yet another young doctor came to him to report that Bailly had cornered him and questioned him extensively concerning the number of his lady patients, the cost and source of the perfumed incense they used, the effect of music on sexual response. . . .

"What do you think about him?" Franz asked d'Eslon when they discussed these matters.

"He is a big man in his field, Franz. Surely he is not considering opening a hospital."

This had not occurred to Franz. "Then we have no course except that of awaiting developments," he said.

They did not have long to wait. Before the week was out, the evening *Gazette* printed the most slanderous assault that had yet been made upon Franz. Bailly accused him of practicing immorality mixed with medicine. He did not come out and call the Hôtel de l'Harmonie a house of assignation, but such was the inference in the whole bitter, conniving dénouement.

"Most of the patients are women and are not ill; many of them come out of idleness or to be amused; others, though not entirely healthy, have retained their freshness and vitality; they have the sensitivity of their youth. Their charms must affect the physicians; and undoubtedly this is a reciprocal affair, for the physicians are chosen for their virility and splendor."

Bally confessed himself shocked. Piously he threw his stones. "The magnetizer generally keeps the patients knees enclosed within his own. As a result, the knees and the lower part of the bodies are in close contact. The magnetizer touches the hypochondriacal region with his hand, and sometimes that of the ovarian, so that the touch is exerted at once on many of the most sensitive parts of the body. . . .

"The experimenter passes his right hand behind the woman's body and they bend to each other . . . their faces almost touch, their breaths intermingle, physical impressions are mutually felt, and the reciprocal attraction of the sexes must be greatly excited. It is not surprising that the senses are inflamed. . . ."

This whole indictment was so incredible that Franz's senses refused to accept it. He walked home in icy insensibility. He took the paper to Monique. "What do you think?" he asked after she read the offending article.

"Franz," she answered, "I think you had better be at your office early in the morning. All the ladies in Paris will be clamoring for a Bailly treatment." But her kiss was tender with understanding.

Bailly did not let the matter rest. The storm of protest which Franz's supporters unleashed only served to harden Bailly's desire to destroy him. He and a group of his cohorts kept after King Louis XVI until a Royal Commission was appointed. As Franz understood it in the beginning, the Commission was charged with the task of deciding whether or not there existed a universal fluidum—of determining whether or not there was such a thing as animal magnetism.

Franz was pleased. And as name after distinguished name was added to the Commission roster, he became hopeful. Surely such eminent scientists would give him an unbiased hearing. Bailly was on the Royal Commission, but so was Le Roy, who had tried to help Franz. There was Lavoisier, the chemist, and Doctor Guillotin, who had successfully pleaded for humane execution. There were three from the medical faculty, but there was also Jussieu, the celebrated botanist. The final list contained the name of Benjamin Franklin, ambassador from the New World.

"Surely," Franz said to Monique, "surely, now my work will be vindicated."

"There was a man named Vesalius," she said soberly.

Franz looked at her in surprise. "The Flemish anatomist?"

"Yes, Franz." She kissed him on the nose and smiled. "You

see, since my close association with one of the greats of medicine, I have developed an interest in other greats of medicine—dead ones, that is. . . ."

"No need to be jealous?" Franz pretended relief.

"Not unless being jealous would make you love me more," she answered.

"I couldn't," and he pulled her to him.

"I thought not," she said smugly, and then her lovely face sobered again. "Nor could I love you if you were less stubborn. That is why you must promise me."

"Promise you what? And where does Vesalius fit in here?"

"He was the first physician to dissect human cadavers. He proved that the descendants of Adam had no missing rib. He disproved the silly doctrine of the indestructible Bone of Luz from which the body would be resurrected when Gabriel blows his horn."

"He was denounced as a heretic. That was long ago, Monique. This is an age of reason."

"Do you remember who denounced him?"

"No," Franz answered slowly.

"It was not the church, Franz, not the religionists—but the men of his own profession. Then he recanted. Promise me, Franz, promise me that no matter what happens you will never recant."

Franz looked at her closely. Had she read his thoughts? What was this fear in her eyes? His arms tightened around her. "I promise . . ." he whispered against her mouth.

The first surprise the Commission gave Franz was their use of d'Eslon's hospital for investigation of magnetism. Franz could not understand why they had not chosen his place, or at least their joint establishment in the Place Vendôme. He was pleased that the King had ordered an investigation of his theories and not of him personally, but he did not wish to be separated so completely from the inquiry.

Franz considered the matter for several days; then he drove out to Passy, where Franklin made his home. He would make his protest to him.

Doctor Franklin received Franz with gracious hospitality and listened to his complaint. "I understand your feelings,"

Franklin said, "but I sympathize, too, with the attitude of several of the scientists of the Commission. Their belief is that the investigation will be more objective if testing is done apart from the founder of the system."

"Then you approve of their action?"

"The investigation is of the system, not of you, doctor."

Doctor Franklin gave Franz little satisfaction, but he could understand Franklin's position—especially when he pointed out that he would be unable to make the daily drive to Paris to attend the sessions of the Commission. The pressure of his work, plus his gout, would make such travel impossible, and inasmuch as he would not be an active member of the inquiry he could not direct procedures. But until he made the following statement, Franz was still hopeful of Doctor Franklin's support.

". . . There are in every great city a number of persons who are never in health because they are fond of medicines and always taking them, whereby they derange the natural functions and hurt their constitutions. If these people can be persuaded to forebear their drugs in expectation of being cured by only the physician's finger or an iron rod pointing at them, they may possibly find good effects though they mistake the cause."

D'Eslon kept Franz informed of the progress on the investigation. For the first few days, the members of the Commission simply sat in observation at d'Eslon's clinic. Then they came to him with a protest.

"There are too many people in here for treatment. Too much is happening at once and we cannot observe patients individually or as closely as we feel is necessary."

D'Eslon suggested a separate hour for observation, during which time he would limit the group treatment to ten patients. The observers accepted this new plan of action. Within a few days, however, they had another complaint.

"Your patients are prominent people who are not accustomed to being questioned. Some of them show distinct annoyance. Perhaps you might try animal magnetism on us."

D'Eslon agreed. He gave the scientists a number of treatments at the baquet, explaining in detail how to make use of the fluidum and what to expect from it.

"I feel nothing, nothing at all," complained the chairman.

"Have you been ill?" Jussieu, the botanist, asked him.

"I'm never ill," answered the chairman.

"Then why," asked Jussieu, "did you expect a cure from an illness you never had?"

Franz and d'Eslon laughed at the astuteness of Jussieu.

Before long the Commission informed d'Eslon that further experimental work would be carried out at a more suitable location. "We know enough about this system," said one doctor, "to work now on our own."

"I can't say that I miss them," commented d'Eslon to Franz.

Monique brought Franz the next news of the work of the investigators. They were in Passy, conducting experiments in the presence of Doctor Franklin. They were using, they said, ". . . really diseased persons. We chose them from the lower classes."

Franz waited.

It was August 11, 1784, when the Commission made its formal report. This report was issued in the name of the King and of the Academy of Sciences.

". . . The Commissioners have found that magnetic fluid is not perceptible to any of the senses; that this fluid had no action, either on the Commissioners or on the patients subjected to it. The Commissioners are convinced that pressure and contact effect changes which harm the imagination. Finally, they have demonstrated by decisive experiments that imagination, apart from magnetism, produces convulsions, and that magnetism without imagination produces nothing. They have come to the following unanimous conclusions about the existence and utility of animal magnetism: that there is nothing to prove the existence of the magnetic fluid; that this fluid, since it is non-existent, can have no salubrious influence; that the violent effects observed in patients during public treatment are due to contact, to the excitement of their imagination, and to a mechanical imitation which involuntarily impels us to repeat that which strikes our senses. At the same time, the Commissioners feel compelled to add, since this is an important observation, that the contact and the repeated excitement of the imagination which produces the crises may become harmful; that the sight of these crises is also dangerous because of the imitative faculty which is a law of nature; and consequently that all public magnetic treatments must, in the end, produce harmful results."

There was more, much more. The report suggested: ". . . the convulsions might become habitual and even be transmitted to future generations . . . such practices and assemblies might also have a disastrous effect upon public morality. . . ."

Franz was shocked at the hostility of the report and sick at heart over its departure from the true spirit of scientific investigation.

"Franz," said d'Eslon, "Doctor Jussieu did not sign this report."

Franz looked again at the signatures—Franklin, Bailly, Guillotin, Lavoisier, Le Roy, and the three physicians—but not Jussieu.

It was several days before they knew that Jussieu had refused to sign it. In bold, clear words he disagreed with the other Commissioners and published his own report.

". . . They have failed to make use of the positive results of magnetism . . . not investigated thoroughly . . . and I for one regret this negligence . . . because I am convinced that an insight into the force behind animal magnetism would be infinitely illuminating. . . . The human body is subject to influences, like imagination, which must be from within or due to moral causes . . . others, such as rubbing or touch, must be external and physical."

Since it was d'Eslon's hospital which was the subject of the report, he made public response to the attack:

"I think I can lay it down as a fact that the imagination has the greatest share in the effects of animal magnetism. The new agent might be indeed no other than the imagination itself, whose power is as extensive as it is little known."

"If Doctor Franz Anton Mesmer had no other secret than that he has been able to make the imagination exert an influence upon health, would he not still be a wonder doctor? If treatment by the use of the imagination is the best treatment, why do we not make use of it?"

Franz read d'Eslon's report with tears in his eyes. For some weeks they had been in disagreement on basic theory, d'Eslon moving slowly but surely toward the spiritist view of animal magnetism. In this report he had expressed his new convictions concerning imagination—yet his unswerving loyalty to Franz took away all of the vexation Franz had felt. Theirs was an honest and open difference of opinion. It would not affect their friendship. Franz's tears stemmed partly from personal relief and partly from appreciation of the courage and integrity of his colleague. How regrettable that all scientists did not possess these traits.

The medical faculty of the University had declared an ultimatum: anyone practicing animal magnetism would be excluded from the faculty and dismissed from the Academy.

D'Eslon and Franz called a meeting of their staff. Franz read the ultimatum and affirmed his belief in the system. "We leave you to your decision," Franz said as d'Eslon and he withdrew to permit freedom of discussion.

One physician cast his lot with them. The other twenty defected.

In the provinces, Doctor Jean Louis Vernier and Doctor Jean Baptiste Bonnefoy continued to support magnetic healing. Both were openly and severely rebuked by the University. Doctor Bonnefoy was of the Lyons College of Surgeons and he fought back, challenging the academicians with these pertinent remarks:

"How are we to deal with nervous disorders, with diseases of which we are totally ignorant? Hot or cold baths are prescribed; stimulating or refreshing or exciting or calming methods are tried; and none of these poor palliatives has produced anything approaching such marvelous results as the psychotherapeutic methods adopted by Mesmer." Franz read this statement with humble gratitude.

He found writings by another author accusing the Academy of having shirked the real problem. ". . . It does not suffice, gentlemen, that your minds should rise superior to the prejudices of the century. In addition you should be willing to sacrifice the interests of your order for the sake of the common weal."

Bergasse, the clever lawyer friend of animal magnetism, wrote: "Monsieur Mesmer has constructed a great system upon the groundwork of his discoveries. This system may prove to be as untenable as many that have preceded it, for there is always a certain amount of danger in trying to reach back to first principles. But if, apart from this system, he has been able to clarify certain ideas—if but a single truth of importance to man owes its elucidation to Mesmer—then he has a right to our respect. Thus a future generation wil do him honor, and no commission or government will be able to deprive him of his deserts."

On every side of Franz the conflict raged. Time was when an edict published under the seal of the reigning monarch would have put an end to public controversy, but now revolution was in the air of France. Franz knew the people were beginning their struggle against institutionalism, and Franz and his theories were convenient weapons against the conservative elements of French society.

Not that his supporters were all revolutionaries. On the contrary, the Société de l'Harmonie members were intelligent. astute, God-fearing men, and most of them were of the aristocracy. They issued an excellent pamphlet in defense of animal magnetism. This did little, however, to quiet the furor.

Franz was challenged by the press for a statement. He made it brief. "I venture to flatter myself that the discovery I have made lies beyond our present knowledge of physics, just as the microscope and the telescope once lay beyond it."

His medical practice did not suffer. He and d'Eslon were as busy as ever, and the crowds in front of their hospitals were just as great. Monique and Franz were still invited to more social affairs than they could possibly attend. Their private life remained inviolate and infinitely precious to Franz—but something that had sustained him was gone.

The drive within him which had forced his struggle for scientific recognition—that drive had disappeared. The scientists themselves had killed it. "I can no longer value, nor can I long for, fellowship with men who presume to judge me so harshly and without proper investigation," he told Monique.

Franz realized he was not unhappy; he was busy with his work. Too, he had his circle of friends who were loyal and true. And he had Monique. He lived each day with no thought of the day which would follow and no regret for the day which was past.

It was, therefore, with a sense of unreality that he read the name of Fraulein Marie Theresa von Paradis on the theatre billboard. "How long ago was Vienna?" Franz wondered as he stood and looked at the board. He could still hear Theresa's music—but he could barely recall her face. "So she is to give a concert in Paris. We'll go," he decided on a sudden impulse.

He went to the theatre office and procured tickets. That evening he dropped them in Monique's lap.

"Have you seen the *Gazette*, Franz?" she asked.

"No."

"Then listen," and she read from the paper. "Fraulein von Paradis, the blind concert pianist, was another unsuccessful case of Mesmer's. He was evicted from Vienna when he claimed fraudulently that he had cured this young lady with animal magnetism."

Franz took the paper. There was more to the story and it was all vitrolic. They did not attend the concert. Franz made no attempt to see Theresa.

Count Gebelin was another of Franz's patients who was used against him. They had been friends of long standing and Franz had treated him for many years, not only with animal magnetism but also with such chemical compounds as were recognized treatment for the kidney ailment with which he suffered.

The Count had played the musical glasses himself, and had seemed to enjoy hearing Franz perform on them. Franz had been fond of the Count and felt a great sense of loss at his death. His sorrow knew no bounds when he was accused of neglecting him and actually hastening his end. He knew of no answer to such an accusation.

Where once he had been adored, he was now frequently scorned. Where once he had received respect, he now became the occasional object of jibes and jokes. Yet through it all, the voices of a few were loud in praise.

Father Girard, an army chaplain, wrote of the cures he had performed using animal magnetism, "the honor of which goes to Doctor Mesmer," he said.

Nevertheless, Franz felt caught in the middle, as if he were being torn apart painlessly—for neither the criticism nor the praise touched him. He could still cry for others, but not for himself.

He wrote Haydn:

My Beloved Friend:

It would be good to sit quietly and visit with you. Music-wise, I know your every move, but only Wolfgang writes me of your personal life—and this but seldom. He is grateful for your help and encouragement.

In many ways my life is blessed, but even as you have seen beauty through tears—so I now have reasons to weep, yet I do not.

I am not the first man to be so convinced of the truth of my vision that I am willing to give myself utterly to this Truth. Whether I personally ever gather recognition of my theories or die a reject of society is a matter of vast indifference.

Nevertheless, Paris evenings are still touched with their own special magic. Should you come here, you would find new melodies praying to be written.

Affectionately your servant,
Franz Mesmer

CHAPTER XXVI

FRANZ KNEW his friend Count Puységur and his brother, the Marquis Puységur, had returned to the family estate at Buzancy. Both men were now free of army duties, and they were spending much of their time in the pursuit of new knowledge of animal magnetism.

In the beginning, the brothers were interested only in curing the many peasants who so desperately needed help, but the Puységurs kept records of their cases. They had shown them to Franz. The recorded cures grew, and slowly the men were drawn into a more serious investigation of the miracles which were occurring daily on their own estate.

In the heat of the controversy over the report of the Commission, Franz was not surprised that the Puységur brothers had published a pamphlet on somnambulism which could be produced by animal magnetism. They had written this pamphlet in support of Franz's cause; yet he was not at all sure that such information would help. "Even in Vienna I observed phenomena such as they describe here." Franz had the pamphlet open on his desk. "I called it magnetic sleepwalking," Franz told d'Eslon and handed him the pamphlet. "I never thought it had anything to do with cures, so I avoided mentioning it. Too, public knowledge of this condition might occasion even more misunderstanding of magnetism itself." D'Eslon nodded his head as he scanned the pamphlet. "Naturally, they are seeking to help," Franz added.

He decided to drive to Soissons to visit the Puységurs, and he invited Lafayette to accompany him. It was a pleasant trip and both brothers were on hand to greet them when they arrived.

"I know why you have come," said the Count, "but we will dine before we talk of work."

"We have much to tell you," said the Marquis as they made their way to the manor house through the pack of fine hunting dogs that milled about their feet and bayed a welcome.

It was a hearty meal, served with vintage Puységur wines. The men lingered over the table with talk of crops and hunting and local social conditions. There was no mention of animal magnetism until the brothers led the way into a small study at the rear of the house.

"Our people would not feel at ease in the other rooms," explained the Count. "We work with them here or out in the open under the trees."

Except for the shelves of records, a table, and several old chairs, the study was bare. The Marquis leaned back in his chair.

"Our people are extremely superstitious. They fear evil spirits. We have circumvented their fear of magnetism by practicing it only in broad daylight. Evil spirits do not wander about in the light of day, you know," he explained with a humorous smile.

"I am comforted by this bit of knowledge," smiled Lafayette.

"In the center of our village green," continued Count Puységur, "there is an old elm tree. It is hallowed by age and by use. For generations the elders of the village have gathered around it to discuss crops; the young people have courted under its sheltering arms; and the lonely have sought the solace of its shadow."

"We magnetized this tree," the Marquis Puységur broke in.

Franz listened without speaking. He had no words to express his bewilderment, and he didn't want to hurt his friends.

The brothers talked together as they warmed to their subjects. They began pulling out records of the amazing cures which had occurred under the old tree. They described how they had built benches in a circle about the base of the tree and tied strings to the branches to carry the flow into the patients who waited below.

"Your patients reach the crisis easily?" Franz asked. He was all interest now.

"Some easily; with others it takes longer. But wait, you have not heard the exciting part."

"One day," broke in the other brother, "Victor Race, a peasant lad of twenty-three summers, came to the tree and asked for treatment. He told me that his difficulty was with his breathing and that after a hard spell he sometimes spit blood. I tied one of the strings from the tree about the lad's chest."

"Immediately he said he felt the flow. . . ."

"But he did not have a convulsion. . . ."

"He went to sleep with his eyes open."

"Yet it was not a true sleep, for he spoke and moved in accordance with my brother's directions—and he heard nothing but my brother's voice."

"Others tried to talk to Victor?" Franz questioned, his medical interests aroused.

"Oh, yes," answered the Marquis, "I tried and some of the lad's young friends tried. He heard only my brother's voice, none other."

"How long did he sleep thus?" Franz asked, leaning forward in his eagerness.

"Until," said the Count, "I untied the cord, told him to walk to the tree trunk, to touch it, and awaken feeling cured."

"He did just that?"

"He obeyed my brother to the letter," said the Marquis, looking at the Count with admiration.

"But was he cured?" Franz had to satisfy himself.

"It took three such treatments. Meantime, however, the rest of our people began asking us to put them to sleep and make them well. We obliged, and now they all ask for sleep. They like it better than convulsions—and they hear nothing but the magnetizer's voice. Nor do they feel anything. We have tested them with the needles and hot pokers."

"And they are cured?" Franz asked again.

"Most of them are cured. Even the hopeless cases find surcease from pain."

"What do you think?" asked Count Puységur.

Franz smiled. This was Puységur's classic question. Franz recalled that even in Paris, when Puységur was directing affairs of the Société de l'Harmonie, he proceeded according to his own ideas, accomplished his objective, and, after the matter was done, asked, "What do you think?"

"I think," Franz answered him, "that the ebb and flow of the fluidum is very powerful under your hallowed old elm tree. But there is another matter of which you have not spoken."

The brothers Puységur looked at one another and then at Franz. "You have heard?" they asked together.

Franz nodded.

"It was Victor who started this, too," said the Marquis. "Perhaps my brother should tell you."

"I cannot remember, Doctor Mesmer, just how it started. Surely it was by accident—yet we have tested and affirmed the phenomenon repeatedly. When Victor is in this state of somnambulism, he is able to diagnose the ills of anyone present. The lad walks over to the other patients and points his finger at the afflicted parts of their bodies. Sometimes he speaks and describes the inner condition. Sometimes he merely points."

"And since Victor first exhibited this talent," added the Marquis, "two more of our patients have developed the same ability."

It was as Franz feared. Laymen were now in possession of yet another facet of the power of animal magnetism. Certainly the Puységurs were well intentioned in their zeal, and certainly one should try to ascertain what truth somnambulistic phenomena might teach; yet Franz was apprehensive at the prospect of this knowledge falling into the hands of charlatans.

He warned the Puységur brothers, but it was with a heavy heart that he started homeward with Lafayette two days later. Lafayette questioned Franz closely. Finally Franz admitted to him that he had a patient in Paris who exhibited unexplainable behavior after treatment with animal magnetism.

"This woman always falls into a cramp-like sleep in which she is able to talk and to write," Franz confessed.

"Please tell me," Lafayette begged.

"She lives alone in a small apartment, with a tiny dog on which she lavishes a heart full of love. One day the little dog disappeared and the mistress was inconsolable. She cried so hard and so pitifully that her maid came to fetch me."

"Yes, yes. Go on."

"I gave the grief-stricken woman a treatment and she fell into her usual sleep. It was hours later that she awakened and discovered that she had written herself a note. It said, 'Calm yourself, you will find your dog in eight days.'"

"And did she?" asked Lafayette.

"She sent the note to me along with a letter of explanation. Of course, I was curious. I called at her apartment again on the eighth day."

"And—" Lafayette prompted.

"Even as I greeted her, she dropped again into her magnetic sleep. As one talking in a dream, she addressed her maid. 'Fetch the gendarme on the corner.' The maid ran to do her bidding."

"The gendarme came and my patient addressed him. 'Go to the rue Saint Sauveur.' This street was about a fifteen-minute walk from the apartment of my patient. 'There you will meet a woman carrying my dog. Take my little dog from that woman and bring him home to me.'" Franz paused, then continued.

"The gendarme obeyed. Within thirty minutes he returned with the dog. In my presence the furry little animal cried and barked his greeting to my overjoyed patient."

"But what do you make of it?" demanded Lafayette.

"My friend," Franz said, "one should realize that from childhood onwards it is necessary to guard against those pests—superstition and fanaticism. One should study the strange faculties of human beings very closely, and one should realize that man's nervous system causes him to be constantly in tune with the ebb and flow of nature—but should one ever jump to conclusions?"

CHAPTER XXVII

IN SPITE of Franz's concern at the spiritist or animist turn which the Puységur investigation was taking, the trip was good for him. Lafayette and Franz had enjoyed a rapport from their first meeting, but on this trip they established a closeness that would endure forever. Franz felt that Lafayette sensed without his saying so that his fight for medical recognition was over. Lafayette only made this comment: "We do what we must do; history writes the verdict . . . right or wrong."

Lafayette dropped Franz at the Hôtel de l'Harmonie, where he retired to his office. Karl had stacked newspapers, notes and letters, and on top of the letters was one from Franzl. It had been several years since Franz had heard from anyone at Landstrasse, except by word of mouth. "No doubt they feel as far removed from me as I do from them." He was almost startled at this reminder of his former life. He opened the letter and read:

BELOVED FRIEND:

It grieves me to write you this sad message, but I hope you have been prepared for it in some measure by my dear husband's letter last week.

Yes, Marie Anna died shortly after Junge wrote you, and we buried her yesterday. The services were as she would have wished. Beautiful and solemn. We used the Limoges ornaments you sent her on her shroud. She looked lovely, as though she were asleep.

We will continue to look in here at #261 Landstrasse until you return. And the servants will keep things in perfect order as Marie Anna taught them.

Hoping you are in the best of health, I am your devoted daughter-in-law. . . .

Franzl von Bosch

Marie Anna dead. Franz couldn't believe it. Marie Anna didn't belong to death or to heaven; she was too well situated on earth. Franz sat with the letter in his hand, trying to feel something—remorse, pain, grief—but nothing came. No flood of remembered joy in their companionship . . . there had been no companionship to recall. He returned to the letter and reread it. The letter from Marie Anna's son. . . . ? Where was it? He rustled through the neat stack of letters, but there was nothing else from Vienna. He stood up and walked about the room; Marie Anna dead! "I can't register the thought; it's all outside of me; nothing enters my heart; nothing stirs my emotions." With a feeling of guilt, he realized he had no tears.

Franz didn't know what impulse prompted him to ring for Karl and ask him to go to Monique and give her his regrets for the evening. As Karl started from the room, Franz called him back and told him of Frau Mesmer's death. His reply startled Franz, "Now you will be free to marry Madame Montarre."

So it mattered to Karl. Outwardly Karl had accepted Monique's and Franz's alliance, but evidently he had worried. "Dear Karl—but perhaps I, too, have wished for legal acceptance of our status. Now it might be arranged."

Karl was at the door when he turned to ask, "Will you arrange for masses to be said for the repose of her soul?" Franz nodded.

In the months to come, d'Eslon and Franz worked as hard as ever. They conferred often and held their regular staff meetings. New pupils sought them, and they accepted those whose education and intentions qualified them for training. Never for one moment did their belief in animal magnetism waver. They were in touch with medical men in other parts of the world. Their reports were gratifying. The Puységur brothers called frequently. They kept accurate accounts of their patients and in their enthusiasm won many converts to the cause. Their friendship sustained Franz in these trying times, and he worked hard to keep the brothers in line with the "fluidist" school of thought.

Gluck had been ailing for some months. He was twenty years older than Franz; and though his youthful mind and love of beauty made him seem younger than his years, his body was failing. Franz recognized it reluctantly. When they at last talked as patient and physician, Gluck recounted to Franz the fear he had of losing the use of his hands. "I feel it coming; there is a numbness here," he touched his fingers together, "and at times I have great difficulty walking."

He was right; there was all the evidence of body degeneration. Franz sat back, trying to find the words to tell him, but Gluck, ever sensitive declared, "If it is to be, I'd rather be in Vienna. There my roots are. . . ." Franz nodded. They, who had always spoken so freely, now found words unnecessary.

Franz knew that Marie Antoinette loved Gluck with great tenderness. He thought her farewell party for Gluck was one of the most lavish banquets of all time. She presented him with gifts, and in her farewell speech she told charming little stories of Vienna when Gluck had been her childhood music master. "Here in Paris he has been my friend and confidant; and since the death of the Empress, he has represented a part of home, my childhood home which I am losing again in losing him." Gluck kissed her hand and Franz felt his throat ache.

When Marie Anna had been dead for a year, Franz asked Monique to go to church with him. She was in her small courtyard, sitting flat on the ground with her gardening paraphernalia gathered about her. "I am potting these bulbs," she greeted him and bade him sit on the steps near by. When he asked her about going to church, she looked up, a tiny frown between her eyes. "Why, of course, Franz, anything wrong?"

"No, dear Monique, but we could talk to a priest."

"But, why Franz . . . I talk to priests all the time . . . at parties."

"Monique, Marie Anna's death has left me free to marry again; I want to discuss an annulment for you; then. . . ."

Monique resumed her work. At last she looked at Franz again. "You haven't been happy with our arrangement?" she asked.

"Oh, darling, yes. But to have you my wife. . . ."

"Franz, the contract we made—it has been a marriage to me."

"I know," Franz said. "I do know," he insisted, "but Monique, think, dear one; we could live together openly— one home, one name. People would know that you belonged to me—and I to you."

"Is that important, Franz—that people know?"

"Yes," Franz answered slowly, "I believe it is. That and the blessing of the church. . . ."

"I am a freethinker." Her soft voice was stubborn.

Franz could find no answer. He waited. Monique finished filling all her little pots. She stood them in a row in front of her. She gathered her tools into a basket. She examined her soiled hands. Then she turned back to her row of little pots and spoke to them, "My dears, our friend, the good doctor, wishes us to marry him. Shall we?"

She laughed, and half rising she flung herself against Franz. Slipping her arms around his waist she said, "Franz, do you want me to clean up a bit or shall we go right now?"

The plea for annulment was entered. Monique started class instruction. Their relationship had always been a wonderful thing for Franz, but now it took on a tenderness and depth which was almost religious in nature.

Count Puységur visited the hotel with a new report. Franz and d'Eslon listened with interest as he told them of the work being done by Doctor Ostertag in Strassburg.

"The Doctor is primarily interested in somnambulism, and he uses something new in his inducement." Puységur paused to enjoy their attention.

"Yes, yes, go on," d'Eslon exclaimed.

"He uses a small glass ball. He has the patient stare at it, telling him to keep looking until he feels a sense of nothingness, of quietness, until all he can hear is the doctor's voice. The patient goes into a trance-like state, just like that produced by animal magnetism. It's hard to believe. What do you think?" Always Puységur's classic question, "What do you think?"

Franz had no precise answer to the question. There was no doubt in his mind that the fluidum was reflected like light from a mirror. The same phenomena could conceivably occur with a glass ball. If Dr. Ostertag himself were strongly magnetized or imbued with the flow—"Nevertheless," Franz said, "I should feel easier about the matter if the doctors who use animal magnetism would confine themselves to investigating new ways to cure with it—rather than inventing new ways to magnetize."

Animal magnetism, as Franz had discovered it and tried to establish it, was taking many new turns and twists throughout the world. He was powerless before the spread and degeneration of Mesmerism into cults.

The conflicting philosophies grew and adopted new titles. Franz and his followers were referred to as the "Fluidists," but gradually their system lost ground to the bizarre and occult practices of the other "schools." Reports were being made all over the continent, and now as often as not Franz's name was omitted.

The annulment had not come through. Franz had been assured that it would, but there was the understandable delay of papers from the New World, the tortoise-like pace of church investigation in its never-ending protocol—and the pressure of the government on the church was well under way.

Paris was changing; there was a tenseness, a sense of waiting. A deluge of sharp-witted journalism stirred the populace. Criticism of the court was heard on all sides, and Franz, from the vantage point of a physician to rich and poor alike, saw much to deplore and little to commend in all the factions. There were small uprisings which were promptly cut down. Streetcorner politics seemed to deepen in meaning and vehemence. The bourgeoisie from the countrysides were voicing their complaints; they spoke in bitterness of the old feudal law still in effect, the *corvée*. "I know what they mean. I treat peasants whose years are young; yet fifteen hours of hard labor each day of their lives has robbed them of their God-given right to age with nature," Franz told Monique. Then there was the salt tax, the *gabelle*. This was a very sore spot. Franz tried to remain free from politics, but it was like standing by a waterfall and hoping one would not get wet.

Franz received a message that Christoph Gluck had died of paralysis on November 15, 1787. He had died in his beloved Vienna. Franz and Monique wept together. Leopold Mozart also died in 1787. "Two of my dearest companions gone," Franz thought. However, the pressure of work gave him little time to mourn. Apparently Wolfgang, too, was working off his grief. Franz did not hear from him until some months after his father's death. Finally Wolfgang wrote:

My Dearest, Best and Truest Friend:
I am at present working on an opera, Cosi fan Tutti. When it is finished it will be produced for Emperor Joseph II, who com-

missioned it. I am dedicating the opera to you with a heart full of love for the priceless gift you gave a small frightened lad so many years ago. Perhaps you will enjoy the following lines from the libretto—"This magnetic stone should give the traveler pause. Once it was used by Mesmer, who was born in Germany's green fields and who won great fame in France."

I am tired, too tired to live at times, but the music plays constantly in my mind and in feverish haste I write it down. Beauty should not be stilled because the body is tired.

I wish you could see my little ones; they are charming. Tell Monique I can father a child with much less effort than fathering a concerto and the child is every bit as noisy!

Wolfgang

The annulment was granted at last. In gratitude and joy, Monique and Franz knelt to pray in the quiet church. Franz never knew why he opened his eyes and looked at her. The curve of her cheek, the sweep of her black hair, the beads in her hand . . . how unforgettable the picture she made. In his joy he suddenly felt an anguish. He almost cried out in pain—for what, he knew not, unless it was the pain of loving so much. Monique opened her eyes and turned to him. Briefly their eyes held, and then she returned to her prayers.

The day was hot. As they came from the cool interior of the church, the heat assaulted them. It was July 14, 1789. In addition to the heat, there was an oppressive quiet in the streets of Paris. Clumps of people were gathered on the corners; others stood in the doorways of the shops, but no one spoke. No carriages were about.

They walked to Monique's little cabriolet. Franz helped her in and kissed her hand. She leaned to him and smiled, "Dear Franz, I love you."

Her little vehicle rolled away and Franz stood gazing after it. As it reached the corner, he noted that the people gathered there were all carrying bricks or stones or stout clubs in their hands. He glanced at the clusters of men in the doorways. They were similarly armed. Their ominous silence was suddenly fraught with meaning for him.

Monique must have sensed his fear—or else she became

aware of the danger at the same moment—for she whirled her horses in the middle of the street and turned the little cabriolet back in his direction.

At that instant the church bell began to clang. Immediately its clamoring was taken up by all the bells in Paris. Their wild, harsh cry was swelled by a din of human screaming. From every side came the shout, "Liberty! Equality! Fraternity!"

The clusters of people were transformed into mobs—unruly, vicious mobs, intent upon destruction. Stones flew through the air, windows shattered, and in the midst of the milling crowd Franz saw Monique's horses rear up, plunge forward, and break into a run.

He dashed out to catch the frightened beasts, but at that moment a group of mobsters rushed into the street waving flags and beating drums.

Avoiding the flags, the frenzied horses swerved and dragged the little cabriolet across a vacant lot and into a pile of bricks and lumber. The light carriage swayed; then it overturned.

Franz saw Monique hurtled into the air. For only a moment she seemed suspended there—and then she dropped to the bricks below.

Franz rushed to her—but even as he knelt by her poor little twisted body, he knew. He lifted her. Waves of horror swept over him, and his mind kept screaming, "No—no—"

A ragged little urchin stood beside him. His eyes were big in his pinched face. Among all the people that gathered on the scene, this child's white face was the only one Franz saw. "Doctor Mesmer," he said—and Franz heard his words repeated as the crowd parted to make a corridor for him. He moved on, carrying her to his hospital.

The bells continued to ring out and he could hear screams and shouts from all sections. He could hear it all, even inside the hospital; yet he was too numb with pain to care. He placed his precious one on the emergency table—but there was no emergency, he reasoned. He straightened her dress; he bathed her face with a pad dipped in an astringent; he removed a torn shoe; her little foot was broken. He covered her with a sheet as though she were asleep; then he sat down beside her in a stupor. He tried to reason, to think. . . . He found himself doing little things for her. He smoothed a bit of lace on her jabot. He placed her hands in a more comfortable position. Her hands were getting cold; he found a blanket . . . but no. . . .

Karl came in. He didn't speak. Sometime later he took Franz to his apartment. Franz didn't sleep; he didn't think. Later he went to Monique's home. The servants were red-eyed from weeping. He felt that he should speak to them, but no words came. He went into her boudoir; he touched her toilet articles; he lifted a bottle of her scent; "she was so sweet." He opened her cupboard. Her lovely frocks. . . .

Karl made all the necessary arrangements for the funeral.

"We have been so discreet. No one comes to me to embrace me, to speak words of condolence to my broken heart. Oh, no, no one speaks except as friends who have lost a friend. 'Dear Monique, we shall miss her.' 'Precious Monique, always so lovely.' Oh God, oh God!" Franz cried in bitterness to the night.

In the days that followed, Franz, who had never known pain, knew it now. He who had wept with emotion over a beautiful sonata, who had cried at the misfortunes of his friends, could find no tears to ease the torment of his body. Karl filled his days with patients and there were many wounded among them, for the zeal of the revolution was in every Parisian heart. The new song "Ca ira" was on every lip. Franz was caught in a nightmare of living. He moved as an automaton. He spent the nights at Monique's. He lay on her bed. He couldn't pray. He couldn't weep. He slept but little.

The days stretched out, banded in mourning. They held no peace for Franz. Nor for Paris, for the new regime was here. All over France violence had broken out. Chateaus were burned, property destroyed, people killed; Lafayette was commander of the Parisian National Guard and as such was probably the most powerful man in France—yet even he could not restore madmen to sanity.

Many of Franz's friends were fleeing Paris. He, as a doctor, stayed on, helping as best he could. His hospital in the rue Montmartre was ransacked and burned. At last he knew—he, too, must flee, for he was classed with the aristocracy. He went to Monique's home for the last time. Karl was to pick him up there. He had already loaded a lorry with a few of their treasures and sent them out in the night to Austria.

Franz didn't know what disposition to make of Monique's things. "I have no legal right to do anything, anyway." He walked through her home for the last time. The gay little garden she loved so well . . . her herbs in their allotted space spoke eloquently of her.

"Should I take a few souvenirs for remembrance?" In her boudoir he selected a fan, a lacy affair. He opened it and recalled her eyes smiling. Next a glove that had shaped to her hand. Then the miniature by Saint Germain. He looked long at the face. "Do I need a souvenir to remember her? Remembering Monique will be as automatic as my heartbeat and will last as long." Gently, he returned the fan to the desk, the glove to the drawer, and the miniature to the table. He stood for one last moment of farewell and walked away.

CHAPTER XXVIII

SIGNS OF the advancing revolution were everywhere. As Franz and Karl drove along, they noted the change in clothing of the people they passed. The vogue of the "bonnet rouge," symbolizing the new era, was much in evidence, as were the long, flopping pantaloons affected by the Revolutionists. Robespierre, the apostle premier of Rousseau, was rising to power. In this, the Year of our Lord 1792, violence befitting the darkest ages was rampant in France. Franz was glad when they crossed onto German soil. The France he knew and loved was writhing on her deathbed. He sought escape from her cries of pain.

They put in at an inn. Franz and Karl went to refresh themselves with a draught of ale. As they sipped their drink, a group of traveling musicians came in. Among them was a violinist Franz had known in Vienna, Karl Phillip Mayerbeer. It had been years since Franz had seen him. They embraced and Franz invited him to join them and plied him with questions of Vienna—the gossip of the theatres, the opera, the musicians. Franz admitted that he hoped to visit Salzburg and Vienna, too. "I must see my beloved Wolfgang Mozart." Karl Phillip's face saddened.

"Then you don't know?"

"Know?" Sudden fear touched Franz's heart.

Karl Phillip placed his hand on Franz's arm. "Wolfgang died in December. I'm sorry, my friend, that I say it so abruptly."

Franz and Karl sat mute with shock.

"We didn't know," Franz finally said. "But, of course, the revolution. . . ." To his ever-present suffering in the loss of Monique was added this new grief. Wolfgang had been a joy to him always. "He was like a son."

Karl tapped his chest and through glistening eyes said, "That lad had joy here in his heart. He was a merry lad, a noisy one, 'tis true, and not always respectful to his elders but . . ." and Karl's dear old face brightened, "but he made his elders feel as young as he."

"He has joined the immortals," Karl Phillip consoled. Then he asked, "Since you do not know of his death, you possibly do not know of the story of his Requiem Mass."

They ordered another ale and Karl Phillip told the story: "One day a man dressed all in gray knocked on Wolfgang's door. When Wolfgang admitted him, the man in gray commissioned Wolfgang to write a requiem mass. Wolfgang told him he was very busy working on an opera but that he would do it as soon as he was free. The man made a payment on the commission and left, telling Wolfgang to write it as he had time. Wolfgang called to him, 'What is your name and where do you live?'

"The man answered, 'I shall return when the Requiem is ready . . . you must never ask my name.'

"The man came back some months later, but Wolfgang had not written the work. Again the man in gray refused to give his name, only telling Wolfgang to write at his leisure.

"Wolfgang told Constanze, his wife, that he thought the man was a messenger of death and that the Mass would be for its composer. This idea took shape and filled Wolfgang's every waking thought. He talked to several of us about it. He finished his Magic Flute; that was the opera he was working on.

"The Magic Flute is sublime. To hear it is a religious experience. In the last act the prince meets the tests of life to rescue his beloved. He goes through the roaring fire and fierce torrents of waters." Karl Phillip stopped to imitate a violin. He lifted his imaginary bow and hummed the music. "At last the Prince comes to the Temple of Light. There he is united with his beautiful princess."

"Highly symbolic!" Franz said, for he recognized Wolfgang's beloved Masonry. "But do finish the Requiem story," he reminded.

"He began on the Mass. He finished the Requiem and Kyrie movements. I saw them. I also saw a few passages of the Lacrimosa; he had most of the Mass in outline. You know how he worked?"

"How well I know," Franz nodded. "I can see him now." Franz's throat tightened and he felt tears smart his eyes.

"I hope Constanze will be able to assemble the Mass. There

is great writing in it. The Dies Irae is chilling in its telling. Wolfgang shows a horror of death in this movement, and in passionate agony he cries out against the inevitable."

Karl and Franz were already moved beyond talking, but Karl Phillip added one last heartbreaking touch. "He died December fifth. Constanze was too ill to leave the house, so he was dressed in his black shroud and his bier was placed in his study almost touching his piano. Constanze never left him until we took him to St. Stephen's. You won't believe how poor they were. Constanze had no money, and of course we had none. We arranged for a third-class internment. Constanze was too ill to go to the church; the doctor forbade it. Only a few of us were there. The weather was the worst I've ever seen in Vienna—snow, wind." He shuddered. "We tried to follow the bier to its final resting place, but the storm was so great we finally gave up." They sat in silence for some time, then Karl Phillip added, "Would to God I had followed, for three weeks later no one could show us his grave."

"You mean you don't know where he is buried?" Franz asked, aghast.

"No one knows, no one at all."

The despair of it all kept them silent; then Karl Phillip said, "The saddest thing anyone ever said to me were the words Wolfgang spoke at rehearsal a few months before he died. 'I feel a kind of emptiness, which hurts me dreadfully . . . a kind of longing, never satisfied, never ceasing!'"

"Oh, Wolfgang, Wolfgang," Franz's heart cried out within him, "Wolfgang, my brother—my child."

They supped with Karl Phillip and his fellow musicians, and then Karl and Franz found their way to their separate rooms. Never had Franz felt so worn. The big feather bed was inviting. There was also a grate fire to keep him warm. He put out the light and stretched out on the bed. He was tired and he hurt all over. Until now he had protected his thoughts from Wolfgang's death, but now they swept over him and increased the ache in his very bones.

"Wolfgangrl, my merry lad who never walked if he could dance; where is he now?" In his memory Franz could see Wolfgang at the piano. His hands were lithe and confident. The thin, white fingers moved across the keys, at times stroking them as a lover; one felt the tenderness. Then there would be a jest, and laughter would sparkle his melody. But the times his hands touched the keys in prayer, when he caressed the notes to cry out in supplication—these were the times he showed his greatest artistry.

Franz turned his pillow. He felt as if it would suffocate him. He got up and walked to the window. The ceiling slanted downward. He knelt to keep from striking his head. He pulled back the curtains and opened the window. The cold, moist air rushed in.

Franz knelt there in the dark, looking out into the brightness of the stars. How long had it been since he had seen them? He had laid aside his rosary after Monique's funeral. Why? He had to know. He was a stranger to himself. Where could he find Franz Mesmer again? Somewhere there was a place of reckoning . . . an examining room for his soul.

It was then he knew. Long ago Karl had driven him to Ignanz to visit Papa and Mama. They had stopped by a monastery for a brief rest and to care for their horses.

Franz shut the window and found his way to the bed. The feathers closed around his chilled body. Before he had finished planning, he was asleep.

Karl was at breakfast when Franz went down the next morning. Karl greeted him, "Your musician friends asked me to bid you adieu for them. They left but a short time ago."

Franz sat down with him. "Karl, do you remember the monastery we visited many years ago, the one near Ignanz?"

Karl frowned, chewing his food slowly. Then he asked, "The one with that view of the mountain peak? I remember that one. Why do you ask, sir?"

"Karl, I'm going there."

Karl looked at him. He placed his fork back on his plate. He seemed to be searching for appropriate words. At last he asked gruffly, "Will you become a monk?"

Franz had to smile, but he answered seriously. "No, not just yet anyway, but I need a time for contemplation . . . so much has happened, so much has been lost. . . ."

"I understand, sir," Karl's voice was comforting. "What do you wish me to do?" he asked.

"If you will take our carriage and go on to Vienna. Stay

at 261 Landstrasse. The servants are there. I will come when I have found some plan for my life."

"But, sir, why don't I take you? Then I could go on. The stagecoaches are uncomfortable."

"The distance isn't far, Karl; I will be all right. With this trouble between France and Austria, it will be best if you do less traveling. Do not worry if I tarry long. There is much I do not know—much which I must resolve before I can go on. I am tired, Karl. For the first time in my life, I am tired; and I know it is a weariness of spirit—not of body."

The first days at the monastery were spent in adjusting to the simple, frugal life of the place. The food was ample and hearty. Franz's cell had a narrow cot and a small table that held a bowl and pitcher. There was a shelf for books, but he had no books. This was not the time to read, to pursue the reflections of others. This was his time of reconciliation.

In his profession he had known the dizzy heights of fame and drunk the bitter dregs of rejection. In his personal life he had lost those who were dearest and best. As a physician there had been times when he recognized death as the great healer, putting a stop to the torment of pain when medicine failed. Death had dealt gently with his parents. They had gone to sleep as had Father Emmanuel. Even Gluck's death he could comprehend, but the day he saw the precious body of his beloved hurled into the street . . . to lie there broken and lifeless . . . he could find no comprehension . . . no words to formulate a question. Now with Wolfgang gone . . . the genius lad of love and laughter, young . . . so young. . . .

He spent hours there in the cell, lying on the cot, rising only to eat, to take a walk, and to return to the cell. The days slipped by. He didn't count them. The sun came up; it went down; day or night . . . did it matter?

A gentle monk, in age nearing heaven, touched his arm and questioned, "Son, have you tried the chapel?"

He looked through his valise. "My prayer book and rosary are somewhere here." Finding them, he went into the chapel.

This was a chapel built of love by great artists, of that he was sure. The holy water font might have been a Cellini; the stained-glass windows were wondrous. There was a side altar for the Infant Jesus of Prague. Franz had once seen the original . . . this was a beautiful and holy replica. The compassionate Mother was a joy to his eyes. She was life-like and real. Franz saw her beauty, for the art was great; but he saw her only as art. At last he sat in a pew. He read a bit. He clutched his beads and knelt to pray. There was no response from his heart.

He sat back. "Here is the appointed place, the communion of saints, the ebb and flow of the Eternal. Why am I missing it? There is no response anywhere, no sorrow, no tears, no pain, no joy, no laughter, no hopes." Franz rested his tired eyes.

He returned to his cell and the days drifted by, as noiseless and remote as clouds passing over the moon.

The seasons changed and yet he waited . . . no voice spoke, no challenge came. At last he aroused himself from lethargy. He announced to the monks that he would be gone for several days, maybe a week. He took heavy clothing and a blanket and placed them in a back-pack. He set out the next morning about an hour before sunrise.

He stumbled along in the darkness, down the road a bit, then turned toward the peak. He climbed and climbed. Soon a glimmer of light brightened the steep, rocky path. At times he would use both hands to lift himself from one shelf to a higher one. The snow clung in shallow patches but grew deeper as he ascended. His breath was explosive from the climb, though he tried to keep it deep and even, as his father had taught him in his childhood. He stopped for a brief rest. The light of a new day was full upon the tiny village, and to the left the monastery gleamed and sparkled. They looked remote and toy-like. In the canyons, clouds came up from the earth. Like ghost balloons, they floated heavenward. He drank deeply of the air, scented by pine and fir. More trees were walking with him now. They came closer and closer; the foresters had not cut as many here. . . . He passed the timber line; he reached the top. There were only the ice-capped peaks, solitude, and himself.

The foresters had erected a small stone hut. This was not unusual. Papa had built a number of such huts in his district. Franz pushed open the door. It was shelter for a climber, and fuel was stacked for his use. He shrugged off his back-pack and walked out into the awesome silence. Like an ancient priest awaiting a sign, he wrapped the blanket about him and sat upon a large stone that served as a step into the hut. He leaned back against the door of the hut. The sun had left the mountains, but a touch of rose light remained for a little while . . . and then darkness fell.

Franz was grateful for the shelter of the hut, but hunger assailed him. There was water, but no food. He had determined to fast and pray for one week . . . in complete isolation. He was bone-tired; sleep came early. He awakened thinking of breakfast; all day he fought the thought of food. There would be momentary lapses of hunger when his soul would feast upon the glory of the mountain top, but hunger again demanded attention. The next day was even worse. He felt nausea, and he could judge that he had a slight fever. Toward evening of the third day the illness left, but he was weak. That night he did not sleep. He sat out under the stars. They were near to him. The great trees below whispered in the night. The stars and Franz listened for their secret. "Do they know why man is born to wonder, to struggle, to grieve?"

The wind came moaning from across a chasm, its voice hoarse—as though it had wept for a long time. It touched his face and he grew cold. He gathered his blanket and trembled, and then a great light flowed down from the sky. It shone all about him. He felt an upsurge of being, a giving of himself into the light. They joined and became one. He cried out in joy; tears, unbidden, wet his face. He was embraced and held fast in love. The Voice spoke and he listened with his soul, "Come unto me, give me your burdens . . . your sorrows, give me your unshed tears . . . the questions that coil themselves like vipers around your brain . . . give them to me." How gentle, how persuasive the voice.

Slowly the Light ebbed. Franz leaped from his stone; the blanket dropped from him. He reached for the ebbing Light. He tried to lift himself to it, but it was gone. A great peace flooded his soul, dampening his eyes with tears.

Four more days passed. Reluctantly he left the hut and started down the mountain side. He had heard the voice of his Master. The God of his heart had spoken. "I will return to His work, and giving Him my burdens, my sorrows, I will live as He chooses for me. As simply as a child takes direction from a parent, I will listen for His voice." Franz held his rosary in both hands.

"The moment in the light might never come again, but I know there is a Light. I know that my Redeemer liveth." Franz sang Handel's great song of faith the rest of the way back to the monastery.

He tarried only long enough to make his confession and receive the Blessed Sacrament—for this was the outward and visible sign of the inward and spiritual grace.

CHAPTER XXIX

VIENNA AFTER fifteen years! Two-sixty-one Landstrasse had not changed. Karl greeted him, "Sir, it has been a year!" They embraced. Karl looked at Franz closely. "You are healed," he announced. Then as they supped together, Karl told Franz of worldly events.

"Lafayette fled Paris the day it fell to the enemies of the King," Karl said. "He was caught and imprisoned by Austrian forces, war having been declared by then."

"And where is he now?"

"Still in prison," answered Karl.

"Can't we help?"

"Sir," said Karl, "Lafayette is safer in the hands of the Austrians than he would be in the hands of the French rebels. And there is so much hard feeling in high places these days—one can't be sure—perhaps we had better stay out of it." Karl shook his old head sadly.

"You are right, Karl—and we are going on to Switzerland as soon as I can settle things here."

In a short time, Franz had Karl pack and they left for Fruenfeld, a small town not too far from Zurich.

Franz bought a chalet "with a view," as Karl expressed it. "Where could we find a chalet here without a view?" Franz asked him.

A middle-aged Swiss woman came to cook and tend the homemaking. Karl hung out Franz's medical sign and they were busy again.

The lorry arrived from Vienna. The musical glasses were brought in. Franz touched them in tender remembrance. Gluck had composed on these very glasses. Wolfgang had once desecrated them with a village jig and laughed in boyish glee at his father's displeasure. In later years Wolfgang had composed some lovely pieces for the glasses. "Monique, my beloved, stood beside me when I played them, urging, 'Just one more melody, Franz.'"

"Oh, Monique, Monique, my darling, how barren those years would have been without you," he whispered.

" 'When I go, don't pray for me . . . just talk to me.' " Over the years he heard her voice.

"Monique?" he whispered, and he knew he heard her laughter in the answer that came.

"Franz, talk to me."

He talked to her.

The village people also talked to Franz. He became one of them. He had time for long walks—for hours spent prostrate on the ground, listening to the earth's song and the voice of the brooklet.

The years passed gently. Karl, too, went to sleep. Even as Papa and Mama, he found death tranquil. God was very close the day Franz laid him to rest. As he knelt there and listened to Father Alfonso's final Amens, Franz felt others listening with him—Wolfgang and Monique. "Life is wondrously kind and beautiful—and death can be so, too," Franz thought.

Through the years, he had kept notes on all his cases. Karl recorded them as long as he lived. Franz continued the use of animal magnetism, and his interest in it stayed as fresh as when first he had discovered this force.

"I never seek the world now except as it comes to me by post. The newspapers and periodicals and a standing order at my favorite bookbinder keep me informed," Franz would tell visitors.

In the year 1812 he was urged to return to Germany, with the promise that the Berlin Academy, the King, and all of Germany wished to honor him. When he refused so touching an honor, a Professor Wolfart was dispatched to fetch him if possible; if not, to learn all he could of the Mesmer methods.

"After thirty years they are coming to me to learn. Blessed little children," Franz laughed. "I have my records. I'll get them out." Franz and Professor Wolfart went over case after case. It was stimulating. When Professor Wolfart insisted that Franz should return to Berlin for honors, he only smiled. "I could not make him know that I have what the world cannot give," Franz told the stars.

Professor Wolfart sat with him during his office hours. He

was with Franz when grumpy old Grandfather Shultz came in with all of his complaints: "My legs cramp, my back hurts, Mama nags me all the time. Gretchen, my daughter-in-law, is raising a house full of hellions; they tromp all over my feet. See my bunions—" His vehemence and breath gone, he sat back satisfied and awaited Franz's doctoring.

Franz gave him iron filings, with directions for taking them in wine three times a day. He also gave him a small vial of extract of opium, with explicit orders to take only a few drops when his back and leg cramps were very bad. Then he told him he must walk down to the river every morning at eleven and take a bath.

When he left, Wolfart questioned Franz, "Why did you send your patient to bathe in the flowing waters of the river and not in the village springs nearby?" His young face was so serious that Franz could not resist teasing him a bit.

"Because the sun shines on the flowing waters of the river," Franz said, "and I magnetized the sun twenty years ago." Franz laughed heartily at his joke.

Berlin sent him a copy of Wolfart's report: "My expectations were exceeded when I made the personal acquaintance of the discoverer of magnetism. I found him fully immersed in beneficial activities. In view of his advanced age, all the more remarkable to me seemed the comprehensiveness, clarity, and perspicacity of his intelligence, his indefatigable and vivacious determination to impart the information I needed, the ease and brilliance of his diction—characterized as it was by a great facility of metaphor—the refinement of his manners, and the marked amiability of his behavior. When I add that he showed an abundance of positive knowledge in all branches of science— an over-all knowledge that does not usually come within the compass of one individual, together with a kindliness of heart, as manifested by his whole personality, his words, his actions, and his environment; when I add, further, that he showed the most amazing power to influence his patients by his penetrating glance or by the quiet raising of his hands, and that all these qualities were intensified by an aspect which inspired the profoundest veneration . . . I hope I shall have succeeded in giving the main outline of the picture Mesmer presented to me."

Franz tossed the report on top of his records and closed the drawer. "That Wolfart's a nice lad."

There was a talented young musician in Zurich. Sometimes he would drive out in the evening to play Franz's piano or the musical glasses. "I love them. There is no sweeter sound on earth than my glasses," Franz said and thanked him. Franz had time to listen to the cry of the untamed wind racing through the firs, to the laughter of school children walking by his door, to the whisper of snow falling on his window pane . . . to Monique's voice saying, "Franz, I love you."

It is good to be old . . . with all fires dead. . . . Then one can know . . . the ebb . . . the flow.

WITHDRAWN FROM FREE USE IN CITY CULTURAL AND WELFARE INSTITUTIONS. MAY BE SOLD FOR THE BENEFIT OF THE BROOKLYN PUBLIC LIBRARY ONLY.

Pd 6/17/86